Copyright © 2022 Jaclin Marie
All rights reserved

The characters and events portrayed in this book are fictitious. Any similarity to real persons, living or dead, is coincidental and not intended by the author.

No part of this book may be reproduced, or stored in a retrieval system, or transmitted in any form or by any means, electronic, mechanical, photocopying, recording, or otherwise, without express written permission of the publisher.

ISBN- 9798408344895

Cover design by: Acacia Heather
Editing by: Antonia Salazar
Library of Congress Control Number: 2018675309
Printed in the United States of America

To my readers who have supported and showed me kindness through my writing journey. Will always be grateful.

Trigger Warnings

This story contains mentions of Physical and Mental Abuse.

PTSD:
A disorder in which a person has difficulty recovering after experiencing or witnessing a terrifying event. The condition may last months or years, with triggers that can bring back memories of the trauma accompanied by intense emotional and physical reactions.

Gaslighting:
A form of emotional abuse that's seen in abusive relationships. It's the act of manipulating a person by forcing them to question their thoughts, memories, and the events occurring around them. A victim of gaslighting can be pushed so far that they question their own sanity.

Non-Consensual Sex/Relationship:
Touching of intimate body parts such as genitalia, groin, breast, buttocks, or mouth or any clothing covering them, without consent; the removal of another person's clothes without consent; touching a person with one's own intimate body parts without consent; etc.

Domestic Violence:
Violent or aggressive behavior within the home, typically involving the violent abuse of a spouse or partner.

Verbal Abuse:
An act of violence in the form of speech that decreases self-confidence and adds to feelings of helplessness. It is "an act that includes rebuking and the delivery of harsh words".

Some people go through this in real life, and I don't appreciate when people talk down about it or what they have been through because I think they are some of the strongest people out there.
Just wanted to mention this.
Other than that, enjoy the story.

Playlist

*"Pull your long hair
And watch your eyes roll
To the back of your head
From my kisses down low"*
**Fucking High
- Adrian Daniel**

Bad Decisions **ARIANA GRANDE**
Feel Me **SELENA GOMEZ**
Sex With Me **RIHANNA**
Earned It **THE WEEKND**
Crying In The Club **CAMILA CABELLO**
Can't Remember To Forget You **SHAKIRA**
Talking Body **TOVE LO**
Die For You **THE WEEKEND**
Best I Ever Had **DRAKE**

Needed Me **RIHANNA**
Beware **BIG SEAN**
Don't Wanna Fall In Love **KYLE**
The Heart Wants What It Wants **SELENA GOMEZ**
Pillowtalk **ZAYN**
Unforgettable **FRENCH MONTANA**
Drunk In Love **BEYONCE**
Let Me Love You **ARIANA GRANDE**
Love Hurts **PLAYBOI CARTI**
Anxiety **JULIA MICHEALS**
Grenade **BRUNO MAR**

One

"Do you have anything to say at all Aria?" my dad, George White, asks sitting in the chair opposite from mine.

I lean back in my chair and play with the bracelet around my wrist. "Not really," I say bluntly.

Long story short, my friend, Layna and I were sneaking out to go to these tracks where you can race cars and drink, but my dad ended up catching me right before I could get out of the door.

I'm turning twenty-one but am still treated like a child.

My dad rubs his forehead as some sweat starts to form.

He is always stressed out when it comes to me.

I am not the golden child like my older brother, Alex. He is crowned to be next in line for the position of the "boss" as everyone calls it.

To me, he will always be an annoying little shit.

"Aria, you can't keep doing this," he states.

I raise my eyebrows at him. "I'm turning twenty-one soon and you're still treating me like a child while you treat Alex as if he is a saint. He is only four years older than me," I almost laugh while explaining.

"He isn't like you."

I furrow my eyebrows at him. "How so? Because I'm not going to be the 'boss'?"

My dad sighs loudly. "Go get ready for dinner, Aria. I will talk to you more about this after."

I don't say anything. Except I stand up from my chair and walk out of the office.

He is being unfair.

He always is when it comes to me.

Even when I go on dangerous missions.

When I get downstairs, I see my mother, Layna, and Elena, Layna's mom.

"Aria- "

"If you are going to yell at me, dad already did," I cut my mom off before sitting next to Layna on the stool.

"I'm not going to yell at you. But you could have gone through your window," my mom winks at me and a smile lit on my face.

She always has my back.

Even when my dad yells at me for not being careful when going on missions. My mom, Lisa White, thinks I am strong and independent. My dad on the other hand thinks otherwise.

"Next time you girls sneak, give us a heads up so we know not to freak out," Elena says.

"I understand," Layna nodded her head.

Layna has always been a goody-goody. She always tries to be

the perfect daughter for her mother ever since her father died. Elena stresses out a lot and still misses her husband.

His name was Adrian. He was my father's second in command and that's how I ended up meeting Layna and becoming best friends with her. Adrian died from a gunshot wound and I remember Layna getting nightmares every time she slept over at my house.

"Well then, now that we got that covered. Let's start on dinner."

While helping my mom and Elena with dinner, Calla, my brother's wife, comes in the kitchen with her daughter, Ariel on her shoulders.

He and Calla have been together for about six years. Long story short, Calla was running from her father, and she ended up meeting Alex. He brought her in and helped her while also falling in love with her. A few months after, he got her pregnant and had to tell her the truth of what he was involved in. And that was all when he was around twenty years old while Calla was seventeen turning eighteen.

But Alex loves her, and Calla and Alex make a great team with taking care of Ariel.

While everyone cooks, I sit next to Ariel to keep her occupied, so she doesn't get bored.

"So, what are you going to do?" Layna asks as we start putting the plates down for dinner.

"For what?" I ask Layna while doing the same as her, putting plates down.

"About your dad. I want to go to the tracks tonight."

"He said he wants to talk to me after dinner. If he finishes in time, then we can go."

Layna and I finish setting the table.

We do have maids and workers to set the table and clean the house, but my mother wants us to be able to do things ourselves. Like instead of having a maid clean my room, I clean it because she wants me to have a sense of responsibility. I don't mind, though, because it is my room so it should be my responsibility to clean it. Plus, my room is rarely dirty.

The family always tries to have dinner together. We have a lot of people living in this house, so we have an excessively big table for people to be able to sit and a lot of dishes to set.

Once Layna and I are done setting the table, my mom sets the food down in the center. We all have kind of an assigned seat because each of us claimed a seat to sit in permanently.

I go to sit in my seat which is right next to Layna. She takes her seat while my mom and Calla finish getting the rest of the food from the kitchen. My mom also cooks a lot of food. The food she makes is mostly her homemade mashed potatoes or her famous meatball soup.

I see my brother Alex walking in with Ariel on his shoulders and Cole following behind him.

Cole Reyes is Alex's best friend and the second in command of the *Family Business*. Cole was always like another big brother to me. He was always annoying me and Layna when we were younger. Alex met Cole through training. I don't know much about Cole's old family life but when he met Alex, they instantly clicked and, long story short, he moved in with us.

It's crazy how alike these two are. They are like twins. Cole is always there for me when I need him to be. I never liked him in a romantic way, though, and I don't think I ever will. He likes Layna believe it or not and she likes him, but the two never made a move to start a relationship. They flirt though...a lot.

I can see why she likes him as well.

Cole is an attractive guy. He has dirty blonde hair and a sharp, strong, prominent jawline. He is tall, which is a plus for Layna because she is tall just like me, standing at five foot eight while Cole stands at six foot three.

Alex takes his seat with Ariel still on his shoulders and Cole takes his seat next to him, across from Layna and me.

"Alex put Ariel down. She is going to fall like last time," Calla scolds Alex as she walks towards him.

"Babe she's fine. She is a fighter. She always gets back up. Right, princess?" Alex asked his daughter as he set her down in the chair next to him.

"I'm not a princess," Ariel pouts.

"You're always going to be my princess," Alex says, squeezing her cheek, leaving a red mark.

Calla smiles at the two and walks towards them to kiss them on their cheeks before sitting in her seat next to Ariel.

Soon Layna's mom, Elena, walks in and sits next to Layna. A few minutes later I see my father walk in the dining room. Before he sits in his seat, he kisses my mom on her cheek and squeezes her hand three times.

That's their silent way of saying 'I love you'.

I'm lucky to be able to live with the family I have now because I know some other families aren't so kind towards their loved ones. For example, some girls in the families are forced to marry while I get to choose the kind of career I want for myself. But, since my dad started training me as a child, I have always been interested in this business, same with Alex.

Once everyone puts food down on their plates, they start to eat. After a few minutes of eating everyone dives into a conversation.

My mom, dad, and Elena talk about politics and the food she made, which is just chicken, asparagus, and potatoes. Ariel is just playing with her food. Alex and Cole are talking about some other family, they both love to gossip and talk shit on the other Mafia Families.

"Dude, I'm telling you. I have a feeling it's these fucking Italians. They are always good at sneaking around. The Mexicans make it obvious when they try to steal shit. And the Russians have been quiet. So, it's got to be the Italians for sure." Cole tells Alex as he tries to get Ariel to eat her food.

"What happened?" I asked Cole.

Cole turns to look at me, "Alex told me there are some shipments being stolen."

"Like what? Drugs?"

"No, weapons. Alex thinks it's the Mexicans because they were asking for some sort of rifle, but your dad refused."

"Okay, but why do you think it's the Italians? Don't they have enough weapons?"

"They have more than enough. But Cole thinks they are bored

and just trying to piss us off which doesn't make sense," Alex said while rolling his eyes.

"But I thought they had an alliance with us?"

"No that's the Mexicans. We used to have an alliance with the Italians and a long time ago we were just a joined group, but the new capo got rid of all the alliances he had because he couldn't trust anyone. That's what our mole told us before he got killed. They are smart and play a good game but them stealing our shit doesn't make sense." I nod my head at Alex's response.

"But I heard your dad is going to have a mole in their household to see if they can get any information," Cole explains.

"When did you guys find this out?"

"Just right now," Alex answers and then turns back to Ariel. "Baby you got to eat your food," Alex scolds.

"Are you going to ask him?" Layna asks, making me look at her.

"Should I?" She shrugs her shoulders. I let out a sigh and turn to look at my dad. "Dad?"

The table goes quiet, and everyone looks at me.

Why can't everyone mind their own business?

Do they think I'm just going to blow up or something?

"Can Layna and I go out tonight after our meeting?"

Everyone looks at my dad as he finishes swallowing his food.

"I'll talk to you about it after dinner."

He didn't wait for me to reply and went back to eating and talking with my mom and Elena.

I looked at Layna and then I shrugged my shoulders.

"It's okay, Aria. We can go out when you get back."

"You guys are going out?" Cole asks looking at Layna.

"I don't know because Aria has a meeting with George. We were going to go racing and get some drinks," Layna states looking at Cole.

Cole just nods his head and goes back to eating.

I turn my attention back to my food and finish eating as well.

Two

"So, what is this mission that I have?" I ask as my father as I walk inside his office. My father sits in his chair right in front of me and takes out a file from his desk drawer and puts it between us. I lean forward and take the file to look through it. I see pictures of a guy with dark brown hair with glasses covering his eyes, and a hat on in a warehouse that looks familiar. "Is this our warehouse?" I ask my dad.

"Yes," my father states coldly.

"Okay and who is it? Who does he work for?"

"Alex and Cole have suspicions that this individual is an Italian."

"Well, what do you think?" I ask putting the file back on his desk.

"I think I need someone to go deep undercover and figure out what the hell is going on with those Italians," my father says while resting his hands on the desk. "I need a mole to go undercover and figure out if they are actually stealing shipments."

"Alex and Cole said you need a mole." I state. "Am I doing this all by myself or is Layna coming with me?"

"No. You are doing this alone. I am having Layna stay here and go through all of our staff to make sure we don't have a mole."

"Well, what's the plan then?" I ask, smirking.

"I want you to go to this warehouse they have in Pasadena. They have warehouses everywhere in the world but the only one they have here in California is Pasadena. The address is in the file," Dad says while bringing out another file with papers in it. "I want you to purposely get kidnapped and then I want you to have them trust you and make amends with them. If you can, I want you to try and sneak into their office and hack the mainframe."

"I don't specialize in hacking, Dad," I deadpan.

"That's not a problem. Layna will be on it once you text her."

"How am I going to text her if they take my phone? I doubt they will let me keep my shit, Dad."

My dad shrugged his shoulders. "Steal a phone for a second and contact Layna from there. Shouldn't be hard."

"Okay should be simple. How long am I undercover for?" I asked.

"As long as you can stay undercover."

The first thing I see when I open my eyes is my ceiling. I sit up from my bed and look around my room. My blinds are open, and I see a beautiful view of the city.

I get out of bed and head towards my bathroom. I don't bother showering because I showered last night, and my hair is still kind of damp.

I change into a black tank top and some black pants. I put on my oversized leather jacket that has pockets for me to put my mini knives and other small weapons that are helpful for missions.

After I put my clothes on, I pull my long brown hair in a high ponytail and head downstairs.

Last night my father explained my mission and what I was going to do for it. All I have to do is try to take a crate they have in their warehouse and hopefully they'll catch me.

When I walk into the kitchen, I see my mom making breakfast and Elena sitting down on one of the stools.

"Hey, baby. Are you ready for the mission?" my mom asks when she sees me.

"Yeah. I'm just going to eat a banana and make a coffee or something."

"Okay. I made a breakfast burrito for you so take that with you. Make sure you are careful out there. You never know who is working on the job when you go to this warehouse," my mom scolds while Elena just listens in.

"Yeah, make sure you come back home in one piece, please. I don't want Layna coming to me to complain that her best friend died," Elena jokes.

I laugh while making my coffee. Once I'm done, I take the banana and breakfast burrito and I kiss them both goodbye before walk out of the house to the garage.

I wonder if my dad revealed my actual mission because they made it seem like I would be gone for just a day.

When I walk outside towards the garage, I see our collection of cars. I personally like sports cars while my dad likes the classy cars like Rolls Royce, Bentley, and Mercedes. Alex and I have always liked fast cars though.

I unlock my black BMW I8 and get inside the car. I start the engine making it roar before pulling out of the estate.

The warehouse is around thirty to forty minutes away. We live in between Hidden Hills and Calabasas so Pasadena is thirty to forty minutes when there is no traffic. I'm lucky that there is no traffic right now because LA traffic is the worst.

While driving I listen to music with my windows rolled down to let some air in while eating my food. I love blasting music while my windows are down.

Once I get closer to the warehouse, I turn down my music and park my car where no one will be able to see it. I get out and make sure I have everything I need and start walking towards the entrance where the gate is locked.

The guard they have is clueless. I don't know whether to kill him or knock him out. He is on his phone watching porn, I can see the screen through the glass window.

I grimace before shooting my gun at him. I would be decent and just knock him out, but he was lacking on the job, watching porn.

Who does that?

I walk inside the little area he was sitting in and take his keys from his pockets. I could mess around with the cameras, but my plan is to get kidnapped, so I don't even bother.

I take out the map my father put in the files to see where the crate would be located. It shows that it's in the back of the warehouse.

I continue walking through the warehouse. After a bit, I hear footsteps and some mumbling nearby.

I stop walking and hide near a crate so that I can't be seen. The voices are getting closer and closer. I take out my knife once they are close enough and step out of my hiding spot and stab one of them in the neck and roundhouse kick the other making him fall to the floor.

I take my knife out of the person's neck and he instantly falls to the floor. I turn to the other guy who is still standing. I take my knife that still has some blood on it, and I throw it, making it fly towards the guy's neck so he doesn't make any sound.

His knees go weak and then he falls to the floor. I take my knife out of him and step over his body. I continue walking and make multiple left and right turns.

When I finally get to the crate, I make sure it's the right shipment that my father wrote down for me. I also make sure that there are weapons in there. There are assault rifles and multiple snipers and handguns.

Nice.

"Who are you?" I turn around and see two men who are dressed in all black, with their guns raised at me.

I raise my hands in the air and smile. "Now I'm not here to start any trouble."

"I'm not going to ask you again. Who are you?" They demand in a sterner tone.

"Fine, we can do this the hard way," I say with a smile before taking my gun and shooting both of them.

A few more men walk out from the corner, and they turn their heads to look at me.

They take their guns out and start shooting but I move out of the way and run towards them. I take out my knife and stab one of them in the eye while kicking the other in the stomach. The guy I stab screams loudly.

Before I can go after the other one, I feel arms wrap around my waist. I nudge the person behind me in their lower region making them release me and groan.

I turn around and grab my gun pointing it to the last guy before shooting him in the head.

I find the person I nudged on the floor whimpering while holding his groin. I walk towards him and look down at him.

Seeing him like that made me feel kind of bad but oh well. I lift my leg and step on his face, knocking him out cold.

I was about to turn around to check if I had missed anyone, but I feel something shoot into the back of my neck making me hiss.

I turn around and see no one in sight.

I feel my legs go weak making me fall to the floor and then my eyes fall making me see nothing but darkness.

Three

"Dude, you wake her up."

"No, you do it."

I hear voices talking as soon as I start to wake up. I feel all my senses set in motion once I gain consciousness.

The voices continue to argue back and forth about who is going to wake me up. I open my eyes but all I see is black. What the fuck? Did I even open my eyes? I try to bring my hands up to my face, but they are chained down.

"You guys can stop arguing about whether to wake me up or not."

I don't hear any more talking. They rip the cloth off my eyes. I see two guys that look like they are in their mid-twenties. One of them has dark brown hair and the other has dark black curly hair and they both have dark brown eyes.

"Oh, good you're awake. Josh, go tell the *capo*." The one with brown hair says while turning his head to look at the other guy who I am assuming is Josh.

"Okay well while Josh is getting him, mind telling me why I'm chained up and not in my beautiful car?" I ask the guy who is still standing in front of me while Josh leaves the room.

"Oh, don't worry, the *capo* is going to tell you everything and handle you perfectly."

"Lovely, but I would rather go home now. You see I have somewhere to be so if you don't mind-"

"Yeah, I don't think so. Do you know what you're doing here? Why are you here?" the guy questions, cutting me off while also walking closer so that he's right in front of me.

"Um, no clue. Just a mindless little girl, right?" I say, while giving him a small innocent smile.

Of course, they know what I was doing. What idiot wouldn't know?

"Funny. You got an attitude. Make sure you keep that in check before you meet the *capo*." He backs up and goes to lean on a wall.

"You keep mentioning this *capo*, but I have no idea who it is. Would be helpful if you gave me some info, yes?"

I already have the entire plan ready in my head. I thought about it during the drive here and now I am just playing everything out.

Make amends with them, Aria.

I hear the room door open making me look away from the guy who was leaning on the wall and towards the doorway. I see a very tall, muscular frame walk in. I can't see his facial features because there is only one light in the room, and it's dim and right above me.

I focus my attention back on the man who just walked in.

"*Capo*." The brown-haired guy who was leaning on the wall straightened his posture and greeted the tall figure who walked in.

This man screams confidence and intimidation. "Leave, Jared." The man speaks with a hint of a strong Italian accent.

His voice is deep, smooth, and captivating.

Jared leaves the room without another word and closes the door.

"So, you're the *capo* I'm assuming?" I ask as I narrow my eyes at the man. He doesn't answer me. It looks like he is just observing me. Even though I can barely see him I feel nervous under his gaze. "Are you going to tell me why the hell I'm in here?" I tried to see if he would fucking talk or not. "Look I don't have all day. I have things to do so if you don't mind letting me go-"

"What the fuck were you doing in my warehouse?" the man says cutting me off.

He sounds powerful and strong. His voice seems so controlled.

"So, he does speak?" I smirk.

The man starts to walk further out towards me and with each step he takes, his facial features become more clear and vivid.

Fuck me.

Why'd he have to be attractive?

"I'm going to ask again and I expect an answer. What the fuck were you doing in my warehouse?"

I can finally see his face. Still a little dim but I can see him.

He has bright green eyes and a very sharp jawline. His lips look very plump and smooth. His dark brown hair looks like he hasn't cut it in weeks, but it works for him. It is messy but it looks good on him. I notice that he is wearing a dress shirt and black pants. I can see a snake tattoo crawling up his arm and what also looks like a dragon and an ace card cover his other. The rings on his hands aren't dramatic like the ones I've seen other men wear, they are bands and some other rings with different designs on them.

He looks extremely intimidating and good looking. Too bad I'm going to have to kill him after I get out of here.

"What's it to you?"

"Because no one ever steps in my warehouses," he says while walking closer to me. "I know for a fact you aren't an innocent little girl who just wandered into my warehouse because no innocent little girl can kill over twenty of my men with just a small little knife and a handgun." He leans down so that his hands are on the arm rest of the wooden chair, his face right in front of mine. "So, I'm going to ask you one more time and you better fucking tell me or else I'll just have to force it out of you."

"I have no clue what you're talking about." I bluntly state.

He looks like he is getting frustrated but he is trying to control his temper. I notice the way his fingertips turn white from holding onto the chair too tight.

"You aren't a naïve little girl. You came into my warehouse and attempted to steal a whole crate filled with assault rifles, handguns, and snipers. I know for a fact you're working for something so what is it?"

I stay quiet and just stare at him.

"Who are you?" I ask ignoring his question.

"Excuse me?" He looks shocked that I asked him that question.

"Who are you?" I repeat.

He chuckles and gives me a dark smirk. "Ever heard of the Italian Mafia?"

I keep a smirk on my face. "Of course, I have."

"Where are you from?"

"The fuck you mean where am I from?"

"What fucking organization do you work for?" he asks, his controlling voice fading away slowly.

I pull on the chains so that I can break the wood from the chair. "Who said I was from an organization?"

I hear the mystery man let out a deep chuckle, but it was anything but sweet and sincere. "You're either from some sort of crime orginization or an assassin for one."

"But how do you know?" I repeat my question.

I am just trying to stall.

"Because *amore*, not everyone can kill twenty men who are trained assassins with a small little knife and gun. You are really testing me so stop the bullshit and speak."

I don't answer his question. Instead, I break the chair handles making the whole chair crumble and fall to the floor. Before he can react, I jump up off the floor and kick him in the face making him stumble a little bit.

I go to punch him in the ribs and face, but he catches my wrist and pushes me against the wall.

"Not smart. You really have no idea who you're messing with," he says in my ear while holding me against the wall.

I feel his hot breath on my neck sending shivers down my spine. "Then who are you?" I ask while struggling against his grip.

"Ace. *Ace De Luca. Il capo della Mafia Italiana.*"

They can't keep me in this stupid ass room forever.

Fucking assholes.

After Ace put me up against the wall, he had that Jared guy put me in one of the rooms they had here. I ended up giving him a black eye. I was close to running away from him but the other guards caught me and locked me in the room I am currently in.

I don't even know where I am.

I have been yelling nonstop.

I've been in this room for probably about a day, I think. They don't have anything in here. They only had a bed and a bathroom. No TV, no windows, nothing. Ace had maids come in and out of the room to give me food and water, but I didn't eat anything.

Do you think I'm really going to eat food from the enemy? I have been trained to not eat food for longer than a week. My father was always super strict with my training.

It was a hard week but good thing I didn't die.

The maid gave me clothes to wear as well. I did take those because I wanted to be comfortable. I'm wearing a black sweater and some shorts that they gave me.

I thought they would treat me completely differently. I thought they would put me in a cell like what we do with our prisoners.

I have tried to escape so many times but there is no way out. I have made a complete mess of this room as well. I made multiple dents in the wall and even smashed some vases from the room and a mirror.

I got bored, so I walked to another vase they had in the room and threw it to the floor.

There were cameras in here, so they knew what I was doing. They probably also saw me change.

Sick fucks.

Just as I'm about to throw an art piece on the floor the door opens revealing Ace. He's wearing a black suit with his hair styled the same as yesterday.

"Come," he says, making me furrow my eyebrows.

"Huh?"

"I said come," he repeats. "But if you try anything, I'll kill you without any hesitation."

I roll my eyes at him, making Ace clench his hands into a fist. I walk out of the room and follow him. While walking through the house I see all kinds of photographs of a family and some artwork hung up.

I have only seen a little snippet of the downstairs from when Jared was leading me to the room I was just in. So, I didn't really get to see the living room and kitchen.

I see the living room come into view. It looks like a regular living room. There are multiple cloud couches, a TV hung up and a long wooden coffee table in the middle on top of a very luxurious rug.

After I finish scoping the living room, I catch up to Ace who turned a corner. I bump into him.

He turns around slowly, towering over me.

"Do you know how to walk?" he spat.

"Well asshole, it wasn't my fault that you were standing in the way."

He comes closer to me, and I swear my heart skips a beat for a second, "Let's get one thing straight. I'm the boss here. I don't care if you're the queen of fucking England. Don't disrespect me. You have no idea what I'm capable of." He doesn't wait for my response. He turns around and opens the door he's standing in front of. He walks in and I follow in after him. "Sit."

"You sound like my dad," I say, while walking to the chair in front of his desk and sitting down.

He sits in his chair and pulls out a file. "Your dad? George White?" Ace says as if it was just a normal name. I freeze when he mentions my father's name. My dad is the head of the American Mafia. Not a lot of people know that he has a daughter. Ace notices me freeze up and my face pale. His lips lift in a small smirk. "So, Aria White, why did my men find you in my warehouse trying to steal my shipments?" Ace asked while putting his hands on the desk leaning towards me.

I gulp, "How do you know me?"

"It's not hard for me to find information that I need. Now if you answer what I ask of you then I will consider not killing you after I'm done with you."

"Why?"

"Because I've heard a lot about you believe it or not. You have remarkably interesting torture methods, and you could be extremely useful to me. That's why you are not dead yet. But if you don't agree I will simply just kill you now."

"You're bluffing."

"You really want to know if I'm bluffing or not?" he raises his eyebrows while questioning me.

I don't answer and he pulls a gun out of his drawer and aims towards me. I don't flinch or move a muscle. I just stare at him with a bored expression.

"If you're going to do it just do it," I state.

"Answer the question." Ace states.

"Damn, relax," I say, before talking again. "My father disowned me. He doesn't want me anymore, so I saw your warehouse and went in there to stay. Closest thing I could find," I lie. "Now since I answered your question tell me what the hell I'm doing here and where I am." I demand.

"Italy."

Four

"ITALY?!" I scream at the top of my lungs. "You're crazy if you think I'm just going to stay here in Italy until you let me go. Do you even know who I am? I can kill you in an instant right now."

My father never told me about this. I thought I was at least staying in the state or the country at least, but I am literally miles across the world from my family.

Ace turns to look at me. His lips start to tug into a smirk.

He doesn't think I can kill him right now.

Sure, he is a made man and muscular, but he can't do anything.

Right?

"Go ahead, try it," Ace says, throwing the gun he was holding, onto the table.

I make a move to get the gun and stand up aiming it at him.

"You really think I'm not going to kill you?" I ask, pushing the gun towards his head.

He looks so calm. "Do it." Ace says looking up at me.

I press my finger against the trigger, and I hear a click, but nothing comes out.

Ace grabs the gun from my hand, "You're stupid if you think I would actually let a loaded gun near you. Now, go sit back in the chair like a good girl." I go and sit back in the chair I was sitting in before. "Just letting you know I have guards surrounding the perimeter so even if you try to leave, you can't," he says smugly.

What an asshole.

"Why am I in Italy?" I ask.

"Are you really that dumb or do I need to spell it out for you?" He waits for my response, but I don't give him one. "You're in Italy because I can't have you at one of my bases in the U.S. I need to keep a close eye on you."

"Okay, what do you want with me?"

"I need you simply for leverage. I need something from your father and until he gives it to me, you're staying here while also helping me with other things."

"He won't care." I shrug. "What do you need anyway?"

"That's none of your concern. What you're going to do is go up to that room of yours and stay put. You're not going to make a mess in that room because if you do, I will just put you in the cells downstairs where it's dark and smells like rotten blood. You aren't allowed to leave the estate. I always have security out. I have maids and chefs to do what you need them to do so take advantage of that. I will have Jared or Josh show you around," he answers coldly.

"You do know my dad won't care because he disowned me, right?" I ask with raised eyebrows.

"You really have no clue what I can do," Ace smirks.

I roll my eyes at him. "What about clothes? I'm not staying in an oversized sweater and some shorts the whole time I'm here."

"I don't know *amore,* you kind of look good in my clothes, *sì?*" he says with amusement and trails his eyes down my body.

I roll my eyes and get up from the chair and walked towards the office door. The guards who were standing in front of it were blocking my path and before I could push them out of my way, Ace mutters 'let her go'.

I walk past them and go out of the hallway Ace led me through. Instead of going back to that room, I decide to explore the house a little bit.

I walk through the house and see multiple photographs of him up on the wall. I walk close to one of the pictures and see a mini-Ace and another boy who looks around Ace's age in the picture. He had hazel eyes and dark blonde hair.

"Hey." I turn around and see Jared with a smile on his face. He still has the black eye I gave him. But he still has a smile on his face. "Sorry if I scared you. Ace said that he wanted me to show you around the house?" Jared asks.

"Yeah, I guess. Is he always that moody?" I ask as we start walking out of the hallway.

"Yeah. His dad taught him to be like that from what I heard."

"Oh," I answer without saying anything else.

Jared shows me the rest of the house. He tells me where to go and where not to go. After the tour, we go to the kitchen to get something to eat and when we walk in, we see three incredibly beautiful women sitting down on the kitchen stools talking.

"Hello, ladies. This is Aria. American Mafia Princess. She is going to stay with us for a while. Aria, that is Emma Russo," Jared says pointing to one of the girls. She looks around my age. She has beautiful dark blue eyes and dirty blonde hair. She looks like a model. "Mia," Jared says, pointing to another girl. She has dark brown hair and dark brown eyes. She kind of has a baby face, but she is beautiful none-the-less, "and Alicia, Ace's mom." He finishes while pointing to an older woman.

She has brown hair with brown eyes. She kind of looks like that one actress, Ashley Judd.

I look at them and back at Jared who shrugs his shoulders. Why should I trust them? I was taught to trust no one, and they expect me to trust them?

But I have to blend in and try to get them to trust me.

"Nice to meet you. If you need anything, please just ask," Alicia says and then looks over at Jared, "Mind telling me why this beautiful girl is standing in our kitchen and not at her own home? No offense dear."

She doesn't seem too bad. I still have to show respect because my mother taught me how to show respect to people who were older than me no matter who they are.

"Ask your son. He is the one who made Josh and I kidnap her," Jared said shrugging while sitting next to Mia on the stools.

"Well, now I have another person to talk to in the house. It was getting boring." Emma says while walking towards me.

"How old are you, honey?" Alicia asks looking back at me.

"Twenty. I'm turning twenty-one in a month though," I answer.

"Oh, well if you're going to be here for that long we have to celebrate. We love to have parties and celebrate birthdays around here," Mia said.

"I don't even know what I'm doing here." I lie.

"Well, this is a plus for me 'cause now I have someone else to talk to besides Mia since she is always at school," Emma says while rolling her eyes at Mia.

"Not my fault I want an education. Not all of us are going to be in the freaking mafia forever. I need to pay my own bills," Mia said, making me chuckle a little.

A few seconds later I see a guy with dirty blonde hair. He looks like the one in the picture I saw in the hallway. Emma starts walking towards him and they share a kiss while he wraps his arm around her waist.

They break away and Emma turns towards me, "Aria, this is my husband, Leo. He is also Ace's best friend and second in command."

"Oh. Thought you looked familiar," I say, studying his face.

"What do you mean?" Leo asks as he tilted his head a little.

"I saw a picture of you and Ace in the hallway. Tell me, was he always such a jackass?" I ask.

Leo laughs, "Careful. Not a lot of people who call him names like that get to live and see the next day."

"Then I should be dead right now. I called him multiple things and all he does is threaten. I even put a gun to his head. He is all bark, no bite."

"My son isn't the kindest person ever. But that's because of his father," Alicia says with sadness laced in her tone. "Speaking of Ace?" Alicia asks Leo.

"Last I saw Ace, he was in the office."

"Okay well, dinner is going to be ready soon. Lana is making pasta carbonara." Alicia says.

Everyone in the kitchen leaves and I am soon left alone.

What time does dinner even start?

After everyone leaves the kitchen, I go to explore the house a little more. I go to the backyard they have and let me tell you, they probably paid millions for this house.

The backyard looks like it's the size of the mansion itself and the mansion these people live in is huge.

But I need to find a phone so I can call Layna and see if she can hack into their mainframe. I also need to find a way to sneak into Ace's office.

Dad said once I am in his office, I need to find whatever dirt I can on them. I also need to see what kind of deals they are making with other organizations.

Anyway, dinner is starting soon, and Alicia is calling everyone to the table. Jared sees me outside looking around the backyard and he tells me that dinner is ready.

So here I am sitting at the dinner table with Mia on my right and Emma on my left.

There are five other people here that I haven't met yet. The table we are sitting at is awfully long. There are five seats on each side and two chairs at the end of the table.

The side I am sitting on has Leo, Emma, Me, Mia, and Alicia. On the other side of the table are Valentino and Marco.

Valentino and Marco are Mia's brothers. I already knew for a fact that Mia and Valentino are related because they look so much alike. I soon figured out they are twins. Marco looks like he is around Ariel's age. He looks just like his brother and sister except he has lighter hair and blue eyes.

They seem nice and Valentino seems like a cool guy.

Sitting next to Marco are his mother and father, Ana and Antonio.

I see where Marco gets his blue eyes from; his father's eyes are almost as blue as the sea.

Emma told me that Antonio is a close family friend and was the underboss before Ace and Leo took over those roles, so that is how they are all super close and know each other well.

It's a lot to process.

At the head of the table is Ace and there is an empty chair on the other side next to him.

"So, you must be Aria?" Ana asks, looking at me as we start eating dinner.

"Yes," I say while showcasing a fake smile.

"Well, I am Ana. I am sure Mia already told you that," Ana states with a smile on her face. "That is my husband Antonio and my boys Val and Marco."

"Yeah, Mia told me a little about you guys."

"She did?" I nodded my head. "Well, I wish I could have introduced myself." Antonio claims.

I can't help but wonder if Ace has a father or not because last time I heard about the Italian Mob there was a boss named Angelo but where is he?

Seconds later I see a very tall and beautiful girl walk inside the dining room. She has platinum blonde hair and bright blue eyes. Her skin looks flawless, but I don't know if it's because she's wearing makeup or not. She has a very slim but flattering figure.

I study her as she walks to the empty chair in between Ace and Valentino. She messes with Ace's hair which makes Ace return a glare at her.

After she sits down, Lana, the chef, brings in food. She serves me a plate and I thank her. Once everyone has their plate everyone starts eating.

"Who is she, Ace?" the girl sitting next to Ace asks in a hushed tone.

Ace looks at her and then to me, "Don't worry about it."

"Come on Ace, tell me," the girl asks in a flirty tone while touching his arm with her manicured finger.

"Lexi, if you don't stop talking, I will slice your throat right now in front of everyone," Ace mutters and that shuts her up quickly.

"So how long am I staying here for?" I ask after a moment of silence.

"Don't worry about it. If you didn't want to be here, then you shouldn't have gone inside my warehouse," Ace mutters.

"Well, I had nowhere else to go. I would rather go inside a warehouse filled with weapons rather than staying the night out in the woods."

"Well then that's on you. Don't get pissed at me for your actions. Should have thought before doing so."

"Bet you would do the exact same," I argue.

"See the thing about me is that I am not impulsive, and I think before I do anything," Ace drops his utensils and looks at me, "You simply just do and that's where you end up dead."

"You know nothing about me," I narrow my eyes at him.

Ace raises his eyebrows. "Really? Wanna bet?" I give him a challenging look. "You are physically strong, yes, but you are also a very stubborn girl. But because of you being stubborn you do things your way and if you make impulsive, stupid decisions then you will end up dead."

I chuckle, "You have no clue what I can do."

"Yeah, but I am going to find out."

"Find out?"

"I am going to figure out what makes you tick and what made you so angry to the point of insanity. I am going to find what makes you weak and vulnerable. I will figure you out, Aria, and figure out why the hell your father would disown you, one of the best trained assassins in the world."

He really thinks I am disowned.

If he does then this will be easier than I thought.

Five

I open my eyes and instantly see a very bright light making me close my eyes, so I can't see the light anymore.

Who the hell opened the blinds?

I open my eyes again slowly and it's not as bad as before. Once my eyes get used to the light, I turn to the side and look at the clock which reads eight-thirty a.m.

After the argument with Ace last night, everyone during dinner kept quiet. After dinner was done, I helped Lana wash the dishes and clean the table. She told me I didn't have to, to which I replied that it was not an issue. She is an old lady and I feel the need to just help her.

Lana's food is delicious, but I felt bad for her doing all the work, so I assisted her. She told me about everyone who lived in the house.

I learned that Ace and Leo knew each other for almost all their lives. They met when they were just four years old. I guess they met because Leo's father had a deal with Ace's father, who I am still trying to figure out if he is around or not. Ace and Leo are both twenty-three.

When Lana told me Ace's age, I was shocked. He seems so much older and mature.

Emma and Leo have been married for two years but they have been together since they were seventeen.

I also asked Lana who the girl who kissed Ace on the cheek was and she told me her name was Lexi Romanov. Ace and Lexi, I guess weren't dating just messing around.

I mean people have their needs.

Who am I to judge?

I have my own needs as well. But she is bold for going after the boss.

After I finished helping her, Jared took me to my new room since the last one I was in was damaged by me. The new room he put me in was kind of similar to the other one but had some small differences. Like for instance there was a window, and I didn't feel like I was being held captive.

I stand up from the bed and go towards the bathroom. I walk in and see a bunch of lady products for me to use to freshen myself up. It had toothpaste, a toothbrush, a hairbrush, hair ties, deodorant, and perfume.

I quickly brush my teeth then my hair and put it in a high ponytail. I walk out of the bathroom and walk towards the closet wondering if they left clothes in there.

They did.

They left a lot of clothes.

I walk inside the closet and inspect them.

They left some designer brands like Dior, Louis Vuitton, and Chanel.

I find a pair of leggings and a sports bra to change into. Surprisingly, they fit me well. I grab some black sneakers and put them on before leaving the room and going downstairs towards the gym.

Jared showed me where the gym was when he gave me a tour. They had a punching bag and I've been wanting to punch something lately.

As I walk closer and closer to the gym, I start to hear grunts. I furrow my eyebrows wondering what or who is grunting like an animal.

Once I'm in front of the door I open it and see a tall muscular back with sweat dripping down facing me. I look in the mirror and see that it's Ace beating the punching bag. He is going at it hard. His movements are quick and strong. He has a very toned body. You can tell he works out a lot and keeps his body healthy. I also notice more of the tattoos that were hidden underneath his shirt from when I first saw him. I see a skull that had roses surrounding it, a sword, and a outline tattoo of a girl.

He looks so-

"Done staring?" Ace says facing me now.

I feel my cheeks heat up and I can't hide it 'cause all my hair is in a high ponytail.

"I wasn't staring," I argue.

I try to not let it faze me and walk towards the punching bag

that is a few spaces away from him. He turns back to his bag and starts punching it again. Same movements as just a few seconds ago.

I ignore his presence and start to wrap my hands and knuckles. I always struggle with it. Usually, my brother or someone else would wrap my hands but they aren't here. I try so hard to do it, but I always mess up.

Funny right?

A trained assassin who can kill people and sneak around can't wrap her own hands.

Ace could probably hear me struggling because he walks over to me after taking his gloves off. He takes the wrap from my hands and comes closer to me while taking my hand in his and starts wrapping it.

He is so much taller than me. He is maybe six foot four. He doesn't say anything. He just wraps my hand up. His touch feels gentle, not how I thought. I would expect him to be rough, but he is being gentle, and his fingers are soft against my skin.

I didn't realize how close we really were until I feel his breathing on my skin.

He drops my wrapped hand and picks up the other one from my side, "You don't know how to wrap?" he asks.

"No, I do. I just always have trouble with it," I say softly while watching him.

He grabs my other wrap from the floor. "Hook the thumb strap over your thumb," he says softly while putting the strap over my thumb. "Wrap your wrist and forearm a few times," he does exactly that while touching my forearm sending a million chills throughout my body. "Bring the wrap to the heel of your palm and wrap your thumb," he wraps my thumb now holding onto my hand, "and your palm. Then you loop the wrap around your knuckles two times," he says while also inspecting my hand that has some scars on it. "Pass the wrap between each of your fingers," he passed the wrap between each of my fingers. "Then you spread your fingers a little and wrap your knuckles twice," he wraps it around my knuckles making them tight. "Then you secure it by passing the wrap around your wrist and then Velcro it," he finishes by pressing the cloth and Velcro together.

I look up at him and see him still towering over me just a few centimeters away from my nose.

I can see all his features up close now.

He has a few faded moles on his nose and scars on his cheeks and forehead. I look down at his lips and see they're plump and puffy probably from waking up.

I look back up to meet his eyes that, I swear, sparkle when they look down at me.

After what feels like hours of just staring at each other, Ace backs up, "Wanna spar?" he asks while walking towards his gloves.

"What?" I'm still a little fazed from a few seconds ago and I don't know what is real and what's not.

I'm not going to lie and say Ace isn't good-looking or handsome 'cause he is. Curse his good looks.

But I can't be distracted from what I am here for.

"Wanna spar?" he asks again looking at me.

"I guess," I say walking towards the ring they had installed in the gym.

I really like the layout of their gym. They even have a bathroom and a fridge. They have weights in all different sizes and then a huge mirror along an entire wall, they also have a floor to ceiling window on the side of the gym so you can see most of the city and the beach that is close by.

I climb in the ring and wait for Ace to appear. I see Ace walking in the ring with his gloves on. He has black gloves on while mine are red.

He got onto his side of the ring and into his position. "Ready?" he asks.

I get into my position. "Ready when you are."

"First one down for five seconds wins." Ace says while circling me.

"What do I get if I win?" I ask while following his movements.

"You can leave."

"Deal," I say before I go towards him.

The first move I make is a kick to the throat that makes him fall back a little.

"So, we're doing illegal kicks now?" Ace chokes out.

"You never said anything about rules," I say before lunging at him and kneeing him in the stomach.

He groans before regaining his strength and standing to his full height. Once he is close to me again, I punch him in the face and then throw another at his ribs but that doesn't do much damage.

He's about to punch me in the face, but I dodge it and throw a combination of punches to his face and chest.

He backs away but keeps his defensive position.

"You're good," he pauses before speaking again. "But not that good."

Before I know what's happening, he charges towards me and slams me down on the floor. He punches me lightly in the ribs and then holds me down by my hands.

"Seriously? You can't even punch me hard. If you're going to punch me at least do it with a little force so I feel it."

I then feel Ace punch me in the ribs much harder.

I wince and lift my hips making him loosen his grip on me. I then slide my legs out from under him and lock them around his neck and flip his body to fall on the other side of the mat hard.

I stand up and get back to my position while he is kneeling. I take his chin into my hand and make him look up at me. "This is a good position for you. I like seeing you on your knees." I smirk.

Ace swipes his feet under mine making me face backwards. "You play dirty," he speaks.

"Well, what did you expect me to do. Play by the rules?" I get up and now Ace and I are both standing.

He circles me as if I was his prey.

I see he's about to knock me down by sliding his feet under mine, so I jump up and throw a kick to his chest making him fall to the ground on his back.

Next thing I know I feel his hand on my ankle. He pulls my leg down making me fall on the ground next to him. And we are back in the position we were in before. He's straddling my hips and tightly gripping on both my wrists.

I try to lift my hips to get him off, but he stays put. I keep trying to lift them, but it's no use, he just keeps pressing his lower half against mine.

"If you think you're getting out of here anytime soon, you're wrong."

"Why? You like my presence that much?" I ask, struggling against his grip on my wrist.

"You know I kind of like this position," he smirks while staring down at me. "Wish it was under different circumstances."

"Sorry, I don't fuck my enemies," I spit.

"You know you should be thanking me for not putting you in a cell with all of the other prisoners. You wouldn't last ten minutes with them."

"Then why didn't you put me in there. It's not like I asked to come and stay at this luxurious mansion. Although I do love it and I'm not complaining."

He comes closer to my face and still has a good grip on my wrist, "Because, Aria, you amuse me. You're the only one here that talks back to me. It surprises me because usually, people who do that type of shit get killed in an instant, but you don't care. You test me," he said in my ear.

"Then why not kill me?" I challenge him.

"Because I think one day, you're probably going to do something that could make me loose my control."

"You're control?" I mutter out.

"Stop being so nervous," he says softly.

"I'm not nervous," I argue.

"Yes, you are. Your breathing increased and I could hear your heartbeat just from being this close to you."

I don't say anything. I just stare at him.

What am I even supposed to say?

Ace leans down towards my ear slowly. I could feel his warm

lips on the hood of my ear. I try to stay as still as possible so he knows that he couldn't affect me.

Why does he suddenly affect me?

I've barely known him for a week. He has been so moody every time I talk with him.

"I win," he says in my ear and then suddenly he completely lets go of me and stands up.

Six

I sit down next to Alicia who is drinking coffee in a white mug. She turns her head to look at me and I see her lips lift in a smile.

"Good morning, Aria. How did you sleep?" Alicia asks.

"Pretty good." I shrug.

I had been up all night trying to figure out a plan to get into Ace's office. He had guards and lock combinations for his office. I need to get in there so that I can get the information I need and get the hell out of here.

"Can I be honest with you Aria?" Alicia asks me and I look at her.

"Of course."

"I think you being here is good for us. For some reason I just have an amazing feeling about you being here and that you are going to do amazing things for us."

I don't know how to react to that. No one has said something that nice to me before. Plus, I have no clue how she thinks I could be a good influence around here. I mean, I literally snuck into their warehouse.

"Thank you, Alicia, but I don't know. I don't see how I am going to make a difference in your life."

"Things have been horrible for the past few years and nothing has been the same. Ace hasn't been the same. He used to be such a happy boy," Alicia says while smiling, probably reminiscing about a memory.

"What happened?" I ask trying to find a way to get information about the family.

It seems wrong but it's my job.

"Well, seven years ago, Ace's father died. It was a very tragic death." Alicia says with a sad look on her face.

So that's why he isn't around. He died.

But how?

"What happened if you don't mind me asking?" I ask.

Alicia sighs. "Ace's father was never the best at showing kindness or feelings but when I first met him, he was different. He showed kindness to me. I thought he was the most charming man ever. Soon I was pregnant, and he used me. He wanted an heir for the empire he built and then Ace came along," Alicia says. "When he was just a kid his father used to abuse and torment him. He made Ace's life a living hell," Alicia says, shaking her head lightly. "When Ace got older, he started to learn the ways of fighting, the ways to run his father's empire. But one night, Ace's father almost beat me to death and when Ace found out he went ballistic, and he killed him."

"Who?"

"Ace killed his father," Alicia admits and I see that she is almost about to cry.

I put my hand on her shoulder to somehow comfort her.

"I am so sorry Alicia. No one should ever go through that."

One tear falls from her eye. "I am telling you this Aria because I trust you. Maybe it's wrong of me but you have a good heart and I know that I can trust you with this information. Just please don't ruin it." She wipes a tear that had fallen. "Well, I have things to do," Alicia sits up from the stool. "If you need anything Aria don't be afraid to ask," she says smiling before she gets up and leaves.

Well, now I have more information about what happened to the original *capo*.

Yes, it's a shitty thing to use Alicia like that but I'm not here to make friends. I'm here for one thing and one thing only and I can't let Ace's trauma get in the middle of what I should be doing.

Yes, I feel bad for him and shitty but that's what this kind of job requires.

I look at the clock that was hung on the wall and see that it is six-thirty.

Perfect.

I get up from the stool and walk towards Ace's office. Better to do this now rather than later.

I can't stop thinking about what happened between Ace and his father. He killed his father when he was just a teenager, no wonder he acts all cold and emotionless. I hate him more than anything but that doesn't mean I can't feel bad for what he had to go through.

I am lucky enough to have a mother and father in my life who love me, even if my father doesn't know how to show it.

I see a guard in front of Ace's office. I let out a deep breath before hurriedly running towards the guard, acting terrified.

"I saw a man out in the backyard. I think he was trying to get inside," I say, acting terrified.

The guard looks worried, "Uh aren't there guards outside?"

"No, I didn't see them anywhere but please, you have to get him. He looked like he was trying to sneak in, and I saw him holding a knife and gun in his hands."

The guard nods his head and runs past me.

Way too easy.

I chuckle lightly before walking closer to the door. I take out my lock pickers and put them in the keyhole. There is a keypad, but I have no clue what the combination is so luckily there is a keyhole.

Once I pick the lock, I open the door and get inside. I walk towards Ace's desk and sit in his chair. I pull out one of his drawers and see it filled with burner phones, so I close it. I open another and see it is filled with small handguns. I open another drawer and see different files in there.

Bingo.

I look through the files and find one with my name on it. I open the file and see multiple pictures of me along with information about who I am and where I live.

He has our house address.

I look through more files and see the name of our mafia, so I take it out and look through it. It has everything you need to know about our mafia.

But how?

I have to contact my father and tell him that we have a mole because this is all just too much information about us and what we do or have done. It has money transfers, information about our alliances, shipments; everything.

I look at the rest of the files and see one for the Italian Mob.

Bingo again.

I grab the file at the same time I hear the door open. I put them under my shirt and turn around only to see Ace with a furious look on his face.

"What the fuck are you doing here?" Ace asks, giving me a dirty look.

I walk out from his desk, "I thought I saw someone in here. The door was open and then when I walked in, I saw your drawers open," I say pointing to the open drawers.

Ace walks closer to his desk and then he looks at me and furrows his eyebrows, "Where's Francisco?" Ace asks with a raised eyebrow.

"Who is Francisco?" I asked.

"The guard," Ace states and walks closer to me.

"He went to go check if anyone was out in the backyard."

Ace walks even closer and I back away from him making the back of my legs touch the desk.

"I am going to ask you one more time so you better answer," Ace states. "What were you doing in my office, Aria?"

"And I am going to tell you the same thing I told you a few seconds ago. I saw someone come inside here."

"You're a shit liar," he claims. He moves his face closer to mine. "If you step one foot inside of here again without me knowing I will make sure you feel as much pain as possible before I kill you," he whispers huskily. "Get the fuck out of my office."

I didn't waste another second before slipping away from him and leaving.

Seven

I'VE BEEN STAYING AT ACE'S MANSION FOR PROBABLY two weeks now.

Ace and I haven't talked since the little moment we had in the office. I've seen him in the hallways, but we didn't say a word to one another. During dinner, we sometimes glance at one another but that's it.

I've been spending most of my time with Emma when she isn't with Leo. But Leo is always working with Ace. Mia and Valentino are at school most of the time, so I don't get the chance to talk to them. Jared and Josh rarely come to the house but when they do, they always make sure to come and say hi to me.

Sometimes I spend time with Lana and help with dinner and just other jobs she needs help with even though she doesn't want me to.

I have also spent time with Ana and Alicia. I have gotten some more family history from them. They told me about how Ace was when he was little but that's it. I want to know more about Angelo though and what the deal with him is.

I miss my family as well. I miss them a lot. I miss hanging out with Layna and Cole. I even miss arguing with my brother. I also miss Ariel and all the stories she would tell me about Jack from school.

I have tried to contact Layna but when I did, she didn't answer. I called her phone off a burner phone that I found in Ace's office. But I think I'm going to ask Ace if I can call them. I feel lonely especially while staying in an unknown country with people I barely know.

Don't get me wrong I like everyone here, especially Emma. She has been so sweet, but I still don't know anyone here. My birthday is next week, and I'd rather spend it with my family. That's why I have to get all the information I can and then get out of here.

I have been trying to find a way out of here, but I can't escape. There are guards around the house 24/7 and then cameras everywhere.

Currently, I'm sitting on a stool in the kitchen while Lana is making food. She told me not to help because she doesn't need it. It looked like she was making spaghetti. Not hard so I didn't argue with her.

"What's wrong, Aria?" Lana asks.

I look at her, "Nothing. Just thinking."

"You know Ace has that same look on his face when he is stressed about something or nervous. So, I'm going to ask again. What's wrong?" Lana narrows her eyes at me.

"I just miss my family that's all. It's my birthday soon and I would've liked to see them. Don't get me wrong I like you guys a lot, but I just miss my family from back home."

I look away from her, not wanting to see her reaction.

I hate it when people see me being weak. It makes me feel unsafe and exposed to where anyone can hurt me. I would rather have physical pain than mental pain. Physical pain just goes away with time, but mental pain, that's always with you. It never leaves and I had to learn that the hard way.

"Well, I think you should ask Ace if you can call them. I don't know why you're still here. Now I would love to have you here for your birthday, but you miss your family," Lana says while chopping up onions. "Okay, dear. Go on now. Ask Ace," she ushers me away.

I get off the chair I was sitting on and walk towards Ace's office. I somehow manage to remember where everything in the house is. I walk towards his office door and freeze before knocking.

Is this a good idea?

I shove that question to the back of my head and twist the knob, opening the door.

I walk in and see Ace at his desk with his tie loosened around his neck and then the sleeves of his shirt pulled up his arms revealing his tattoo covered forearm.

I walk towards his desk and sit down on one of his chairs.

"You can never learn how to knock," Ace says as he looks at the screen of his computer. "What do you need, Aria?"

"I was wondering if I can call my mom or someone from home? I've been here for about a week or two. I just want to talk to someone," I say calmly.

"You have Emma to talk to." He muttered.

"Yeah, but she isn't my family."

He puts the paper he was holding down on the desk and looks up at me. "Why?"

"'Cause I want to," I answer harshly.

"Didn't your father disown you?" Ace raises his eyebrow at me.

"Doesn't mean the rest of my family doesn't love me."

He doesn't say anything. He scoots a little out of his desk and pulls one of his drawers out and takes out what looks like a burner phone.

"Speaker. You only get one call," he says as he tosses the phone on the desk.

"Okay."

I pick up the phone and dial the only other number I recognize. I put the phone on speaker like Ace asked and wait for the other line to start talking.

"Hello?"

"Layna?" I say into the phone.

"Hello? Aria? Is that you? Where the fuck are you? Everyone is freaking out!" Layna yells on the phone.

"Yeah I know. Look I just need to talk to you, okay? Tell me what's happening at the house."

"Okay well, Alex is worried shitless. Your mom is barely eating. She is worried sick about you and wondering if you're okay. Your dad-it doesn't matter what your dad thinks. You never liked him so..."

I wonder if she knows about this whole mission or not. I wonder if she is acting or if she is worried.

I look at Ace who is in front of me with a hand on his jaw as if he is trying to figure something out. "Layna what about my dad? Tell me. I want to know."

She doesn't talk for a bit. I first thought she hung up, but she was just thinking and then had a 'fuck it' moment.

"Your dad doesn't seem to care that much, Aria. Sorry but everyone misses you and they are worried. Alex is going through hell and back to get you to come back. Where are you even at? I answered all your questions but now you need to answer mine?" Layna demands.

Ace gives me a look as if saying 'tell them and I will kill you on the spot'.

Asshole.

I turn my attention back on the phone.

"Did Alex tell you anything?"

"No, he just said that on the mission you were kind of being held hostage but like he didn't say by who."

Oh Layna.

You just ruined everything.

Ace raises his eyebrow at me, but he doesn't seem mad which makes me kind of worried and a little scared because of what he might do.

"What do you mean mission?" I ask, trying to sound confused.

I don't hear anything on the other side of the phone for a few seconds. "Mission? I didn't say mission," Layna chuckles. "Anyways, where are you?" she asks trying to divert the conversation.

I look at Ace and see him giving me a look that says, 'tell her and I will kill you.'

"Italy. It's actually beautiful here," I deadpan while looking at my nails, picking at them.

"What the fuck Aria?!"

Ace then glares at me.

Oh, I am so going to get it after this phone call.

"Layna calm down. I'm fine. At least I'm alive. I called you because I miss you. I wanted to just tell you guys I'm fine and to not worry. I won't be gone for long."

"Okay, but if he or anyone lays a hand on you, I'll go batshit and find you."

"Okay Layna," I chuckle. "Look I have to go but tell mom I love and miss her. Make sure she eats. As for Alex, make sure he doesn't go crazy either and make sure he knows I'm fine. Don't forget to give a big kiss to Ariel for me and tell her I'm coming home soon."

"Of course. Ariel misses you a lot. We were supposed to go racing, Aria. Why did you have to get kidnapped? You have the worst timing," Layna says, laughing a little.

"Yeah, I guess I do. But hey, I am living in this luxurious mansion instead of camping in the woods, right?"

Layna chuckles. "Sure. I love you. Miss you too."

"Love you too," I say before hanging up and tossing the phone on the desk and looking at Ace who is glaring at me. "Are you just going to stare at me all day or are you going to say something?" I ask Ace.

He sits up straight now, "You really love tempting me."

"I'm not just going to call my best friend and not tell her where I am. I'm going back home. I may not be able to escape but I'm not staying in here forever."

"Yeah, you're not getting out of here anytime soon. By the way you probably would have gotten away with this whole mission you had going on if she didn't say that."

Shit.

"What mission?"

"Stop playing pretend. I knew you were lying a few days after you came here," Ace says in a bored tone. "Now, want to tell me what you are really here for?"

"Nope," I say with a small smile.

"I can get it out of you Aria if you don't tell me. So, either you tell me, or I will just have to make you," Ace threatens.

I roll my eyes at him, "I'd like to see you try." I stand up and walk towards the door but before I could put my hand on it, I feel a strong grip on my wrist, turning me around and pushing me against the wall. "Ow, you asshole."

"Tell me or die," Ace demands.

"I'd rather die," I smirk.

"Careful *amore* you might get your wish."

"I have been telling you to do it but you're all bark and no bite," I spit.

I knew what I said made him mad because his grip on my wrist tightened and his jaw clenched.

Ace leans closer to my face, I feel his breath on my ear. "Trust me, I will kill you Aria. But not until I get what I want from you. And I will make sure that your death will be the most painful one yet."

I push him away from me, "I'd like to see you try." I smirk before leaving his office and going to the kitchen.

When I walk inside, I see Emma on her phone, but she lifts her head and smiles at me. "Hey, I was wondering where you were." Emma says putting her phone down so she can give me her full attention.

"What's up?" I sit in the chair next to her.

"I was thinking that since you haven't been out for a while. We should go to the club. Me, you, Mia, Valentino, maybe Jared and Josh if they can? It'll be fun."

I know for a fact I am not allowed to leave the estate but with Ace pissing me off I don't give a flying fuck. It will also give me a chance to escape. I already have what I need which is a file that tells me all about the Italian Mafia and their secrets.

"When are we going?" I ask.

"Tonight."

Eight

Currently, Emma and I are on our way to Ace's club. I was kind of worried about Ace seeing me there, but Emma told me it was fine. If he sees me then it will ruin my plan to escape. I got what I needed so now I just need to get the hell out and go back home.

Plus, now that he knows what my plan is, I *need* to leave Italy.

One of the drivers is taking us to the club right now. Emma said that it would be better for us and our safety.

I am wearing a red strapless dress that stops at my mid-thighs. It looks very flattering on me. Emma had some dresses in her closet, so she just gave me this one. In my closet, all I had were leggings, pajama shorts, tank tops, and some sweaters because I requested them and then some regular clothes for me to wear. Also, undergarments.

Emma is wearing a pink strapless dress. It hugs all her perfect curves in the right places. She did my hair and makeup because I can't do makeup for shit. Although I do it for missions, I'm still kind of shit at it.

Once the driver stops the car, Emma tells him that she will call him to pick us up. We head into the club and lights are flashing, very few people are dancing, and music is playing.

This is the kind of setting I love to be in.

I feel free.

Happy even.

"Come on let's go get drinks," Emma says, breaking me out of whatever trance I was in.

"When are Mia and Valentino going to be here?" I ask while following her.

"They should be here already. Let me text them," Emma says once we sit down on the barstool chairs.

I order a drink from the bartender. He has black shaggy hair and looks a little pale. I notice he has a black diamond stud earring on his right ear.

While Emma texts them, I take the drink from the bartender.

I'm planning on leaving the club from the back when Emma is drunk enough or occupied with Leo. Valentino seems like the type to get blackout drunk so he shouldn't see me leave. I'll just have to make sure Mia doesn't see me.

Then once I leave, I will just steal a car and drive to the airport, hopefully there is a jet or some way I can get away from this fucking country.

"Hey, guys!" I hear Mia say.

I turn to look at her. I see Valentino standing next to her.

Mia is wearing a black dress with an opening on her torso where you can see her toned stomach. Valentino is just wearing a black dress shirt and some black jeans with his classic chain he wears everyday around his neck.

"Hey. Where were you guys?" Emma says.

"We were dancing a little. But now that you guys are here, we can get some drinks!" Valentino hollers. He looks at me with the drink in my hand, "Hey, you already started drinking." He says with a frown on his face.

"It's one shot. I was getting impatient," I say before ordering multiple drinks for us all.

Probably not smart to be drinking while trying to escape but what can one shot do? I don't get drunk easily, so I'll be fine.

The rest of the group takes multiple shots while I just order a soda to sip on. Valentino grabs my hand while Mia and Emma follow.

I start dancing with the girls and Valentino, getting lost in the music.

The song playing is "Acquainted" by The Weeknd. Layna and I would always sing this song and dance to it when we were drunk at the house.

We're all just singing the lyrics while dancing and moving our hips. Valentino tries to rotate his hips and twerk while all of us stare at him and laugh.

For the past month, I felt so alone and bored. But I don't feel alone anymore. I don't know if it is because I had a drink or two or if it is because I'm hanging out with Emma and everyone but right now, I don't care.

Two years ago, I wasn't the same girl I am right now. The difference between me right now and me before is that I have a backbone and am stronger. And it's all because of him.

He made me feel this way. He made me feel like a monster and more closed off with my emotions. That's the only thing I can thank him for though, making me stronger. But he broke me.

Right now, I feel open as if I'm finally free. Free from him.

But that's probably the alcohol because there is no way that anything could make me want to open up or let my guard down. Alcohol is kind of like therapy but not a particularly good one 'cause then you depend on it. Right?

"I'm going to get more drinks. Anyone want to come?" Emma asked while yelling over the music.

"No, I'm fine," I yell over the music.

"I'll come!" Mia says.

"Well, I need to go take a piss then. Aria, are you sure you're going to be good?!" Valentino asks me loudly.

I nod my head and they go. Perfect timing for me to leave.

I'm about to leave but then I feel hands slide onto my waist. The hands start to go lower and lower, so I slap his hands away. Obviously, the motherfucker doesn't understand because he keeps doing it.

"Okay, buddy I think it's time for me to go," I say, tapping his hands to get them from me.

He still doesn't let go. He only tightens his grip on my hips.

If I had a knife, I would have cut his fucking fingers off, but I don't.

He tightens his grip again before pulling me over to a secluded area of the club where barely anyone is at. He holds me against the wall and holds my hands. I take my knee and shove it to where his dick is. He immediately lets me go and falls to the floor.

Jackass.

Time to fucking get out of this place.

I'm about to leave the secluded area this man brought me too but then I felt his hands on me again. "Fuck, did I give you the wrong drink or something?" I hear the man mutter.

Drink?

He fucking tried to spike it.

I elbow him but he dodges it and pushes me hard against the wall again. "Fucking asshole let me go!" I demand.

I see him dig into his pocket and pull out a pill. I try to punch him again, but he won't let go of my hands. I knee him in the balls again, but he doesn't seem as fazed by it.

The fuck?

How can he not feel that? I just kneed him.

Is he really that desperate?

I try to move again but the next thing I know he puts the pill he was holding in my mouth. Once it hits my tongue, I taste salty powder and feel it dissolve. I quickly spit it out and it lands on his face. He stumbles back a little.

"Ewww. You fucking bitch," he says.

I walk towards him and punch him in the stomach and then knee him again but much harder.

"Asshole," I mutter once he is on the floor.

Now it's time to get the fuck out of here. I turn around to leave but instead I see Ace leaning on a wall watching me.

Shit.

"Ace," I state, before making a move to leave the secluded area, but he blocks me. "You need something or-"

"What the fuck are you doing here Aria?" Ace asks.

"Well people go to clubs because they want to party so-"

"Did I say you could leave the house?"

"I don't need your permission to do anything. Let's get one thing straight. You're not the boss of me. You may have your little whores that you boss around and then all of your workers that will kneel to you, but I won't."

Next thing I know I get pushed against the wall with Ace holding my wrist down and his lower half pressed against mine. I feel heat spread across my cheeks but you wouldn't be able to tell because it's dark in the hallway.

"You are in my club, my country, and staying under my roof. Don't be fucking disrespectful like that. I had enough of your damn mouth. Maybe I should treat you like one of my damn whores, so you show some respect."

"That's rape," I state. "You didn't even help me from that guy who was trying to rape me."

"You can handle yourself Aria."

"Well, you still could have helped me..." I say while my voice starts to trail off.

It's like I start getting tired of talking. I can't say anything that I was thinking. I feel hazy.

"It's your fault that..."

His voice starts to become muffled and I can't hear him. I can see him and his lips moving but I can't hear.

My eyes feel like they are getting heavy and eventually, all I see is darkness.

My head pounds as I open my eyes fully. I put my hand to my

head to try and calm down the headache I have, but it doesn't work.

I sit up from the bed and look around the room I'm in. This isn't my room. Don't tell me I hooked up with anyone.

God, you're stupid Aria.

Really?

You just had to get dick while drunk?

Before I can think of something to do, I hear a door open revealing Ace in just a towel low on his hips with wet hair and droplets of water running down his body.

Oh, fuck.

God, why are you acting like the Virgin Mary every time you're around him?

Wait did I sleep with him?

Before he noticed I was awake I check my body to see any signs if I had sex with him or not and I don't see any. All I'm wearing are shorts and a sweater. I also have my bra on underneath so we can work with that.

Thank God.

"There are pills by the bed. Take them and get out," he says while walking over to what I assume is the closet. "Meet me in my office after you change into something decent."

Damn who pissed in his coffee?

I take the pill and leave his room.

Maybe he will tell me what happened?

All I remember was dancing with everyone. Then me about to leave. That guy trying to rape me. Everything else is a little foggy. But I remember seeing Ace's face at the club.

I go into what is now my room and get changed into a pair of leggings and a white Chanel top. I could honestly not care less about what I look like right now.

I leave my room and start heading towards Ace's office.

I don't know if he's there or not, but I don't care. He said to meet him in his office so I'm going to do just that. I walk downstairs and then head straight to his office.

When I walk in I don't see him.

His office is very boring.

I walk around his desk over to his wall of shelves that look like it would be in a library. He has a few books and some folders on some shelves.

I'm surprised he doesn't have pictures. His office seems so formal. So many files and papers.

I didn't have time to snoop the last time I was here so might as well now.

I see some files on his desk, so I decide to snoop and look at some of the files.

This reminds me of the files I took from before.

Shit.

I hope he didn't go into my room and snoop or any of the maids because if they did then they would find those. But I hid those files under the mattress of the bed so I should be fine.

I go to his desk and sit in his chair. I pull out one file that was in the front and center of his desk. I open it up and it looks like a bunch of money transfers and property information.

It looks like he is buying property from the Mexicans.

Wonder what?

I was about to flip the page of the file until I hear a door opening. I quickly put the file back in the same place it was before.

"What the hell are you doing?" Ace says in a demanding tone.

I look at the door and see Ace standing there with a not so pleasant look.

"Relax, Hulk. I have a question," I state before asking, "Do you always ask the same thing 24/7? I feel like every time we talk, you always ask, 'What am I doing.'" He rolls his eyes and starts to walk towards his desk, towards his chair that I am sitting on. He stands in front of me while I'm just sitting in his chair. "Yes?" I question.

"Get off my chair and go sit in the other ones like a good girl," he demands.

I roll my eyes and stand up. "Your no fun Mr. De Luca," I say while walking out from his desk sliding in between him and the desk. Making sure to tease him. I sit down on the chair in front of him waiting for him to speak. He doesn't say anything for like two minutes and I'm starting to get impatient. "Are you saying something or are we just going to stare at each other?"

I look at Ace's hands and notice he squeezed them twice. I notice he does that a lot when he is trying to control his anger or himself.

He sits in his chair and looks at me. "So, someone is trying to kidnap you."

Nine

"WHAT?"

"You were drugged. At the club," Ace claims coldly.

"You were there?" I furrow my eyebrows.

"Yeah. You don't remember?" Ace asks, sounding surprised.

"I mean I remember but the ending is kind of foggy."

"What do you remember?"

"I remember Emma and I meeting Val and Mia at the club. We got drinks. I only had one shot and then another drink that I sipped on. Then we all started dancing. Emma and Mia went to go get drinks and Val went to go to the bathroom. I stayed back and uh...danced." I'm not going to admit that I tried to escape because that's just stupid. "I then felt this guy groping and touching me. He took us to this secluded area in the club and then long story short I fought him off. I'm pretty sure he tried to spike my drink because he said that he got the wrong drink or whatever. Then he put some pill in my mouth, but I spit it out." This is when things start getting foggy. "I got him off of me and then I think I saw you but that's all I could remember."

"So, you don't remember anything else after that?" Ace asks. I shake my head no and he doesn't say anything. Ace looks up at me again. He looks pissed but also like he's thinking hard about something. "Do you remember what the bar server looked like?"

"Uh yeah kind of. But why would you need the bar server? He isn't the one who tried to spike my drink."

He stands up from his desk and fixes his suit that he's wearing. "Come on. Put some shoes on," he says ignoring me.

I stand up as he walks over to the door. "Where are we going?"

"My club. Meet me in the car. I'll be in the front waiting. Don't take long," he demands before walking out of the office door.

Once we arrive at Ace's club, he doesn't say a word and gets out of the car. I don't know if I'm supposed to stay in the car or not. I get out of the car and decide to follow him inside of his club.

When we walk inside the club, there weren't many people. I see a group of men in suits in a room that's upstairs and overlooking the entire club.

I continue walking forward not watching where I'm going and end up bumping into Ace's back.

He turns around and looks at me. "Watch it," he spits.

"Well, you weren't moving."

He rolls his eyes. "Whatever. This is the last place to start shit with me. I won't tolerate any of the attitudes so keep it in check. Sit down at a table somewhere. Don't talk to anyone here. Just sit and wait for me. *Comprendere?*"

"What am I? A fucking dog?" I say without thinking.

He looks down at me and gives me a dark look. "Aria I swear to God I will not hesitate to show everyone in this club who is the boss between me and you. I'll put you over my fucking knee and make your little ass beat red."

I feel tingles in my stomach and before I could argue with him, he leaves without another word and walks upstairs.

I could try to escape.

Should I?

It's a perfect opportunity though, isn't it?

I look around the club trying to see if there is any way I can leave without being seen.

I'll just walk out the door because who's going to stop me?

Ace?

Deciding I'm going to escape I walk towards the entrance of the club and walk out.

That was easy.

I look over at Ace's car that's parked in the front. Thank God I know how to hot-wire a car. I walk towards his car and break the glass of his window with my elbow.

I unlock the door and get inside the car. I grab the wires from his car and try to hot-wire the car. Once I hear the car roar to life, I start to get excited. I'm finally going home. I'm about to switch gears but then I hear the car door open and I get pulled out of the car roughly.

"Ow, what the hell?" I look up, seeing Ace.

"What part of 'stay put' do you not understand?" He grabs my wrist and pulls me up to my feet and pushes me against the car. "I should kill you right now."

"I've been telling you to do it," I try to get his hands off of me, but his grip is too tight.

"You're lucky that those men up there didn't see you or else they would have shown you how to show some god damn respect or they would probably just kill you," Ace spits.

"I will never show respect to someone like you."

Ace grabs my wrist and pulls me inside the club. He pulls me towards the table in the back and snaps his fingers making two excessively big and buff men walk towards us.

"Watch her and whatever you do, don't let her out of your sight," Ace spits at them before glaring at me and walking away back upstairs.

"So, what're guy's names?" I ask them but they don't answer. Fuckers. "I'm Aria White. Nice to meet you guys. I honestly am in love with the music they are playing right now. I do love R&B music more but I honestly-"

"Would you shut the fuck up girl?" One of the men spit.

"Girl?" I'm sorry but the disrespect. "I have a fucking name you assholes."

"You're just De Luca's whore of the week. You're nothing," the other one says.

Whore?

They think I'm a whore?

I grab the gun from one of their pockets and hit him in the head with it. They both turn around and the one who has his gun aims it at me.

"Put the gun down or I'll shoot."

I ignore him and shoot him where his hand is holding the gun. He drops the gun and holds his hand while screaming in pain.

The other one makes a move to try and attack me, but I sit up from my seat and kick him in the face and punch him. He stumbles but doesn't fall. I stand to my full height and hit him in the head with the gun making him fall to the floor.

While all of this is happening almost everyone is staring and some girls who were dancing are now screaming.

Fucking pussies.

The one who I shot is still holding his hand. I shoot him again on both of his knees so that he can't stand up and catch me.

Finally, home free.

I grab the other gun from the floor and I'm about to turn around, but I notice that everyone is too silent.

No one is screaming or yelling. Instead, they are all staring at me. Or more specifically something behind me.

"Oh, shit."

"Oh, shit is right," I hear from behind me.

I turn around and face Ace.

Shit, what do I do now?

"Are you going to ask me the same question you always ask?" I ask him while gripping onto the gun in my hand. He doesn't say anything he's just glaring at me while his hands are clenched into fists. "Well, I'm going to go. I have somewhere to be. But thank you so much for being an amazing host and letting me stay in your home," I say while walking away from him slowly. "But I got to go." I'm about to walk away but Ace grabs onto my wrist. I turn around and aim the gun at him. "I have a gun that can actually shoot bullets. And it's not on safety so I would be careful if I were you."

"Then shoot me Aria. You shoot me, then you will have a whole mafia after you. Trained assassins and killers. You'll be dead by morning," Ace says calmly.

"Like I give a fuck," I say before pulling the trigger, but nothing comes out.

Fuck.

No bullets.

I quickly make a move to grab the other gun I have in my pocket, but Ace is fast, so he grabs both of my wrists and pulls me forward and grabs the gun.

He checks to see if there are any bullets and there are. He puts the safety on and then lets me go.

"Stop fucking messing around Aria," Ace mutters before walking past me towards a table. "Someone come and get these fucking bodies on the floor!" Ace yells.

Ace and I sit at the table and stare at each other while there are men who help up the two bodyguards who are clutching onto their hands and knees, where I shot them.

"Damn maybe they shouldn't have tried to stop me from escaping and then they wouldn't be in so much pain," I say while watching them leave but one of them turns around to glare at me as someone was helping him stand.

"You're going to be gone by the end of the week. Again, you are just his current flavor." he spits.

I chuckle. "You're just mad that a girl who is smaller than you shot both of your kneecaps. Now run along."

"I'm going to kill you," he says while leaning closer to me and wincing.

"Yeah, get in line," I roll my eyes and look back at Ace who is staring at me. "Are you going to get rid of him, or should I?"

"Kill him," Ace states and then as one of Ace's men pulls the man away, he just screams profanities and curses us both out.

"You have such lovely soldiers, De Luca. Wish I could snag one," I comment. "Anyways, why did we even come here? Or why did you bring me? You were obviously busy."

"Only reason you aren't dead right now is because I still need you," Ace deadpans. "Do you recognize anyone at the bar from last night?"

I look towards the bar and just see a bunch of workers.

There is a girl who is cleaning up the counters, a guy who is talking to a customer, and another guy who is making a drink.

The guy who is talking to a customer looks a little familiar. He has black shaggy hair. He is lean and has a little muscle, wearing a black long sleeve with his sleeves rolled up. I look more closely and see he has a diamond stud on his ear.

"He looks familiar. He is the one talking to the customer. He has a diamond stud," I say to Ace while pointing to the guy with the diamond stud earring.

He looks at the guy and his eyes darken. He gets out of his seat without saying a word.

Oh God, what is he doing?

I get up quickly and follow him.

"Do you work here?" Ace asks once he gets to the guy.

There is a customer right by us just staring at Ace with confusion and fear in his eyes.

"Uh, yeah," the diamond stud guy says.

Ace then turns to the customer. "Leave."

The customer doesn't waste a second before leaving and dashing out the door. Ace walks closer to the bartender while I just stand behind and watch.

"Do you recognize her?" Ace asks, pointing to me.

The guy looks at me. His face reveals that he does because he looks shocked that I'm here. I raise an eyebrow at him.

"Uh no. Why?"

"Bullshit. Now I'm going to ask you another question. Do you know who runs this club?" Ace asks in a menacing tone.

"Y-Yeah," the guy stutters.

"Good, then this will be a lot easier." After Ace says that he picks the guy up by his collar and drags him out of the bar and through the hallways and out the back door.

I follow them out the door and Ace pushes the guy on the floor.

"What the fuck is your problem man?!" the guy says standing up from the floor.

"Last night you were working at my club. I know all my workers because I do background checks on all of them. You, however, I don't know. Now if you lie to me again, I will be *making you wish you were dead*. Do you recognize her?!" Ace yells while pointing at me. The guy looks at me again. He then looks at Ace's murderous face. He shakes his head multiple times. "You know I have cameras? Right?!" Ace says.

"Dude, I didn't mean to. I was just-" the guy says.

"What? You were just what?" The guy doesn't say anything. He just keeps whimpering. "Alright, I'm getting tired of this." Ace then takes the gun out of his trousers and hits the guy in the head with the gun making him close his eyes and fall limp to the floor.

"Harsh."

"Fuck off," he spits as he pulls out his phone dialing a number. He puts the phone to his ear and waits a few seconds before speaking. "Francisco, I need you to come here and pick up this body immediately." After a few seconds, Ace hangs up and puts it in his pocket. "God, you're fucking stupid," Ace mutters.

"Excuse me?" I ask looking at Ace.

He looks down at me. "You're fucking stupid. Do you not pay attention to your surroundings? Because of you, now I have to do another background check on my staff and make sure this doesn't happen again."

"It's not my fault that I attracted a guy!" I yell. "God, you're such a dick," I mutter and cross my hands against my chest.

"You haven't seen anything yet, *amore*."

"Stop calling me those stupid pet names. I'm not one of your little girlfriends."

"If you think I actually bother having a girlfriend then you're stupid."

"I know you don't have a girlfriend. With an attitude like yours, I'm not surprised you don't have one," I say to Ace. "You say I'm the one who doesn't show respect when you're the one who treats me like a dog instead of a human being."

"Says you. You're the one who doesn't listen to simple directions."

"I'm not a dog, De Luca. I'm not anyone's pet and I never will be."

Last time I was someone's pet it almost got me killed and I will never ever put myself in that kind of position again.

Ten

"Now, I'm going to ask you one more time. If you don't answer, then it's another finger," Ace says while circling Damien.

Damien is the guy with the diamond stud. It's the bartender who drugged me or at least helped try to. He admitted he recognized me but that was after Ace cut off his pinky finger.

After Francisco picked us up, Ace dragged me to his car, and we met up with Francisco at the house. We took Damien to the basement for torturing and interrogation. Ace told me to just follow him and watch. Kind of wish I could do something because I am bored of watching Ace do the work.

But I do want to see why so many people are afraid of him.

Ace asked for his name and that's the only question he answered easily. Ace then started asking questions about me and he started with very simple punches to the face but then he got frustrated and brought out the knife and started slicing fingers and stabbing him.

And here we are.

Ace has been asking questions, but Damien is not cooperating. He's just staying silent.

"Do you want another finger cut off or maybe I should just start with the eyes?" Ace asks, getting into Damien's face.

We wait for Damien's response, but he doesn't say anything.

Ace pulls out his phone making a call.

"Come to the basement and get this asshole out of his clothes. Make sure he is chained up tightly. Cut off his clothes and don't let him get away," Ace hangs up and puts his phone in his pocket.

"You know I don't think you're going to get the information you need by just cutting his fingers off," I state but Ace ignores me and turns towards Damien.

"You better be ready 'cause this is going to be a hell of a ride for you."

Without another word, Ace leaves the room and I follow after him. "What are you going to do?"

"He has a tattoo somewhere so I'm going to find it."

"How do you know?"

"Because my men did a background check on him."

"Why do you need to find the tattoo though?"

He looks at me and places a smirk on his face, "You will see, *amore.*"

His men come into the basement and go into the room Damien is in. We hear yelling and a lot of unpleasant words from Damien.

After they are done Ace and I go back into the room and we

see he is fully unclothed. Along with his dick out. I try to avoid staring at his dick. It looks like it hasn't been shaved for weeks or months even. Doesn't look clean either, wouldn't be surprised if he had some sort of disease.

Ace looks at my disgusted face and chuckles a little.

Ace walks around Damien's body looking for the tattoo. Once Ace finds it, he takes the knife in his hand and starts to cut it off, skinning him. All you can hear is Damien's screams and him pleading for mercy.

His tattoo is on his bicep area, so it has got to hurt. There is blood dripping down Damien's arm and there is some blood on Ace's suit.

"Good. Now that you aren't branded. Fucking. Talk."

Damien still doesn't say anything. He is just panting. He has sweat droplets running down his forehead.

Ace shrugs and walks over to the table where he keeps guns, knives, matches, gasoline; just torturing tools, I guess.

As I lean against the wall near the door, I take in Ace's appearance.

Blood on his white dress shirt, sleeves rolled up making his tattoos visible, and him inspecting different weapons on the table. I swear I can feel my pupils dilate as I take him in.

I understand why so many people are afraid to be on his bad side.

Ace walks back with a smaller knife and he gets closer to Damien's face.

He holds the knife up to Damien's eye and holds it open, so he doesn't close it.

"Alright! Alright! I'll talk!" Damien yells making Ace stop.

"Speak." Ace demands.

"I was sent to watch after you and her. Boss said he wanted me to send a warning to you and her," Damian says with his voice shaking in fear.

Definitely put the wrong man on the job.

"What else? I know there is something else?"

Damien doesn't answer Ace. Ace shrugs and starts moving the knife forwards.

"Stop! Okay! I'll tell you!" Damien yells out. "He is coming after your empire. Your entire Organization. Also, the Americans. He doesn't want anyone to stand in his way for what he has planned," Damien answers.

"Why is he coming after me and her?" Ace demands while folding his arms over his chest making his biceps look bigger.

Jesus.

"He is trying to get rid of you all one by one."

"Who?"

"D'yavol."

"So, you're Russian?" I ask coming closer.

Damien nods his head.

"What else?" Ace asks.

"That's all I know man. I swear," Damien answers with a shaking voice again.

"Why you?"

"I'm the best assassin on the team," Damien claims.

Sure doesn't seem like it with all of his whimpering. Ace got information out of him quickly.

Ace stands up from his spot. He walks over to the table and I see him eye the flame gun.

He picks it up along with the gasoline. He walks towards Damien and starts to cover him in gasoline, making Damien whimper and scream in terror because of the gasoline touching his fresh cuts and under the skin.

"Do you know what I can do?" Ace asks. Damien looks as if he is going to pee himself. Damien nods his head. "Then why have you decided to fuck with me?" Damien doesn't say anything making Ace chuckle. "Ah, I'm getting frustrated. *Saluta Satana da parte mia.*"

After Ace says those last few words, he turns on his flame gun and makes contact with Damien's skin. Damien's whole body lights up with fire and his bloody screams are louder than before. He looks unrecognizable. He looks like something you would see in a horror movie.

As Ace holds the flame gun to Damien's body, I see his eyes sparkle again. I can see how much he loves fire. The way the red and orange compliment one another as it spreads on Damien's body.

I never used fire for killing someone. I usually used knives and skinned them. They were my favorite weapon. I trust knives a lot. I have no clue why.

Ace's men come into the room after Ace calls them. They are wrapping Damien's now burned body. You can even see part of his bones and organs that were burned. It looks gruesome.

Sometimes I wonder if what I'm doing is right. But I know the people I kill are all bad. I know I'm not a bad person but being in this kind of business isn't good either. It's hard to be a good person and being an assassin. My mom is a good person. I know that for sure. She just got pulled into this life unexpectedly.

"Now what?" I ask Ace as he comes towards me after talking with his men.

"We call your father."

"Sit," Ace demands as soon as we walked inside his office.

I roll my eyes at his command. "Why are you always so demanding?"

He doesn't respond, he just goes and sits in his chair.

He pulls open a drawer from his desk and takes out a burner phone and throws it on the desk. "Do you know your father or brother's number?" I nod my head. "Call them."

I pick up the phone and start to dial Alex's number.

On the third ring, he picks up. "Hello?"

"Hey, Alex," I say.

"Aria? What the fuck?! Are you okay? I swear if that fucker touched you-"

"I'm fine Alex, chill." I pause and mouth to Ace 'what do you want me to say'.

He makes a gesture with his hand signaling me to give the phone to him. I roll my eyes and give him the phone. Why make me call him if you're just going to take the phone?

"Alex," Ace states.

"Ace," I hear Alex growl from the other side of the phone.

"Look now I'm not here to argue or fight. We have a little issue."

"No, you fucker. You took my sister away from me. What makes you think I'm going to help you?"

Again, I can't tell if he is acting or not but if he is then he is a hell of a good actor. I mean my cover with Ace is blown so he has no reason to act anymore.

"Because if you don't, Aria is going to die along with your wife and kid so fucking listen," Ace roars on the phone.

"Okay, what is it?"

"Bratva," Ace states.

"What about them?"

"I got into it with one of their assassins today. He drugged Aria the other night while she was at my club. He is dead now, but he said he worked for the Russians. So here is what is going to happen, you're going to get your ass down here along with your dear father and we're going to figure this shit out. Cause if you think I'm going to have Russian fiche threaten me, you're wrong," Ace says in a threatening voice. "Dimitri is planning something, and I want to get to the bottom of it."

I am guessing Dimitri is the leader of the Russian Bratva. I don't really focus on other Mafias so I wouldn't know much. That's more of Alex's specialty.

Alex stayed silent for a minute probably thinking before he spoke up. "Okay. I'll meet you in three days. Where is Aria?"

"Next to me. She's fine."

"Let me talk to her," Alex states. Ace rolls his eyes and hands me the phone. "Aria is this you?"

"Yes, Alex this is me. I'm fine. I'm not hurt or staying in an ugly cell. You forgot that I know how to handle myself."

"I know you know how to handle yourself Aria, but I don't trust Ace."

"He is fine. He is a dick, but he hasn't touched me," I say while making eye contact with Ace.

"Okay I got to go but I'll see you in a few days, sis. Your birthday is coming up? Isn't it?"

"Yeah why?"

"Just making sure. Love you." Alex says and then hangs up.

I throw the phone on the desk and look at Ace. He stands up and starts to take off his white dress shirt that is covered in Damien's dried blood.

"Your brother is super annoying, you know, that right?" Ace states coldly.

"He is just worried. He is always like that," I say while watching Ace strip out of his shirt. "So, what now?" I ask while trying not to stare at his bare, tattooed chest.

"What do you fucking think?" He growls.

"Sorry I was just wondering. No need to be a bitch about it."

"Says the one who needed my help when she was about to get raped," Ace says while walking to the back of the room.

"I didn't need your help. I said it would have been nice to have your help instead of you just staring. And are you ever going to not bring that up every time we talk? It's fucking annoying and I don't need someone bringing that up all the time. Especially you."

Ace doesn't say anything. I'm about to stand up and leave but I hear Ace wince. I turn around and see that he is wiping a burn that he had.

How did he get that? I didn't even see him burn himself.

Should I help him or leave him to suffer?

Curse my mother for raising me to be a decent person.

I walk over to Ace and move his hands away from the burn so

that he can't touch it. It's on his chest. It looks like it hurts a lot. I didn't even know he got burned.

I look at Ace and see him already staring at me. I walk closer to him and inspect the burn.

"It's going to get infected if you don't clean it now," I state. "Where is your first aid kit?" I ask him while looking around the office.

"I can do it myself," Ace growls.

"Then why were you whimpering like a little girl?" I ask and raise my eyebrows.

"Just fuck off Aria," he says and pushes me out of his way.

"What the hell is wrong with you? I'm just trying to help and be nice to you. Something you obviously know nothing about."

"I don't need you," Ace says while looking through the cabinets for the first aid kit.

"Obviously," I mutter.

I walk over to where he is looking for the first aid kit. I push him back a little and try to find the first aid kit and when I do, I turn around and hold it so he can see I found it.

He tries to grab it but instead, I throw it into my other hand.

"Stop fucking around Aria. Give me the damn kit."

I smirk at Ace. "Fine," I throw the first aid kit across the room. "Fetch."

Ace looks at the kit and back at me. "The fuck did you just say?" The look he's giving me is priceless.

"Fetch," I repeat.

Ace then starts walking towards me and I take a step back. Every time I step away from him, he just takes a step closer. Eventually, I feel my back touch the wall. Ace is now right in front of me. His face is a few centimeters away from my face.

He puts his hands on top of the wall on each side of my head, trapping me.

He leans his face closer to mine so that his nose is close to touching mine. "You love testing me, don't you?" Ace asks. I feel his hot breath on my cheek making me breathe a little harder. "Mhm?"

"Treat others the way you want to be treated right?" I whisper back and look up at him.

I see Ace's eyes divert to my lips and back up to my eyes. I look down at his lips and back up at his eyes. His green eyes are darker than before.

It's like there is magnetic energy pulling us closer towards each other.

It's not long before I feel Ace's lips on mine.

Eleven

"Good morning," Lana beams as I walk inside the kitchen.

"Morning," I smile at her and sit down at one of the stools. "What are you making?"

"Crepes. Haven't made them in a while so just thought I should. How are you doing? Did you sleep okay?"

"Yeah. My dad and brother are coming in a few days. Ace and I talked to him yesterday."

"That's exciting. Are you excited to see them?" Lana asks.

"Yeah. Hopefully, I get to go home," I shrug.

My mind then goes back to yesterday.

Ace and I kissed.

And I liked it.

A lot more than I should have.

And finally, his lips met mine.

His lips caused a shock of electricity throughout my body once he placed them on my own. His muscular ascent consumed my sense and I kissed him back. His tongue grazed my bottom lip. He bit my lip softly and a moan escaped. He used this as an opportunity to plunge his tongue inside my mouth.

The kiss was frantic and filled with lust and need.

Just a few seconds ago I was treating him like a dog and wanted to beat the shit out of him and now I'm kissing him? I'm kissing the enemy. This is wrong on so many levels, but it also feels so right.

I feel Ace's hands on my hips. Because I was wearing thin leggings, I felt his warm touch through the leggings.

"You piss me off so much you know that?" Ace said while trailing down my neck and kissing me there.

"Well, you're not the easiest person to be around," I grabbed his jaw and make our lips touch again.

This is wrong. I can't be kissing him. I'm supposed to hate him.

Before I could pull away from the kiss, I heard the door open making Ace remove his lips from mine and lift his head up to see who it was.

We both see Jared walk in and I push Ace off me, hoping that Jared didn't see anything but I'm pretty sure he did.

"What Jared?" Ace said and I look down at his hands and see that he is squeezing them.

"Uh, you have a phone call sir."

"About what?" Ace asked.

Jared looked at me and back at Ace. "It's private."

"I'm going to go," I stated and started walking towards the door.

"Leave, Jared." I heard Ace say as I walked out of the office.

That kiss shouldn't have happened. It won't happen again either. Never again.

"Good morning, Lexi," Lana says, making me break out of my thoughts and look at Lexi who walked inside the kitchen, wearing only a white dress shirt that was basically drowning her.

"Good morning, Lana," Lexi says in a very chirpy voice.

She walks more inside the kitchen and sits down next to me. I notice that she isn't wearing any pants.

I don't need to guess why she is dressed like that. It's obvious, especially with that grin on her face.

"How did you sleep dear?" Lana asks.

"Pretty fantastic actually."

"That's amazing. I'm glad that both of you girls are well rested," Lana smiles.

"Very well rested," Lexi smirks before looking at me.

The fuck is she looking at me like that for?

"I need to get some stuff from the pantry. I'll be right back."

"I can get it for you Lana," I say stopping her while standing from my seat. "What do you need?"

"Eggs and some more flour," Lana says and I leave the kitchen and walk down the hallway into the other kitchen.

So, the De Lucas have two kitchens. One small one that is connected to the dining room and then another for when there are bigger dinners and when everyone is cooking.

At home we just have one big kitchen, but the De Lucas like to be extra.

I walk over to where the pantry is, and I look inside for the flour. While looking I hear footsteps walking inside the kitchen making me turn around.

I see Lexi with a small smirk on her face and her arm crossed over her chest. She was just observing me.

Weirdo.

I turn back around and grab the flour before turning around, seeing that Lexi is right in front of me.

"Can I help you?" I ask, raising my eyebrow.

"You know Ace is really good in bed," Lexi claims with a smirk still present on her face.

"And I care why?"

"Just thought I'd let you know."

"I could have gone on with the rest of my day without that information you just disclosed but thanks anyways," I move past her and go towards the fridge that is on the opposite side of the room.

"I also wanted to tell you to back off."

I turn around and place the flour bag I have in my hand on the island that's in the middle of the kitchen. "Excuse me?"

"You heard me. Ace doesn't want you. So, back off and go back to wherever you came from," Lexi threatens.

I raise my eyebrow at her, daring her to say that again. "I don't want that baboon trust me. You two deserve each other anyways. You're both stuck up princesses," I roll my eyes.

"I would watch it if I were you. You have no clue what I am capable of," Lexi says while walking closer to me. I lightly giggle before walking away from her and towards the fridge. "What are you laughing at bitch?" Lexi sneers. I look past the fridge and see a silver knife. She really shouldn't be testing me right now with an object like that so close to me. "Are you going to say something or are you just going to act like a mute freak. Speak bitch!"

I grab the knife and turn around before throwing it an inch

away from Lexi. She winces as the blade cuts her shoulder before it hits the wall behind her.

I turn around and grab the eggs from the fridge. I grab the flour and walk straight up to Lexi.

"And you have no clue what I can do," I sneer at her. "Next time it won't be your shoulder that gets cut," I say before leaving her.

―――――――――

It's officially been three days and Alex is coming today. Time went by so fast it's crazy.

But I'm excited to see Alex and have someone that I know and someone who is familiar to me rather than being in a house with people I met over a month. I love the De Lucas and have spent a lot of time getting to know them, but I miss my family.

My birthday is also tomorrow. I don't know what I'm going to do. Especially with this Russian issue we have going on and with Ace and Alex working on fixing this issue. I doubt they will let me out now that we are targeted.

Besides Ace and I haven't talked since we called Alex which was also when we kissed. I still can't get that kiss out of my head though. Now I have kissed and fucked many but for some reason, that kiss with Ace won't leave my mind. It shook my nerves.

I also haven't seen Lexi since the little incident in the kitchen which is good. She needs to learn to leave me alone.

"Hey, Aria. Lana made some food. Want some?" Mia asks as she opens my door.

"Sure," I shrug and get off the bed and follow her to the kitchen.

In the kitchen are Alicia, Mia, Emma, Ana, and Lana who are setting the sandwiches on the plates.

"Hey, guys. Where are Valentino and Marco?" I ask sitting down on one of the chairs.

"They are outside with Antonio playing football," Ana says.

"Oh okay."

"So, Aria. Your birthday is tomorrow," I look at Lana who is talking. "I was wondering what your favorite cake flavor is, favorite kind of breakfast, and dinner dish is."

This puts a smile on my face. "Lana, you don't need to make me anything."

"You must be high if you think we aren't going to do anything for your birthday, Aria," Emma says.

"Yeah. Don't you remember when Emma and Val said they had something special planned? That is still going on," Mia says.

Yeah, Val and Emma said they had something planned for me, but I have no clue what.

"You guys really don't have to do that though. I'm perfectly fine with just hanging out," I say to Mia and Emma.

"Well, we are going to do it anyway. You are basically family now. This is going to be the best birthday for you yet," Emma says coming over to me and slinging an arm over my shoulder.

I feel warm inside from them thinking about me as family. It's weird 'cause I barely know them, but they act like I am literally a part of their family.

"Thanks, guys."

"Good, now that we got that covered. Pick your favorite flavor for cake," Lana says talking to me.

I laugh before answering. "Chocolate. I love chocolate. I also like mousse too."

"Perfect. Breakfast?"

"Anything. I'm not picky with breakfast."

"Okay, then I'll surprise you. Dinner?"

"I like pasta and any dinner you make is good."

"Awesome. Tomorrow is all about you Aria," Lana says rubbing my shoulder and leaving the kitchen.

Once she leaves, me and the girls just talk about what I did for my past birthdays while Alicia and Ana just talk amongst themselves.

"So, me and my friend Layna actually one time pulled an all-nighter the night before my birthday, and we ended up almost halfway across the country. Layna can drink. Like she is a heavy drinker. During that whole night she was full-on naked. The only thing she had on was a strapless bra that was lace," I explain the story while laughing.

Me and Layna had so many adventures. I'm explaining to Mia and Emma about my twentieth birthday last year. Layna thought it was a bright idea to take my dad's Rolls Royce and have a joyride with it. We ended up in New York two days later and my dad was not the happiest.

Usually, it takes three days to get across the country, but we drove super-fast and skipped all the red lights.

My dad was pissed.

"Damn when can I meet this Layna? She sounds like a mini-Emma but crazier," Mia says laughing.

"Oh, shut it. I'm not that bad," Emma says slapping Mia in the shoulder.

"Hopefully, you can meet her soon. My brother is coming today so you get to meet him and maybe my dad."

"Speaking of your dad, what's up with him?" Emma says.

The smile that was on my face wipes off and Emma notices.

"If you don't want to talk about it-"

"No, no, it's fine. Me and my dad have a weird relationship. Before I was eighteen it was the perfect relationship. We used to do everything together. He didn't yell at me as much. He trusted me. But now it's different. He is more of a hard-ass on me. He and Alex are closer cause Alex is going to soon be the head of the Mob. My dad just isn't the same with me anymore."

I don't know if Ace told Emma and them what my real cover is, but I wasn't going to say anything about it. And I am telling the truth about my father. We don't have the same relationship we had before.

They are silent for a few seconds.

"I'm so sorry, Aria. You don't deserve that. Besides who needs a man in their life? I don't need one," Mia says.

"It's fine. I'm used to it now. I still have my brother and now I have you guys and Val," I smile at them, and they both come towards me and embrace me into a hug.

We continue hugging until we hear the opening and slamming of the front door.

"Aria!" I hear from a familiar voice. I let go of the girls and walk out of the kitchen. "Aria!"

I walk around the corner, and I feel my eyes tear up. I see Alex in the doorway with the front door wide open.

I don't think twice before I run towards him and embrace him into a tight hug.

He hugs me back instantly and puts his face in the crook of my neck. "I missed you so much, Ari," he whispers into my ear.

"I missed you so much, Alex," I say back with a smile on my face. We continue hugging until we both let go. I wipe my tears away from my eyes and laugh at my behavior. "Is dad here?" I ask.

"Yeah he is in the other car. We all went into separate cars."

"We all?" I question.

Just then the front door opens, and I see my family.

Twelve

"How are you guys all here?" I ask as I go to hug all of them. "I missed you guys so much. You have no idea."

I let go of all of them and I swear I try not to cry from seeing all of them together.

Ever since the incident two years ago my separation anxiety hasn't been the best so the separation with my family for a whole month was hard.

"We missed you too," Calla says while hugging me back.

"Where is Ariel?" I ask Calla as I let go of her from the hug.

"She is at Mariana's house."

Mariana is my mother's sister and whenever we aren't able to watch Ariel, we have Mariana watch her.

"So, who is this asshole who kidnapped you? I need to get a punch in," Layna says from next to me.

I roll my eyes. "He is definitely an asshole. But I purposely did what I did to get kidnapped."

"Still. He should die for laying a hand on you."

"Guys it's fine. At least he didn't put me in one of the cells. Also, the family here is amazing. They are super welcoming and kind." As if on cue Emma, Mia, Alicia, Lana, and Ana stroll into the foyer to meet everyone. "I want to introduce you to the people who made things less hell-like for me. This is Emma, Mia, Alicia, Lana, and Ana," I say pointing to each of them. "And guys this is my family. My brother Alex and his wife," I say while facing my family. "That is Cole, Alex's best friend. That is Layna, my best friend and her mom Elena." I say pointing to each of them. "And this is my mom Lisa," I say, finishing them all off.

There were a lot of 'nice to meet you' and other greetings. I'm so happy that I have my family here with me. Especially since my birthday is tomorrow. It makes it all so much better. I only expected to see Alex and my dad.

When I see my father walk in the house, I walk towards him.

"You, okay?" I ask my dad once I'm in front of him.

He nods his head and looks down at me after looking around the house. "It's just weird being in here."

"Trust me, it was weird when I first got here too," I comment. "Sorry if I messed up the mission."

"You didn't mess up. You did your best and you still got the kind of information I needed from them. But since we have the Russians involved, I need to talk to Ace with Alex and Cole about what really happened."

"So, no doing anything to them until we know for sure they were the ones who stole?"

My dad nods his head and then we go back to our family.

Everyone talked and mingled a little bit before we all go our separate ways. The girls and I go to my room while my father, Alex, Cole, and Leo go to Ace's office. My mom along with Elena, Ana, and Alicia are downstairs talking while Lana is making dinner.

"So, Aria what are we doing for your birthday," Layna asks once we get settled in my room.

"Oh, we have something planned but it's a secret, so we have to tell you later or go out for a minute. Val and I planned it," Emma says to Layna.

"Hey, I helped," Mia argues.

Emma rolls her eyes.

"I want to know," Calla states.

"It's not even a big deal. I don't know why you guys are having something planned," I say.

"Because it is an important day," Layna said to me and then looked at Emma. "I hope you have something fun planned."

"Oh, trust me. It is," Mia says with a smirk on her face.

They leave the room so that Emma and Mia can tell Layna and Calla. When the girls come back in, I see Valentino enter with them.

"Hey, I thought this was a girl talk," I say, and Valentino chuckles and then just shrugs sitting down on the floor while all of us girls sit on the bed.

"Well, I am giving you such an amazing gift, so I am allowed to stay. Besides everyone is doing boring shit. I'm not allowed to go with the boys in Ace's office because they said it's between the higher commands or some shit," Valentino claims.

"Also, Aria your birthday is going to be fun as fuck," Layna says with a smile.

"Well, I'm glad you think it's going to be like that."

"Yeah me and Em did a pretty good job," Valentino says cockily.

"Ok calm down. I don't even know what we're doing," I narrow my eyes at Val.

"You will soon, *principessa*," Valentino says and then adds a wink.

"Hey, where is Ace? I haven't seen him all day," Emma asks while also side eyeing me.

Why is she looking at me like that?

"No clue. I think he has been in his office all day," Valentino answers before looking at me.

"Who is Ace?" Calla asks.

"Aria's soon to be boyfriend," Emma says while still smirking at me.

I scrunch my nose. "Ew, no, never. He is the jackass that kidnapped me. Remember?"

And the jackass I kissed as well.

"That's not what Jared told me," Val says smirking at me.

Shit.

What a snitch.

"What did Jared tell you, Val?" I ask, trying to be clueless.

"That you and Mr. De Luca were about to do the dirty in his office," Val says with an eyebrow raised towards me.

"What?! No! I was-we were just talking!" I exclaim.

"That's a lie," Val states.

"Wait, is he hot?" Layna asks.

"I'm not answering that," I feel my cheeks become hotter and hotter meaning they are probably red.

"Aww our little Aria is blushing. When was the last time she blushed?" Calla says while giving me a questioning look.

My smile is wiped off my face and I no longer feel hotness in my cheeks.

I remember the last time I blushed. It's the reason I stopped blushing and started to stick up for myself and not let anything distract me or try to hurt me anymore. It is the reason why my guards are up and have never been broken down.

Layna notices and puts her hand on my knee and smiles.

Layna and my mom are the only ones who know because I came crying to them after the day it happened.

But that's in the past now. I can't let that affect me.

Thirteen

It's my birthday.

I'm officially twenty-one.

Today has been a pretty good day so far.

I have my family here with me and I ate some good food that Lana made. For breakfast, she made her homemade waffles which were delicious! I loved them. For lunch, she just made croissant ham sandwiches. For dinner, she made five-cheese pasta. Best thing I have ever tasted.

I was also woken up in the cruelest way possible. Val decided it would be a bright idea to wake me up with a blow horn. Quite sure I almost had a heart attack, not kidding.

The rest of the day was filled with hanging out with the family and my friends. Emma and Val haven't told me what we are doing yet but Emma said she is going to help me get ready along with Layna.

Dinner was normal. Everyone talked and got to know each

other more. I finally saw Ace after like two days. He barely talked during dinner though.

I also got some gifts from people. I got mostly jewelry and then weapons from my dad and Alex. Emma bought me a dress and she said that she wants me to wear it tonight for the thing she has planned.

One gift that I really loved was what Alicia gave me. It was a pair of red boxing gloves. On the small note she gave me it was signed with her name and Ace's as well which I didn't expect because of how his personality is towards me.

The gloves reminded me of the time we were both in the gym fighting together.

But I loved all my gifts. They were so thoughtful and sweet. I'm just happy to be here with everyone.

I hop out of the shower and there is steam all over the mirror in my bathroom. I walk into my room but stop when I see Emma and Layna on my bed just talking and I freeze.

"Um, what are you guys doing here?"

"We are here to get you ready. Did you really forget?" Emma states.

"She has short-term memory loss it's not her fault," Layna jokes.

"I don't have short term memory loss," I narrow my eyes at Layna.

"Okay relax. No need for the attitude. Get changed into like a shirt and some shorts. We need to do your makeup and hair," Emma says as she sits up from the bed.

I walk into my closet. "What about you guys?"

"It won't take long for us to get ready. While Layna is doing your hair, I'm going to get ready," I hear Emma say.

"What about you Layna are you not getting ready?"

"No, I'm not going to put makeup on just mascara. For my hair, I'm just going to leave it curly."

Bless Layna for having natural spiral curls in her hair.

I get changed and walk out of the closet and see them with the makeup set up on the floor.

Layna starts to blow dry my hair. We are all just talking about random things while getting ready. Emma starts on my makeup once she is done with hers.

She had glittery eyeshadow on her eyelids and is wearing a bubble gum pink lip gloss and some highlighter on her cheekbones.

Layna finishes my hair. She curled the ends. Emma does my makeup and after she's done, I look in the mirror.

She put some false eyelashes that weren't too dramatic and then added a little highlighter and powder. She made me put on lip balm because she said I don't need lipstick with this look.

Layna puts a little bit of makeup on and then they both go to their rooms to get changed. I go to my closet and go to the dress Emma bought me.

It's a red dress that stops at my mid thighs. The chest area is lace, but you can't see my nipples through the fabric. The dress hugs my body perfectly.

I look in the mirror and put on the jewelry that I got for my birthday. Once I'm done, I overlook my entire outfit. The heels I'm wearing are just black heels. Nothing too special.

The girl in the mirror looks different from two years ago. She looks happy, brave, confident. She looks like she is strong and not afraid of anything.

I smile at myself in the mirror before heading downstairs.

I walk down the stairs and see everyone just waiting for me since I'm the last person who wasn't ready yet.

Layna is wearing a black dress that shows her perfect figure. It came up to her thighs and she is wearing white shoes instead of heels. Emma is wearing a blue strapless silk dress. It makes her look like a goddess. Mia is wearing a purple sparkly dress that is spaghetti strapped and it is ruffled at the bottom as well.

Almost all the boys are basically wearing the same thing. Either suits or dress shirts.

Calla is wearing a white strapless dress that came up before her knees while Alex is wearing a white dress shirt to match her.

Couple goals.

I'm guessing that my mom isn't coming because she isn't dressed up as well as my father, Elena, Antonio, and Ana.

Cole is wearing a black dress shirt matching with Layna.

They better kiss tonight or I'm going to go crazy.

I also see Jared and Josh waiting downstairs too with a shocked expression once they see me.

I haven't seen them in so long.

"Jared! Josh!" I exclaim while running towards them and wrapping my arms around them. "I missed you guys. Where were you?"

"We had to go to one of the bases in the US," Jared says as they both let go of me from the hug.

I turn to look at Val who has a small grin on his face.

Valentino looks so classy.

He is wearing a dark red dress shirt that looked silky and then a golden chain. He winks at me when he sees me.

Layna and Emma come running towards me. "You look perfect Aria," Emma squeals.

"Like a true badass, Ari," Layna agrees.

"Thanks, guys." I chuckle. "Now what the hell are we doing?" I ask.

"Come with me my lady and I'll show you," Valentino comes and takes me by my arm dragging me with him.

We walk outside and see a whole bunch of sports cars.

"You like it?" Val asks once he sees my shocked expression.

"Of course, I like it. Who wouldn't?" I plant a kiss on Val's cheek before winking at him.

"Good, because you get the first pick of the car," Val says with a smile.

I feel a huge smile on my face.

There are five different cars parked in the driveway. All really fast cars.

There are two Ferraris, one black and one white. A black Bugatti which is my favorite car. A black G-Wagon and finally a white Aston Martin.

"Okay, I want the Bugatti," I say to Val.

He showcases a bright smile and gives me the keys, "There you go, *principessa*."

I grab the keys and run towards the car. I see Val walking towards the car as I get in on the driver's side.

I see Emma and Leo go into the white Ferrari and Layna and Cole go into the black one. Calla and Alex go into the white Aston Martin while Jared, Josh, and Mia go into the G-Wagon.

"Follow Emma and Leo. They know where to go," Val says once he gets inside the car.

Once Emma's car pulls out of the driveway, I follow her. Valentino and I listen to music the whole way there.

Once Emma's car stops in front of the valet I get out and give the keys to the valet. It looks like we're at a club or a casino.

Once everyone else gives their car keys to the valet we all head inside.

Music is playing. People are dancing. People are drinking. It seems like your typical club environment.

"Okay, Aria. Emma and I decided on your birthday you should drink and dance as much and as long as you want. Your drinks are all free. You get to pick the music and even dance with the DJ if you want to," Val says.

"Thank you, guys. You didn't have to. I've had enough gifts today," I say while hugging them.

"Time to fucking party!" Val yells making the group cheer.

We walk to the bar to get shots and the beautiful substance of alcohol. We all drink shots multiple times. I feel like I'm flying.

Layna, Mia, Calla, and Emma, all drag me to the dance floor.

The song playing is "Sex With Me" by Rihanna.

The feeling I feel while dancing is euphoric. I'm singing along to all the lyrics, and I don't even know if I'm singing them right or not. I'm swaying my hips along with the rest of the girls.

I have no clue where the boys are at. They are probably still at the bar.

This has to be one of the best birthdays yet.

I have my family here with me dancing.

I'm having fun. I'm happy.

I feel good.

I look good.

Songs keep playing.

I keep dancing.

Val, Cole, Jared, and Josh join in and dance with me. Calla went back to Alex and Emma went back to Leo. But Mia and Layna stay dancing with me and the guys.

I look over at Layna and Cole and see them dancing together. Cole has his hands on her hips while they are swaying their bodies back and forth. I was eyeing them while dancing with Val. Jared and Josh were next to us just swaying and jumping to the music.

Layna and Cole are perfect for one another, but they are both too scared to make a move.

I left the floor so I could get some water and check in with Alex. I walk up to our table and see him with Calla, Emma, and Leo.

"Hey, Aria," Alex says as he has his arm wrapped around Calla's waist.

"Hello brother," I slur.

It's like I can't control my words.

"Man, I'm going to love waking you up tomorrow morning," Alex laughs which makes me frown.

"You're such an ass, Alex. I have no clue why Calla decided to marry your ugly ass."

Calla starts laughing and kisses Alex who is glaring at me. "Don't worry babe, I love you."

I make a gagging face at them while Emma and Leo laugh at my reactions towards them kissing. They then start to make out heavily, so I leave not wanting to see my brother make out with my sister-in-law 'cause that's just gross.

I walk around the club and see that there is a balcony. It's super-hot in the club so I think that fresh air could be good for me right now.

It feels really nice outside.

The sky is clear and filled with stars. I start twirling around looking at the sky and laughing while doing so.

I keep spinning round and round but then I start to feel dizzy and start stumbling. I trip on my own feet but before I land on the floor and fall on my butt, I feel someone's arm around my waist, preventing me from falling.

Their arms are strong as I feel them. "Oooo, you have muscles," I giggle.

"Wow, you are shitfaced," I hear the person say, his voice is deep and sounds a little rough.

I look up to see a very familiar face. I can't place a name to the face, but he looks familiar.

"Who are you again? I forgot." I giggle a little.

He looks at me with those beautiful green eyes. I reach up to touch his face to see if he is real and he is. His face is soft and feels like fire under my skin.

Wonder how his lips feel on my-

"Ace."

Ace?

Why is Ace here?

"Oh cool," I say while nodding my head. "Why are you here?"

"'Cause I needed to talk to Leo, but you won't even remember why tomorrow morning," Ace says.

"You're so hot."

I see his lips lift slightly. "Can you walk?"

"I can try," I say while shaking my head side to side.

He huffs and readjusts me in his arms so that he is carrying me bridal style. He starts walking to the valet and I see a really pretty car come forward.

It's big.

Valet opens the door for Ace, and he slides me in the car in the backseat. He closes my door and goes to the other side and opens his door to slide into the driver side.

I feel my eyes start to get heavy, so I lean my head on the window next to me. "You better not kill me Ace." I mutter.

If he does, I will kill him.

I will kill him and all of his pillows.

Why am I thinking of pillows?

Fourteen

As I start to wake up, the headache I have is becoming stronger and stronger. I open my eyes and try to stand up from the bed I am sitting on.

Before I can assume the worst, I look around the room and see that I am in Ace's room. I remember his black interior and his floor to ceiling window.

I look at his side table and see an Advil and a glass of water. After I am done taking the Advil and drinking the glass of water I get up from his bed and walk to his bathroom. He has a pretty big bathroom. It kind of matches his room except there are some wooden accents. I don't see a shower anywhere though only a bathtub.

I go towards his sink and wash all my makeup off from last night. Whoever changed my clothes forgot I was wearing makeup and they didn't bother to even get that off.

After I'm done, I look at myself in the mirror. I'm wearing

shorts and an oversized shirt that my body is drowning in. My hair is also a mess, so I fix it and pull it back into a low ponytail.

After I freshen up, I head downstairs to see what to have for breakfast. When I come downstairs, I see it's already made by Lana, of course. She is in the kitchen with a big smile on her face while eyeing what I'm wearing.

"What are you smiling about?" I ask as I sit down on the stool in front of her.

"Oh, nothing dear. How did you sleep?" Lana asks dismissing the subject.

"Like a rock."

"How was last night? Did you have fun?"

"Hell yeah! That Bugatti that Val let me drive was so beautiful and fast. Can you believe it?" I exclaim.

Lana laughs. "Yeah, Val told me all about his special birthday plans for you. What are you going to do today? No one else is up yet."

"I think today is going to be a recovery day. I'll probably watch some movies and have a lazy day. I also want to talk to Ace about what happened last night."

"What happened?" Lana asks, worry filling her face.

"I just got way too drunk and the last thing I remember was Ace taking me in his car."

Lana nods her head. "Are you happy your family is here?"

"Yes. I missed them all so much. I'm happy they are here, and Ace let them stay. I'm very grateful he did that."

"Honey I shouldn't be telling you this, but Ace is the one who told them all to come,"

"What?" I ask, shocked.

"Ace told Alex to bring your family along. Think of it as a birthday gift. He also picked out those red boxing gloves from Alicia and him, but he didn't want to give them to you." What Lana was saying was shocking 'cause I could never imagine Ace doing that for me. I never imagined Ace doing that for anyone. "But don't tell him I told you. It will ruin his ego a little," Lana chuckles. "But I'm just letting you know that Ace never helped anyone before."

"What do you mean?"

"I met him when he was around six years old. He was the happiest little boy you could ever meet. He would always help me in the kitchen or ask if I needed help with cleaning," Lana paused and her face showed sadness. "When he started getting older, he started changing a lot. That was mainly his father's doing. He became the man he is today because of his father. Cold, ruthless, manipulative, etc. He never had a normal childhood."

"Lana, what happened between them?"

"That's a story I can't tell you. But in a matter of time, you will know. Not because I tell you but because Ace will."

I furrow my eyebrows. "Why would he tell me?"

"Aria. He is starting to trust again. I can see it in his eyes. He is very fond of you," Lana tells me. "He hasn't been the same since you got here.

"Lana that's never going to happen. Ace doesn't care for me."

"You'd be surprised, Aria. He cares for you. If he didn't then you wouldn't be here right now."

Lana left the conversation at that before I could disagree or ask more questions.

After I finish breakfast, I start to head upstairs but before I reach the first step I start thinking about Ace.

I make a left into the hall away from the stairs and end up in front of Ace's office door. I have no idea why I'm doing this but whatever.

I open his office door and Ace is sitting in his chair while writing things down on the paper in front of him.

"What do you need?" he asks, not even looking up at me.

"Nothing, just wanted to talk." I walk over to the chair in front of his desk, across from him and sit down. It's quiet for a few minutes before I talk. "What are you working on?"

"Some paperwork from the Mexicans. They are asking for weapon shipments from us."

"Don't give it to them. They always ask us for weapon shipments. It's actually really annoying if you think about it."

"You're telling me?" he muttered while flipping through documents.

"What happened last night? I remember falling asleep in your car but nothing after that," I state.

"Nothing. You stayed asleep. I just took you to my room and then had the maids change you so you wouldn't sleep in that dress."

"Do you always have to work?" I ask another question.

"No, not always. I'm the boss. I can do what I want when I want," he answers bluntly.

"Are you busy right now?" I ask starting to get to the point.

He looks up at me from his documents. "Why?"

"I'm bored and I want to watch a movie. Everyone is sleeping. I doubt today will be eventful."

"What movie?" he asks, leaning in his chair, now staring at me.

"I was thinking about Lady and the Tramp?"

"No."

"Cool, then you're going to watch it with me," I say standing up from the chair.

"I have work," he says smugly.

"I thought you said that you can do work when you want. You're the boss, aren't you?" I raise my eyebrow while smirking.

"Watch your tone with me, Aria," he states while still looking at the papers on his desk.

"Or what?" I raise my eyebrows at him even though he isn't looking at me.

"Or you'll regret it," Ace looks up at me.

"Sure." I turn around. "I'll be in my room if you need me," I say before leaving the room.

As I watch the movie Lady and the Tramp I start to get tired, and I feel my eyes start to get heavy but that's until I hear a knock on my door making me feel more awake.

"Come in."

Ace walks into my room which shocks me. "Are you still watching that movie?"

"Yeah. Want to watch?" I ask, trying not to show how excited I am.

"Whatever." He rolls his eyes and makes a motion with his hand for me to move a little so he can sit.

I laugh while moving so that he can sit next to me. It's silent while I replay the movie. Ace comes and sits next to me.

"Thank you," I look at him and I see that he's messing with the ring on his hand. He looks at me questioning why I was thanking him. "For the gifts." He raises his eyebrows in shock. "I like the gloves. Red is my favorite color."

His shock is wiped off his face. "No problem."

"And for bringing my family here. I appreciate it," I give him a small smile.

He looks at me for a while before speaking. "It's nothing. Besides, you have been here long enough," he shrugs, trying not to show any emotion.

"Do you ever smile?" I question.

"No," he states with a straight face, staring at the screen in front of us.

"I bet you have a nice smile. But sadly, you have a stick up your ass so I don't know if that will ever happen."

Ace rolls his eyes and then he looks at me. "There's this…ball thing coming up. They give out awards and do challenges and stuff like that," Ace states.

I look at him. "Is it the yearly Ball already?" Ace nods his head. "Shit I thought it was in a few more months."

"Well, I wanted to know if you would accompany me?"

For some reason, I felt my heart flutter at what Ace is asking. He wants me to accompany him to the ball.

Why would he ask me though?

This ball is super important and going with Ace seemed risky because whether or not we are both from very different families who are known to others that we have a war between us and discontinued our alliance.

I'm surprised my dad and brother aren't fighting with Ace but they're probably not doing it because they don't want to make me or my mom mad. Or maybe they are afraid of Ace.

"I'd love to go with you," I say with a smile.

Ace gives me a half assed smile and then turns his attention to the TV.

I feel myself grow tired again and I rest my head against a really firm pillow. Last thing I remember before falling asleep was watching Lady running into the Tramp.

I open my eyes and lift my head to look around the room. I rub my eyes and see that I am in my room.

The TV is turned off and it's super quiet. I hear light snores from next to me, so I look to my side and see Ace with his arms wrapped around my waist and his head on my chest.

I guess he fell asleep too.

I lean closer to his face to study all of his imperfect features.

His eyes are closed so I can't see those beautiful emerald eyes. His hair looks messy and is sticking up in so many different places.

I touched his hair and it felt so soft. I knew it was always soft because it just looked shiny, probably because of the shampoo he uses. I play with his hair for a little while, not noticing that he is stirring in his sleep.

He looks like he is waking up. I was about to take my hands away from his hair, but he stops me from doing so.

He grabs my wrist and holds it. "Don't stop. That feels good," he says in a raspy voice since he just woke up.

Damn his voice was deeper and just sounded way hotter. I feel my cheeks heat up a little but ignore it.

I relax in his grip, and he lets go of my wrist. I place my fingers back in his hair while his arms are still wrapped around my body but tighter.

It's as if he's afraid to let me go.

I feel my eyes start to get heavier until they finally close and all I see is black.

The next time I wake up, Ace isn't in bed. I don't think anything of it. He probably had work to finish or something.

I get out of bed and go downstairs to see if anyone else is downstairs and I see my mom, Ana, Elena, and Alicia talking in the dining area.

"Hey," I say as I sit down next to them.

Alicia told me to call her Alicia because she hates it when people call her Mrs. De Luca. It makes her feel old but when she said that, it seemed like something else was bothering her.

"Hey, honey. What did you do all day? It's almost five," my mom exclaims while looking at the watch on her wrist.

She doesn't like it when I'm in the room all day.

Mostly because that's what I did when I was depressed for months about what happened between my ex-boyfriend and me.

But I don't like to think about that because it always "makes me feel super uncomfortable.

"I know I'm sorry. Yesterday was crazy. So, we all did a recovery day today."

"Did you have fun?" Alicia asks.

"Yeah. One of the best birthdays yet." I say with a small smile.

"Well, I'm glad you liked it," Ana says, smiling back at me. "Val was super excited while planning the day for you."

"Yeah he's the best," I smile back at her.

"Did you like your gifts?" my mom asks.

"Of course I did but you guys didn't have to get me anything. I had fun hanging out with everyone. But my best gift was probably seeing you all."

"Yeah, Ace is really sweet for doing that. Did you thank him?"

"Yes, I did. We just finished watching a movie actually." They all give me a little smirk. "Wipe those smirks off your faces. Did Lana put you up to this?"

They all laugh. "Lana always speaks her mind," Alicia says while shaking her head.

"Where is she?" I ask.

"Oh, she went home for the day. She lives close by but since no one is really in the mood today I told her she can leave. I mean we know how to make food and we have hands so why not put them to use?" Alicia says.

I nod in agreement. Lana works hard. She told me she has a son who lives with his own family and has a well-paying job. Her husband is mostly working. He works on cars for a living. Lana told me she wants me to meet him one day.

"Are you guys making dinner today?" I ask.

"Yes. Do you want to help?" my mom asks.

"Sure, what are you making?"

"Cheeseburgers."

"Damn that sounds good right now. I haven't had one in forever," I exaggerate.

My mom knows how much I love cheeseburgers. I would always help my mom with making them.

She has a special recipe for making her homemade cheeseburgers.

"Okay perfect. We can start now. Aria, you already know what to do."

Fifteen

It's the night of the ball and I'm getting ready right now.

Ace ordered some makeup artists and hairstylists for everyone in the house so that they could look their best.

He also had me try on some dresses yesterday. There were a lot of dresses that I tried on, but I found one that I think looks perfect on me and for the occasion. The tailor even said that the dress was his favorite choice.

For my makeup, I asked for something a little natural.

They didn't put any foundation on me. They did put a little bronzer on my eyelids and cheekbones to give me some color. For my hair, they didn't do much. They just straightened it because they thought that since my dress was so grand and huge, they should have my hair be simple.

After the hairstylist and makeup artist were done with my hair and makeup, they helped me put on the dress. The dress looked absolutely beautiful. It was the perfect shade of red. Both of the artists were squealing when they saw the full fit.

Usually, I hate wearing dresses, but this is like the one time a year I have to wear these kinds of dresses so I'm not complaining. It's still a beautiful dress.

After they left, I take a minute to really look at myself in the big mirror. I look and feel like a princess.

I feel beautiful and powerful.

It's been a long time since I have felt like this and I'm questioning if this is actually real or not.

When I go downstairs, I see everyone already dressed in their formal outfits. I see Ace walk towards me and away from his mother, who he was talking to before.

He is wearing a black suit jacket with the buttons unbuttoned and the dress shirt underneath is white.

"*Gesù Cristo*" I hear Ace mumble as he walks towards me. "You look decent," he shrugs making me narrow my eyes at him.

"Such a gentleman," I say sarcastically.

"Want me to tell you what else I think in front of your family?" He says in a low voice as he raises an eyebrow at me. He slides his hand into mine. "Because I am pretty sure your brother and father will not like what I will say. But then again, I don't care because they are in my house, and I can kill them in an instant," Ace whispers before he backs away a little bit but still holds onto my hand.

Alicia and my parents all come and walk towards me gushing before I had time to react to what he said.

"Honey, you look fantastic," Alicia says then leans in for a hug.

I hug her back and let go of Ace's hand. God, his family really loves to hug.

"You look beautiful, baby. My baby girl is growing up so fast," I see my mom shed a tear as my dad rubs her back trying to calm her down.

"Mom, don't cry," I chuckle.

"You look stunning, Ari," my dad says and kisses my cheek.

I smile at both of my parents.

After a lot more complementing one another, we take some pictures and head out towards the limos. We all went in three separate limos.

I talked to Cole before we left and told him that he should make a move on Layna at the ball. I told him that he should stop being a pussy and just ask her to be his after like, years and years of flirting.

We are now on our way to the mansion the ball is being held at. This year it is being held in Italy since Ace is basically hosting it this year. Every year a different person from the families hosts the ball. Last year Alex held the ball since it was his first year as boss and my father's last year of being the boss.

"Have you ever been to one of these balls?" I ask Ace who is sitting next to me in the limo.

"Yes, but I didn't participate in the events held at the balls. I usually was there for just the alliances and meetings."

"Oh, that's probably why I've never seen you there then."

"Yeah, but I saw you. I remember last year when you received your award for the best-trained assassin," Ace says with a smirk on his face.

"Really? How come I didn't see you?" I ask in a shocked tone.

"Because I know how to look invisible," Ace jokes but he still keeps a straight face.

"Funny," I chuckle. "I'm surprised that you weren't named best assassin or killer."

"I can't get an award for that because I'm a *capo*. *Capos* or bosses can't receive awards for killing people. The only reward I could receive is getting good alliances and perhaps new and better weapons."

"Makes sense because you aren't an assassin. You're the boss."

"Why? Are you scared I might take your award?" Ace asks with a smirk and raises an eyebrow.

"Funny that you think you can take my place at being the best."

"*Amore*, you have no clue what I can do to you. I can break you without even trying."

"Good luck trying then, Ace."

The mansion that this ball is being held at is very medieval like. It looks like a castle inside. I give props to Ace for picking this place to hold the event.

There are a lot of people here as well.

As we are walking towards the entrance of the mansion, I see multiple people look at Ace and me as he helps me out of the limo.

I feel super uncomfortable with people staring at me because I always feel like there is something wrong with me when they look at me, but Ace makes sure I'm okay as we walk inside the mansion.

As we walk through the entrance, we see many beautiful paintings and pictures hung up on the walls.

Once we get to where the ball is being held inside the mansion, we had to have our names announced as we walked down the staircase. Very extra but they do this every year.

Usually, when I went to these types of things I would also go with Layna because I didn't want to go alone.

"May I introduce Ace De Luca and Aria White."

Once the announcer said both of our names all eyes turned towards us.

"Everyone is staring," I state the obvious as we walk down the stairs.

Ace probably could care less, or he is probably used to being stared at.

"Let them," Ace says as he takes my hand and leads us down the stairs.

I was so afraid I was going to trip and fall but luckily, I didn't.

I stay by Ace's side the whole time and he had his arm around my waist. We talk to a lot of different other mob groups. I'm trying to keep an eye out for any Russians because of what has happened in the last few weeks.

But I don't see any. I'm surprised. Almost all of the crime groups are here; the Mexicans, Germans, French, Japanese, Jamacians, and even the Romanians. But no Russians.

"I'm going to go to the Alliance meeting. Are you going to be, okay?" Ace whispers in my ear.

"Yeah, I'll be fine," I say, nodding my head.

Ace nods his head and then leaves without another word. I turn around to look and see where everyone is at.

I see Layna and Cole walk in with Mia and Valentino. Layna and Cole are standing close to one another, and Cole has his arm around her waist making me smile at them in approval.

I see my parents with Alicia and the others on the other side of the room talking with some people. My eyes go to Emma and Leo who are talking with some older woman. I'm about to go and walk towards them, but I stop when I hear someone call my name.

"Aria? Aria White?"

I turn and see a beautiful blonde-haired woman. She looks like she is maybe in her early forties, but I can tell she has gotten some work done on her face because it doesn't look that natural whatever she was trying to do. She looks also very familiar, but I can't tell from were.

"Yes, can I help you?" I ask with a small smile on my face.

"I just wanted to compliment you on your dress this evening. It's stunning. Did Ace pick it out?"

"Uh no, I did actually but thank you so much. Yours is lovely as well," I compliment while motioning my hand to her long black dress.

"Thank you, dear. My name is Dana Romanov. I don't know if you know this or not, but my daughter actually used to live in the De Luca residence."

"Oh really? What's her name?"

"Her name is Lexi? Have you heard or seen her around before?"

Lexi.

Of course, I have.

She hasn't come to the house in a while though. Last time I saw her was when I almost daggered her eye.

No wonder this woman looks so familiar.

I showcase a fake smile on my face. "Yes, Lexi. I have heard of her before."

"Oh really? Well, she said that she wanted me to pass on a message for Ace, but I don't see him anywhere. Do you happen to know where he is?"

"Uh, not really. He said he would be gone for a little."

"Oh well, then you can tell him? Lexi had to go back to our home country so that's why she hasn't been at the estate for a while. She wanted to let Ace know because she was worried that he would be worried about her."

He doesn't seem that worried.

"Oh yeah, I noticed she hasn't been around. But I will let Ace know," I assure her.

"Thank you so much, darling. Lexi told me a lot about you. I'm surprised you're still here. I thought Ace was going to kill you," Dana giggles as if it's the funniest thing in the world.

"Kill me?"

"Well didn't he have his men kidnap you?"

"Oh, yeah but I think that we're passed all of that now."

"I can tell," Dana says with a fake smile.

I ignore it and just smile back at her.

"Okay! May I have everyone's attention really quick?!" I hear someone yell making me look away from Dana and look at the stage where I see Leo with a microphone in his hand. "So, I wanted to announce all of the award winners tonight, then we can get started with the dance of the evening."

Leo goes towards one of the waiters that has three cards in his hand.

Probably the names of the winners.

"I wonder who is going to win," Dana says from next to me.

I nod my head and look around the room trying to find Ace, but I don't see him.

"Okay well, the first award of the night goes to Ben Shriller for best hacker, so Ben, get your ass up here." Everyone claps for Ben as he walks up to the stage. He looks like he is French. "Next award goes to Rebecca Vladimir for best seductress." Everyone claps for Rebecca. I know for a fact that she was Russian. Not only does she look Russian, but her name is Russian. "And last but most certainly not least Aria White for best-trained assassin with the most kills."

A lot of people clap for me as I walk up to where the man is standing with my award. He has a grin on his face that sends chills down my spine.

Whenever I get those kinds of chills, I always have a feeling that something bad will happen.

"Congratulations, Aria. I'm so happy that you were named best-trained assassin. You deserve it," Leo says while giving me the award.

"Thank you," I say before a photographer comes towards us and asks us to take a picture together.

Sixteen

Everyone goes to the middle of the dance floor while I just stand to the side and watch. I am also holding the award in my hand because I have no idea where else to put it.

Everyone is dancing to the music while also talking to their partners.

"Congrats," I look to my left and see Ace walk up to me.

I look down at the award and back at Ace. "Thanks, what took you so long?"

"The meeting," Ace deadpans.

"It takes that long?" Ace shrugs his shoulders and looks at the dance floor where everyone is dancing. The silence between him and I is unbearable. I want to ask what's wrong, but he looks like he would lash out at me. Fuck it. "You, okay? You seem pissed."

"Don't worry about it," he says while straightening his posture.

"Did something happen?" I ask, looking at him.

Ace finally looks at me. "I said don't worry about it," he says while clenching his jaw.

I open my mouth to say something but instead I get interrupted.

"Why aren't you guys on the dance floor?" I look next to me and see my mother with a small smile on her face. "You two need to go and dance. Now," she says while grabbing my award and connecting Ace and my hands together, then pushing us to the floor.

Curse her.

"You're such a jackass," I say once we get to the middle of the floor.

"That's right *amore*," Ace whispers in my ear. "Better fucking remember it."

"You didn't need to act like an ass. It was just a question."

I don't know what happened in the meeting room but just because whatever happened in there doesn't justify his actions.

"I'm not acting like an ass. If you don't like how I am acting, then leave," Ace bluntly states.

I roll my eyes at him.

We were both doing so good but now I can say it's the complete opposite.

"You are," I scoff. "You are being rude for no reason. I asked you a simple question, but you replied with an asshole type of answer. I don't respect people who talk to me like that," I claim.

I hate when people think they can walk all over me. Maybe a few years ago I was different, nicer, didn't have a backbone, I would let people do whatever the hell they want, and I would let them walk all over me but not anymore.

I am not going to be like that, especially with Ace.

Ace sighs. "In the Alliance meeting I saw a Russian, but it wasn't the leader," Ace says as he starts moving to dance.

I look up at Ace. "How do you know?"

"Because I've seen the leader of their group and that wasn't him. He probably knew I was going to be there."

"Should we be worried?"

"You shouldn't because you could probably kill him in a heartbeat," Ace smirks.

"It would be hard with guards around him twenty-four seven but who knows," I chuckle.

Ace and I continue to dance. It's silent between us but not awkward. He is just staring at me though. Admiring every detail on my face. I feel kind of nervous under his gaze for some reason.

I nip my lip and I see Ace's eyes go straight there. He leans his head down to the crook of my neck and I feel his lips touch the spot below my ear sending shivers down my spine and making me straighten my back a little more.

"Stop biting that lip *amore* or I might not be responsible for my actions."

"What actions?" I challenge and I see something flicker in his eyes.

"Want to find out?" Ace raises his eyebrow.

I don't say anything, instead I look past Ace and see Cole and Layna dancing. Layna smiles widely and Cole looks completely in love with her. I really hope that he makes a move on her tonight.

I can feel their sexual tension from here.

I see Ace turn to look at Cole and Layna and then back at me. "Are they together?" Ace asks.

"No. They do like each other a lot though. Maybe even love."

"I can tell. He looks like he is in love."

"Have you ever been in love, Ace?" I ask Ace.

I can see him shield his emotions once I ask. "No. I don't know what love feels like."

"Do you believe it's real?"

Ace looks down at me and I think his eyes sparkle a little bit. "I don't know."

Ace is about to say something, but I see his eyes flicker to something behind me and I feel him tense up while holding my waist. "Are you okay?" I ask and he averts his eyes back to me.

"Yeah. I'll be right back; I just need to check on something," he says as he lets go of me and walks past me.

I turn around and see a man with an all-black suit outside where the balcony is at.

"Hey, where did Ace go?" I turn around and see Emma and Leo.

"Uh, I don't know. I think to go outside," I shrug.

"Where did you see him go?" Leo asks but he sounds anxious. "I need to talk to him."

I point towards the balcony and Leo says he will be right back before leaving.

"What's going on?" I ask Emma.

"Uh, well between you and I, Leo told me there is someone who is planning an attack and I am guessing Ace is just checking to see if everything is okay," Emma says and I nod my head in acknowledgment. "How are you liking the party though? Congrats on the award."

"Thanks, and for now it's going good. I mean everyone is having a good time," I say while looking around the room.

"Yeah, I even saw you and Ace having a good time as well," Emma says while smirking.

I narrow my eyes at her. "No. He was acting like an ass actually," I state while shaking my head.

"Why?" Emma asked.

"I think something happened at the alliance meeting but I'm not-"

"What the fuck did you do?!" I hear someone yell, cutting me off. Other people's heads turn as well as mine. "What the fuck did you do?!" the person says louder, and the voice is familiar.

"What the hell," I mumble before walking towards the balcony where I saw Ace leave. When I walk outside, I see Ace on the floor with Alicia in his arms. Alicia's eyes were fluttering closed, and she also had blood coming out of the wound on her stomach. "Oh my god," I gasp and put my hands over my mouth.

The man in an all-black suit turns around to look at me. "Oh, look who decided to join us?" he says with a smirk and Ace turns to look at me.

I feel someone touch my arm making me look away from Ace and see Leo with a straight face, but I can see how scared and concerned he really is, "Aria, get out of here. Take your family and everyone else and leave."

Leo looks down at Ace who is still holding Alicia while blood spills out of her, "Hurry the fuck up and get someone to help her Leo!" Ace yells, making Leo run off to get someone.

"What the fuck did you do?" I exclaim to the guy in the black suit.

"Taught Ace a lesson," the man says looking down at Ace. I look down at the man's hand and see a dagger with blood on it. Alicia's blood. "You know Aria, the worst weakness that someone could ever have is loving someone," he says while walking closer to me while I just eye Ace and Alicia. What he is telling me is something I am familiar with. Loving someone is the worst thing anyone could ever do. It's dangerous. "And Ace needs to know that. I just had to teach him how it's done. I mean you understand so I don't need to teach you any lessons."

My eyes go back to the guy who is wearing all black. "Who are you?" I questioned, while I feel my whole body tense.

I know this guy is trouble. I have a feeling.

How does he know?

The only people who know is my mom and Layna.

"Oh, I just had one job to do, and it's done," he smirks. "Dimitri sends his regards."

Russian.

I hadn't noticed anyone else was outside until I hear someone's sobs. I turn around and see almost everyone is outside watching the scene unfold. Some guards come and take Alicia while Ace stands up with blood all over his shirt.

"By killing a weakness that men don't need. Besides all you girls are good for creating heirs for our-" Ace cuts the man off by throwing a punch to his face.

"Fucking *stronzo*!" Ace yells as he throws one last punch and a kick to the face, making the man unconscious. "Get him taken care of. Make sure he doesn't die. Once he is healed, I want you to put him in one of the cells," he tells Francisco who is close to him. Francisco nods his head and takes the man away. Ace looks at Leo who is near him as well. "Get everyone out of here. This party is over."

"Where are you going?" Leo asks.

I see Ace look at me. "The safe house. Aria isn't safe at the house. Dimitri probably has some sort of hitmen out to finish the job."

Leo nods his head making Ace walk past me while also giving me a look. I look at Leo and he motions his head for me to follow Ace.

So, I do.

Ace is sitting next to me while playing with the fabric from my dress. I'm just looking at him trying to figure out what is going through his head.

The image of Alicia's lifeless body on the floor keeps replaying in my mind on and on.

I can only imagine what Ace must be thinking. I'm scared for him. I'm so worried about what he is thinking about.

I have no clue if Alicia is alive or not and I'm scared to know. I can't even imagine what Ace is going to act like if Alicia is dead. Especially since Dimitri did the deed.

As soon as the limo stops Ace lifts his head and looks out the window.

"Come on," Ace says before opening the door.

He walks out and holds it open for me to walk out.

I look up and see a very beautiful, modern black house. I notice we are surrounded by trees and nature.

"Where are we?" I ask.

"My safe house," Ace states before walking forward.

I follow him towards the house and the limo drives off.

Ace unlocks the door and we both walk inside. It's super dark. The only light is the moonlight that surround the house.

Ace turns the light on in the house and then walks further down the foyer. I close the door and follow him towards the kitchen. I see him open multiple cabinets.

"Fucking shit!" Ace yells as he slams the cabinet shut.

I have no clue what to do. I don't want to make him mad or frustrated because he could probably have just lost his mom in the cruelest way possible.

I have never lost a parent or was ever close to losing one, so I don't know what it feels like, and I don't know how to help him. I want to do everything I can to help him though. I know we are supposed to hate each but for some reason, I don't hate him. I did at first but now, I don't know.

"What are you looking for? Maybe I can help?" I ask walking closer to him.

Ace doesn't answer me. Instead, he storms out of the kitchen while taking his blazer off and throws it on the floor. I take off my shoes quickly and follow him as he walks upstairs.

What are you looking for, Ace?

I follow him as he walks inside a room and turns on the light.

The room is very nice. It has a huge window that shows all of the outside and the beautiful night sky. I hear a lot of banging and rustling. I walk to where the sound is being made which is in the closet and I see Ace opening different doors over and over.

"It's not fucking here!" Ace yells as he slams a door from his closet shut. "Where the fuck is it?!" Next thing I know Ace punches the door he just slammed, making it break. I run to him and stand in between the closet door and Ace. "Move out of the way," Ace demands.

"No," I state, not moving.

"No?"

"No. You're going to hurt yourself if you keep punching things. You need to calm down. Go to sleep, rest."

"And how would you know what I need?" Ace asks while leaning closer to my face. "You don't know half of the shit I have been through so you wouldn't know how to deal with it."

"I'm not about to have this kind of conversation with you. Everyone goes through shit Ace, not just you so don't compare other's problems to your own. It's not right."

He has no clue at all about what happened to me in the past. He has no clue what I felt or went through. He doesn't know how hurt and damaged I was when shit went downhill with Dante.

I don't like to think about him though because he scares me.

But everyone deals with pain differently. He takes his anger out by punching things and yelling at people while I hide away and build a wall to protect myself.

"She's going to die," Ace claims, making me look up at him. "And it's all his fault," Ace puts his hands on the closet behind me and looks down. "I could have saved her and-"

"Ace," I put my hand on his jaw so that he can look at me. "It's not your fault. It could never be your fault." I know that Alicia is being taken to the hospital, but I don't want to give him false hope of her being alive. That is the last thing I want to do. "I don't think it's your fault. This wasn't your doing. This was Dimitri's. He did this. You didn't know that this would happen tonight so how could it be your fault?"

"She died because I wasn't there, next to her. She is dead because Dimitri thinks it's fun to play games."

"But it's not your fault. This didn't happen because of you." I say softly.

"I don't want to know if she is dead or not."

"I know," I say as I wrap my arms around him and hug him. "I'm here Ace," I say softly while touching his hair softly.

I don't know how long we stay like this, but Ace lifts his head and looks down at me. I see a dark look in his eyes. It's filled with anger, pain, and it's dangerous.

"Get out," Ace demands while backing away from me.

I raise my eyebrow at him. "What?"

"Get out. I don't need you. I never needed you," Ace states while staring down. "You are just some random-ass girl who thought that you could pick me back up and help me but in reality, you're nothing. You never will be anything, so save the caring act and get out of here." Ace slips his hands in his pockets and stands straight while looking down at me with

He looks so calm and nonchalant.

What he said hurt.

It hurt because it's the same thing Dante used to say to me. He would always say I am worthless and that I didn't mean anything.

"I was just trying to help. I am trying to be a decent person but obviously you know nothing about that." He leans against the wall and crosses his arms over his chest, acting non-chalant.

I slip out from between him and the closet and leave the room.

Seventeen

The sound of banging and cluttering wakes me up. I look at the clock that's hanging on the wall across from the bed I am laying on.

What the fuck is making that sound at four in the morning?

I hear it again along with a frustrated grunt.

Then my mind instantly goes to what had happened a few hours ago.

Ace.

After I left Ace's room last night, I searched the house for a guest room since Ace was busy dealing with his emotions. I ended up finding a room downstairs and it thankfully had clothes inside. There was only a pair of leggings along with some random shirts.

I get up from the bed and walk out of the room and towards where the sound is coming from.

As I get closer and closer, I hear the clashing and grunts clearer.

I turn the corner to the kitchen and see Ace who is opening and slamming cabinets while also grunting. I look near him on the floor and see his phone crushed into pieces. He is wearing nothing but black basketball shorts.

Oh god.

I can't imagine what had happened.

I can't imagine what the person on the other side of the phone said to Ace to make him act out like this.

There are no lights turned on in the house because the natural lightning from outside is peeking through the windows. I wish that I could have been here under different circumstances because it's all so beautiful.

I walk further in the kitchen and that gets his attention because he turns his head to look at me. The look he's giving me made me feel scared and a little threatened. He looks like he would do anything right now.

Perhaps kill me if I said the wrong things.

"May Alicia fucking De Luca rest in peace," Ace says with a small grin on his face, but I can tell he's trying so hard to pull it together. "She was kind, beautiful, caring, and probably one of the only people that I actually gave a flying fuck about in this fucked up world."

I walk closer to him so that I'm right in front of him. "I don't know what to say because I have never been in this situation before but Ace, I am so sorry. I know that might not be the thing you want me to say but-"

"Last time I was here it was snowing, and I brought my mom here for her birthday," Ace cut me off while looking down at me. It's like he's looking at me but not really looking at me if that makes any sense. "All she wanted for her birthday that year was to escape. She wanted to get away from all of this even if it just had to be for a day." As he's talking to me his voice holds no emotion. I see nothing but hurt and anger in his eyes. I never like seeing people look like this, it hurts to see people look this destroyed. "My mom..." he started but didn't finish.

He didn't have to tell me for me to understand what he's trying to say.

They confirmed that she's dead. Dimitri had someone stab Alicia, but she went to the hospital hoping for the doctors to help her but that's not the case.

I didn't waste a second to walk closer to him and hug him. He tenses up before putting his head in the crook of my neck and wrapping his arms around me.

We didn't move for a while. We just hugged.

"I'm so sorry. You don't deserve this," I whisper to him. "You deserve so much better."

"It hurts," he croaks out making me think he's crying.

Hearing him say that broke my heart.

"I know. It's going to hurt. It's going to hurt so much Ace. But you can get through this. I know you can. You are capable of getting through this," I whisper. "You have so many people who care for you and who will be here for you no matter what."

"Why does it hurt?" he lets go of me and now I see that he is trying so hard not to cry.

His eyes are watery but only a small tear slips out and runs down his face.

I reach up to his face to wipe the tear that fell. "Cause you love her. You care and have a lot of feelings for her. You're not emotionless like people think you are. You lost the one person you really cared about. You're going to feel like this for a little while," I say softly.

I see something flicker in his eyes. It was like for a second, he looked at me as if I were the only girl in the world. But that washes away, and it's replaced with that hurt and anger from before.

He drops his arms from around me and backs up from me.

Not again.

"Ace-"

He turns around. "Why do you even care?!"

"Because I just do," I see his face turn in a scowl glaring at me. I walk towards him and grab both of his hands slowly and intertwine our fingers together. His breathing starts to slow down as he looks at me studying my eyes. It's almost like he can see all of me. My secrets. I feel bare when he looks at me like this. "You don't have to pretend to be okay Ace," I whisper to him, making sure he's calmed down. "It's okay to cry."

I pull him closer and wrap my arms around his upper body with one of my hands on the top of his head. This time he isn't hugging me back. He just lets me wrap my arms around him.

"Why do you care, Aria?" he mutters.

"Because I know what it's like to be hurt and feel angry. I may not understand your kind of pain, but I know what it feels like to be hurt and vulnerable and I just want to help." He doesn't say anything. Instead, he hesitantly wraps his arms around me. "I'm sorry Ace. I don't know how many times you want me to say it, but I will say it as much as you want me to," I say softly to him. He buries his face more into my neck while wrapping his arms around me. "She didn't deserve that...you didn't deserve that."

He pulls away from the hug. "No," he shakes his head slowly as I see another tear running down his cheek.

I pretend I don't see it. Until another comes afterward.

"It's okay," I whisper while putting my hands on his face making him look at me. "Cry, scream, fucking punch something."

"It's my fault," he mumbles painfully.

"No...no it's not. Don't ever say that."

"I'm the one who started all of this shit, Ari," Ace pulls my hands away from his face.

God, I feel like me and him are always going back and forth. It's giving me a headache.

Just when I think I was getting through to him and making him feel at least a little better he shuts it down and pushes me away.

"No, you didn't. You could never start something like this."

"Yeah I did."

I can't help but feel guilty for some part of this. If I didn't come into Ace's life, then his mother might still be alive.

A few seconds more pass as we just stand in front of one another. I start to feel tired as he and I stare at one another.

"Come on, you need to sleep. How long have you been awake?" Ace shrugs his shoulders. "Did you even fall asleep?"

Ace looks at me and glares before saying, "Fuck off Aria," before walking past me and leaving upstairs.

One step forward, five steps backwards.

Eighteen

Ace and I have been at his house for the rest of the day. I guess he is having his driver pick us up because he doesn't want to be in this house alone with me any longer. I heard him in his room speaking to Francisco in Italian. He called me a bitch and a stupid cunt in Italian.

Jackass.

After he rushed off to his room after the issue in the kitchen, I stayed in mine until he came into my room to tell me that we were leaving later today and going back to his house. After that he left, and we didn't talk for the rest of the day.

Ace is good at hiding his emotions, but I know he is hurting. I think he is more furious than hurt. I don't know what he is going to do with Dimitri. I know for a fact he will kill him though. No doubt.

Ace and I head out to the car. Francisco is driving because he and Leo are the only ones who know of this house. Also, Alicia as well.

Francisco is Ace's most trusted soldier. He is the only person I see who is always around Ace 24/7.

The drive to the house is silent.

All I can really think about is the night of Alicia's death. That picture won't get out of my head. That's all I could think about while I was in the room. I had nothing else to do at that house so all I did was think.

Once we get to Ace's house, we see everyone start coming out from the front door. They all look tired and drained. I see that there is sympathy in their eyes as Ace and I get out of the car.

"Where have you been?"

"Are you okay?"

"I'm going to kill him."

"My baby."

My family asks once they walk closer to me and from the corner of my eye I see Ace walk inside the house with Leo. "Guys I'm fine. Really," I say as they let go of me.

Who I really want to go to is Ace to see if he needs anything. Yea he acted like an ass but he lost his mother.

We all walk into the house and head towards the dining room.

"What happened?" my dad asks as everyone just listens.

"Nothing. I mean after you know that man killed Alicia, Ace took us where Dimitri men wouldn't be able to find us."

"Where?" Alex asks.

What am I supposed to say?

I doubt Ace would want me to reveal his secret house.

"A hotel."

Everyone then showcases sadness on their faces.

I feel bad for my mom because Alicia seemed like the friend she needed. Although she has Elena it's nice to have another friend to get close to. Alicia had something that Elena didn't. I don't know what that was, only my mother knew.

"I'm so sorry mom," I say softly, putting my hand on hers.

If I can't handle Ace, at least I can handle my mom and have her not be mad at me.

"It's not your fault," she smiles at me softly.

"How are you guys?" I ask Emma, Mia, and Ana.

I can't imagine what Ana feels right now.

She lost her best friend. I know that Ana and Alicia were the best of friends. They did almost everything together. And now she is gone, and she doesn't have that kind of relationship with someone like Alicia anymore.

"I'm fine but I'm more worried about Ace," Emma claims.

"It hasn't really hit me yet," Mia shrugs.

Ana stayed silent.

I didn't push her because I know a lot of people need time to process and grieve.

"What happened when Leo called?" Emma asks.

"I wasn't there when Leo called Ace about her. I was sleeping but when I came out to see him, he didn't say a thing. He was hurt. He is a human with emotions. Alicia was important to him. He was more furious than sad, I think. What do you think he is going to do?" I ask them all.

"Kill him," Alex states bluntly. Calla slaps his shoulder and Alex rubs his shoulder and shoots Calla a look. Alex rolls his eyes at Calla. He then looks at me. "Also, there is something I need to tell you," Alex says. "I know this is really bad timing, but we all need to go back to the house. In LA."

"Why?" I furrow my eyebrows.

"Because we still have work to do in LA Aria. Ace, Leo, your brother, your dad, and I already talked about what is going to happen with Russia. He said he is going to take care of it and already has it handled," Cole says.

"So, when are we leaving?" I ask.

"We," my dad says putting emphasis on 'we', but I know he isn't talking about the same 'we' as I am, "are leaving tomorrow. You, however, are staying here in Italy."

I raise my eyebrows. "What?"

Like hell I am staying here. Especially when Ace is acting the way he is right now with his mood swings. I get that his mom died but I don't want to be around someone who won't show me respect when I am trying to help them.

Yeah, I feel bad for him and help him through it but not if he is being a dickface towards me.

"You have to stay here because Ace needs you for the Russian interrogation and to take them down. That is why he needed you all this time and why you aren't dead."

"I doubt he still wants me here," I chuckle. "I am coming home with you guys," I state as if it isn't up for discussion.

"No, you aren't. As much as I hate you staying here you have to," Alex states.

"Why? What does he need me to do?" I asked.

"Like I said before, for interrogation and to take down the Russians. You are the best assassin Aria, and he wants you to help him with the job. He always wanted you for the job."

"This is stupid," I mutter. "Ace doesn't need me. He never did."

"That's where you are wrong," Emma mumbles.

I doubt anyone could have heard her, but I did glare at her.

"Here's your phone by the way. I got it from Ace the other day and forgot to give it to you," Alex says while tossing me my phone. "Call every day."

"When are you guys leaving?" I ask.

"Plane takes off in the morning," Alex says.

I sigh and scratch the back of my head. "Well, I need to figure out how long this whole Russian thing is going to take because I don't want to be staying here for two whole months," I say before standing up straight. "I'm going to go talk to him."

I am now standing outside of Ace's office, and I feel terrified to knock on the door. But I muster up all the courage I have to knock but then stop when I hear him yell.

"I want him to see my face before he dies! Find Dimitri now!" I hear Ace yell before banging the table.

The next thing I know Leo opens the door and his eyes widen once he sees me. He quickly shuts the door before speaking.

"Aria. What are you doing?" he asks.

"I wanted to talk to Ace. How is he doing?"

I don't know why I asked.

Maybe it's because I do care for this asshole.

"He's Ace." Leo shrugs.

"I'm going to go talk to him."

"Woah are you sure? He is not really in the right uh, headspace," Leo asks while blocking the office door.

"Leo I'll be fine. Go to Emma and everyone," I assure him.

Leo is hesitant but eventually he nods his head and moves out of the way.

I let out a huge breath before going in. I twist the door handle and push the door forward. I see Ace standing in front of his huge window from the side of his office with his back facing me.

He doesn't have a shirt on. His back muscles are tense and somewhat flexing.

He is also smoking a cigarette.

"Those aren't good for you," I claim as I close the office door.

"Why do you think I smoke them?" he says while still staring out the window.

"Well, you shouldn't."

He puts out the cigarette before speaking. "What do you want, Aria? Shouldn't you be packing or some shit?"

"Well, my mom and brother said that I need to stay here to help with the Russians."

"I don't need you now so you can go," he says, still staring out the window.

"Wish I could but sadly this Russian problem is both of our problems. It's threatening my family, so I have no choice but to help."

Now, Ace turns around and I see with a glare present on his face. "Who said I needed you? I don't need anyone."

Liar.

"Okay," I say bluntly, not getting why he felt the need to say that. "Just let me know what you want to do and when you want to do it."

"Whatever," he mutters.

I hope he doesn't continue to act like this while I am here.

"Do you need anything?" I decide to ask.

"Leave," Ace mutters before drinking the rest of his alcohol in the glass cup.

I look up at Ace and raise my eyebrows. "Excuse me?"

"I said leave," he says looking at me dead in the eye.

"I'm sorry, who was there for you for the past two days? Who was the one who cared enough to make sure you actually fell asleep at night? I know you're hurting but you don't have to take it out on me. I'll be damned if I ever let you disrespect me like that. I'm not a damn dog, Ace. I don't know how many times I have to tell you for you to understand. I will never let anyone ever treat me like how are treating me." He doesn't say anything after that he just grabs another bottle of his whiskey and pours it in the shot glass again. "Whatever," I mumble before walking out of his office and towards the kitchen.

Everyone who was in the kitchen before I left, are now gone, and it is only Lana and Leo inside.

"Told you not to go in there."

I roll my eyes at Leo. "Where is everyone?" I ask as I sit next to him.

"Cole is in the guest room. Alex and Calla went to the store. Ana and Antonio are in their room. Val went out to get some things that Ace requested. Emma is in our room. Your mom and dad are outside. And I'm pretty sure that's it."

"Oh. What are you guys doing?"

"Well, we were just talking. I was probably about to make some food or something," Lana shrugs.

"Like what?"

"I don't know, something simple," Lana looks super drained. I know that she has been with the De Luca's for a while so this must hurt her a lot. I wonder if Ace is gonna let her take a break or something or if I should ask Leo to give her some time off. "Are you okay honey? You look mad."

Leo chuckles and shakes his head lightly. "I'm fine," I shrug. "I'm just trying to do what I can for him, but you know how he is."

"Have you given him space at all?" Leo asks.

"Yes and no, but no matter what I try to do he doesn't seem to want anything from anyone. I know that he lost a lot, but it doesn't mean he gets to disrespect me and treat me like one of his soldiers."

"He'll come around. He is already trying to figure out how to kill Dimitri."

"I don't think that's a good idea. I think he just needs time off work or something. He needs time to grieve."

"He isn't used to what he is feeling right now. Someone he loved died. He isn't used to these types of feelings. So, he is dealing with them the only way he knows how to deal with them," Lana states.

"I don't even know what to do anymore. You guys said I needed to stay but I don't see how."

"Because he needs you," Lana states.

Nineteen

I AM STILL IN ITALY.

Lana assured me that I should stay, and that Ace didn't want me to leave and then she ended up saying that everyone will miss me too much including her if I did leave.

Emma was happy that I was staying along with Mia as well. They said that they wanted to show me around Italy now that I'm not technically a 'prisoner' anymore, but I didn't really feel like one while staying here. I just felt trapped.

Those are two different things, right?

Anyway, my parents and everyone else left yesterday. It's been pretty quiet in the house.

Ana has been in her room most of the time. She rarely gets out and the only time she does leave is when Antonio forces her to leave and eat something.

I am worried about her. I don't know how to help her, but

Antonio seems to do a good job at making sure she is taking care of herself.

Valentino has been in and out of the house. I don't know where too, but he hasn't been around in the last two days.

Lana is good company though. Whenever Emma is busy with Leo or just in general or if Mia is just in her room or at school, Lana will hang out with me.

She keeps trying to talk to me about Ace, but I don't want to talk about him. He is still acting cold towards me, so I am just trying to give him his space.

I haven't talked to him since he told me to leave. I did bump into him this morning and he was surprised to see me here instead of in America with my family. But he didn't say anything. He just glared at me and walked out of the kitchen.

Fucking dick.

All guys are dicks.

No offense to some guys that are actually decent but every guy I have had an encounter with has been a dick to me.

"Hey, honey." I look up at Ana who just walked into the kitchen.

I've spent most of my time in the kitchen because it just seems like a very open area to be in rather than the room I stay in.

"Hey, Ana. How are you?"

To be honest she looks like she is tired. I know Antonio is taking good care of her though. As well as Mia and Val.

"Ehh, you know. Good."

"You know if you ever need someone to talk to, I am here, right?" I assure.

Ana smiled. "Thank you, Aria. It's just hard because she was my best friend and knowing I won't ever see her just hurts. And it's all that Russian's fault," I listen to her rant. Ana sighed and poured herself a cup of coffee. "You know she used to be so happy."

"What do you mean?"

"She met Angelo and things got serious between them as they started dating."

"Ace's father?" I ask making sure that Angelo is Ace's father's name because I never knew if it was for sure his name or not.

"Yeah,"

"What happened?"

Ana walks next to me and sits down on the stool and faces me. "Angelo got too much power. They both met maybe in their early twenties. He showed so much affection towards her but one day it's like he turned into a different person," Ana says as she also sips a cup of coffee. "He then started to be more aggressive towards Alicia and you could see that all of the emotions and feelings he had for her were gone."

"Did Alicia try to leave?" I ask.

"Oh, dear god, yes. I had an escape plan for her. But then later on we found out she was pregnant with Ace." I see Ana smile probably remembering a memory between her and Alicia. "She was so happy, Aria. She had always wanted a child." Then I see her smile turn into a sad one. "But then one of the maids in the estate told Angelo about it and once he found out he didn't let Alicia leave."

"Why?"

"Because he needed an heir to his empire that he built. After he found out, he was furious that Alicia kept it from him. Luckily,

Alicia was pregnant so Angelo wouldn't hit or be aggressive towards her."

"Did she still try to leave?" I asked.

"Yes, but Angelo would catch her every time." *I can't believe Angelo would do something like that. But this kind of crime changes men. I would know.* "Ace was soon born and Alicia was so happy that day. She saw something in Ace's eyes the day he was born. It was some sort of sparkle."

I know what she is talking about because I have seen it. I love it when I see his eyes sparkle when they look down at me. It makes me feel important.

"But then-"

Ana got cut off by the sound of yelling down the hall which was also coming closer to the kitchen.

"Get the fucking car ready! What do I pay you for? To sit on your ass?"

I then see Ace walk into the kitchen with a frustrated look on his face.

"Where are you going, Ace?" Ana asks, looking at Ace who was texting on his phone.

He puts it in his pocket and looks at Ana. "To kill the man that killed my mother. I need to find Dimitri and the only way I will do that is if I torture the fucker."

Ana shakes her head lightly before standing up from the stool. "Okay. Be careful." She then turns to me. "If you want me to finish the story then you know where I'll be."

I nod my head and smile slightly at her before she walks off.

I look at Ace who is on his phone. "Who's going with you?"

"Leo, some of my men and you." Ace states coldly without looking at me.

"I never knew I was coming."

"Well since you insisted on staying here you will help kill Dimitri. Faster we find him the better," he mutters.

"Okay what do you need me to do?" I ask standing up from my seat.

Ace then looks at me and I see him glaring at me. "I honestly don't need you for anything. I need you to leave so that I can have some space."

What he is saying is complete bullshit.

I gave him space for the whole day, never saw him once except for bumping into him in the hallway.

"It's not like I want to be here," I spit. "I am trying to be a good person and just help you but you're acting like an ass. I know you are going through a lot right now but that doesn't give you the right to treat me like that. I'm a person with feelings. I think you sometimes forget that."

Ace walks closer to me so that he is standing right in front of me. "It's not like I was a spoiled brat who needs attention 24/7. I don't need you. I can do this myself. Only reason you are still alive is because for some reason my family cares for you. Be thankful you're still standing here breathing because if they weren't here then you would be six feet under, *morta,*" Ace said softly in a threatening voice.

He doesn't scare me. Ace is all bark and no bite.

I roll my eyes at him. "Whatever Ace. Let's go and get this over with," I mutter before walking past him.

I hear him let out a curse before I hear his footsteps behind me.

Right now, we are going to Ace's warehouse that is a few hours away.

Ace went alone in his car while he had Francisco drive me and Leo. The drive to the warehouse is boring. During the whole way there Leo and I talk a little and then I just mostly mess around on my phone and catch up on my social media.

I also am texting Layna while sitting in the car.

Leo told me that Ace was holding the man who killed his mother in his warehouse a few hours away because he didn't want him to be close to the family. They have been feeding him small meals so that he won't die because Ace wants to be the one to kill him.

The car stops, making me look out the window only to see a huge building in front of us.

"Come on," Leo says before opening his door.

I follow in pursuit and open my door, closing it walking behind Leo. I see Ace's car as we walk inside the building. He got here quickly. I remember leaving before him.

Leo, Francisco, and I walk inside the elevator and, on our way up, we all didn't say anything.

I wonder what they want me to do since they made me come.

The elevator door opens, and we all walk out. I see a huge office with floor to ceiling windows surrounding the entire perimeter.

You can see the whole city from up here. I can tell we were very high up.

"Finally, you're here. We can get this over with," Ace states while standing up from his desk.

"Well not all of us have fast sports cars like you to drive to this location," I mutter and I see Ace's jaw clench.

"I am only going to warn you once, Aria," Ace states walking closer to me. "If you disrespect me in my office in front of all of my men, I will make sure to show them how you are supposed to respect me in ways you couldn't even imagine." Ace is now right in front of me, and I am looking up at him. I can feel his breath hit my cheek. "Am I clear?"

I roll my eyes. "Can we get this over with?"

Ace doesn't bother to respond to me. He just walks past me with Francisco following behind him.

"You are the only one who gets away with talking to him like that," Leo mumbles as we all walk inside the elevator.

"I said this before, and I am going to say this again. I will never let anyone, especially a man disrespect me or tell me what to do."

We all walk back in the elevator, and it's quiet. I can feel the tension rising as we all stand next to each other.

Ace and Francisco are in front of Leo and I who are standing next to one another side by side.

I know Ace has been in a shitty mood and I know I should be a little sensitive with what I say but I won't let anyone talk to me like that.

Once the elevator doors open, Ace and Francisco walk forward and I see a dark hallway with stone walls and concrete floors, with barred cells on the side.

"Francisco guard the front," Ace states bluntly.

Francisco nods his head and walks to where we entered from, while Leo and I follow Ace down the hall.

As we walk down the halls, I see multiple people in the barred cells. They are all yelling vulgar things, saying I'm Ace's new whore, etc.

I bit down on my tongue so that I wouldn't argue with them about it.

Multiple men yell as we walk through the hall. I roll my eyes as we keep walking down the halls and hear multiple men yell vulgar sentences.

Ace stops walking, making me stop.

"Aria I want you to come with me and Leo to stay outside of the cell. Don't talk to him," he says to Leo and I before unlocking the cell and walking inside.

I don't say anything, I just walk inside the cage behind him.

"Ahh De Luca, you brought your whore," the man says as he lays against the wall.

Okay that's it.

I walk towards his weak figure and punch him in the jaw making his face go back and hit the wall. I see his nose start to bleed, making me smile a little.

"Say I am his whore again and I will make sure to cut your damn eye out of your eye socket."

"Ah you know how to choose them, De Luca," the man says and I turn around to look at Ace who looks amused, but he isn't smiling.

"Cut the bullshit, Evan," Ace deadpans and walks towards him. "Where is Dimitri?"

Evan gives Ace a wicked smile. "Like I would tell you."

Ace sighs and then looks at me. "You want to handle this, or should I?"

I shrug my shoulder and grab the knife from my pocket and walk closer to Evan.

I move my knife closer towards his eye. "You have such pretty eyes. I wonder how they would look on a silver platter for my dogs back at home," I say while trailing the knife around his eyes making him shiver. "Any clue where Dimitri is?" Evan doesn't say anything, making me cut a spot near his eyes. Evan screams in pain. "Speak or else I will take out your fucking eye!"

"Okay," Evan says in a shaky voice. "Please I want my eye."

"I bet you do. Like I said, you have such pretty eyes. Tell me where Dimitri is," I demand.

"Back in Russia. He hasn't left the estate," Evan looks behind me at Ace.

I feel Ace come up from behind me. "Where in Russia?"

Evan doesn't say anything making me go to stab his hand that is cuffed against the wall.

"Fucking talk," I say as Evan yells, and I even see a small tear roll down his cheek.

"Moscow," Evan sobs.

"What does Dimitri want?"

"He wants power. He wants to be the only group standing. Your mafias aren't the only ones he has threatened," he says breathing heavily. He looks back at Ace. "Now that I told her let me go you fucking bitch."

I look back at Ace. "Want anything else?"

"No," he states, and I stand to my full height and back away from Evan.

Ace walks towards Evan who is still breathing heavily. "Please let me go," Evan begs.

Ace crouches so that he is right in front of Evan, close to his face. "You know you killed the one person I loved right?" he asks Evan. "I don't have a mother anymore because of you," Ace deadpans.

"Please man I was just following orders. Give mercy on me."

"I don't give a flying shit about mercy," Ace says before grabbing his knife from his pocket in his suit. "*Saluta satana da parte mia*," Ace says before slicing Evan's throat, making blood spill out.

Twenty

Ace and I walk inside his office. He goes to his chair while I sit across from him.

He told me to follow him to his office so that we can finish with the whole Russian issue. Leo went to go check in with Emma and Francisco went home for the day. I guess he has a family of his own so obviously he has to go to them.

"So, what do we do now?" I ask once we sit down.

Ace opens one of his drawers and I see him pull out a burner phone.

How many burner phones does this guy have?

"Going to kill Dimitri," Ace states as he types in a number.

Kill Dmitri? How though? Through a phone?

Once he is done typing on the phone, he presses the call button making it ring.

"Hello?" Someone says on the other side of the phone.

He sounds familiar.

"Jared," Ace states.

"Wait, Jared?" I say without thinking and scoot my chair closer so that I can listen in on their conversation.

What the hell is Jared doing in Russia? Is that where he has been lately?

"Shut the fuck up," Ace says looking at me. "I want you to do it right now. The location that I told you is correct. The hostage told me it's in Moscow which I already had a feeling since Dimitri likes to make it known that he is rich by purchasing big houses."

"Right now?" Jared questions.

"Yes. Once you are done, I want you to get your ass back over here."

"Alright, sir," Jared says before I hear rustling and movements on the other side of the phone. "It's for you *Pakhan*," I hear Jared say but it is faint.

"Hello?" I hear a deep voice say with a Russian accent.

"Dimitri." Ace states.

What the hell are you doing Ace?

"Ahhh, Ace nice to speak with you. It's been a while. How have you been?" Dimitri says and I already know he is smiling on the other side of the phone.

I see Ace's jaw clench. "You know, Dimitri. Just cleaning up your messes as always."

"Yes, sorry for the loss by the way. So devastating that such an amazing soul had to die."

"Yeah. What a tragedy," Ace mutters. I hear a ding come from his other phone making him look down and back at the phone he was holding in his other hand with Dimitri on the line. "But I will send you roses, Dimitri," Ace mumbles. "*Saluta Satana da parte mia. Che tu possa riposare in pace.*"

Then I hear a big bang on the phone and the line go silent.

I am in shock. I don't know what to say. Usually when I kill someone I do it in person, but Ace just killed Dimitri on the phone.

Oh my god what about Jared? Was he still in the house when that happened?

"He's dead," I state while still in shock.

"Precisely," Ace states before throwing the phone on the desk. "Now you can leave and live your happy little life," Ace says while glaring at me.

What the fuck did I do?

"What about Jared? Did he get out-"

"Jared is fine. We had an automatic bomb placed in every section of the estate and in his building. They are all dead. Every last Russian scum. I found his estate location with your father and brother, but I needed to make sure that that was his estate before bombing it up. I sent Jared to do the work and make sure everything was going according to plan. He and Josh also went to all of Dimitri's men's houses and kill them and all of their family. He is alive and left the house the second Dimitri touched the phone," Ace spit. "So now that that is over you may leave and never come back."

"Why do you hate me so much?" I ask while crossing my leg over the other.

Ace puts his hands on his desk and leans forward over the desk. "I don't care for you. I don't just hate you. I despise you. I want you to fucking leave and never come back. Your presence annoys me, and I hate that you are breathing," Ace spit.

I don't know why what he said hurt but it did. It made my heart squeeze.

"You can be a real jackass sometimes," I say before standing up.

I make a move to open the office door, but I see a hand come out from behind me and slam the door shut. I turn around and face Ace who is towering over me while making strong eye contact with me.

"Are you saying that because you let me kiss you? Is that why you're acting so hurt and feel like fucking crying all the time?"

My hand collides with his cheek and his face goes to the side. "Stop treating me as if I am one of your whores that will go down on my knees for you. Because that will never happen."

One thing I don't expect Ace to do is wrap his hand around my throat, not tightly, just enough to scare me though.

It feels familiar and it's fucking terrifying.

He leans closer to my ear, "You're lucky that I'm in a good mood today or else I would have shot you right here, right now," Ace lets go of me. "Get out."

I push him away from me and then open his door and leave his office.

So, I'm still in Italy.

My dad says that I need to stay here to make sure that Ace isn't up to anything and to also make sure that the Russians are for sure done with.

I mean it's not the worst thing ever that I am staying here. I get to hang out more with Emma and also piss off Ace because for some reason, pissing him off is some kind of stress reliever.

I also can't get my mind off of what he did the other day. The way his hands wrapped around my neck and squeezed it just a little to make me feel scared.

And I was scared.

First time I have been scared in a while. What he did reminded me of what Dante used to do to me. It just brought back bad memories of how Dante used to touch me.

Speaking of Ace, he left for Russia the other day.

Ace has been gone for almost two days. Leo went with him, and he says that they were on their way back now, but they went to go finish some things first.

I am guessing they both went to go make sure that Dimitri is actually dead, and he is. All of his men are. It seems way too easy for it to be done with them but then again, the Russians were never that good at doing anything. Only getting good revenge and doing sneaky shit.

While Ace has been gone Emma and I have been hanging out more and also shopping around the city. She took me to the beach that was nearby, I had a lot of fun.

I got a lot of dresses, some pants, and also a few workout clothes. I used my card since Alex gave it to me before he left.

Today Emma and I decided to just hang by the pool and relax. Valentino is going to barbecue, and Mia isn't here because she has some classes today. Ana hasn't left her room much and I always go to her room to check up on her. She keeps mentioning small things about how Alicia was like before she met Angelo but she never revealed Angelo and Ace's relationship, which is fine because I'm not asking her to reveal that kind of information. I don't want to push her.

I get out of my shorts and sweater and change into a black swimsuit.

Once I change into the swimsuit I head downstairs to the pool where Emma is already laying on the pool chair.

She has on a blue swimsuit with some black sunglasses protecting her eyes from the sun.

Emma and I just relax and start to tan. I really need a tan because I am starting to look a little pale.

This feels nice. The warm sun against my skin and the sound of music in the background. I can also smell the food Val is making.

While relaxing I start to think about how much my life has changed. I start to think about Dante.

I never like to think about him but ever since being here with Ace I can't help but think about Dante. I have been comparing them two so much.

Ace is better even though he is being a jackass right now. I understand his mother died but there is no reason to act like an asshole to someone.

Dante used to be perfect. He was everything I ever wanted but that was before I knew who he really was. Now all I think about when I see or hear his name being mentioned is to hide. He broke any trust I had. He made me guard myself and my heart. I could never ever trust another man after him.

Towards the end of the relationship, it got super toxic. He started calling me nasty names that I felt uncomfortable with. He would sometimes touch me when I didn't want to be touched. I felt weak when I was around him. This was also around the time I was weak and didn't know much about defending myself around men.

But I still stayed with him because I thought I loved him but in reality, I learned that I just wanted to be loved. He was the only person who did show me the kind of affection I craved but I soon learned it wasn't the good kind of affection.

My mom and Layna saw I was feeling uncomfortable, and they also heard the arguments we would get into, and they said I should break up with him.

Eventually, I agreed with them, and I tried to break up with him but then he punched me square in the jaw. I tried to leave the room after he did that, but he wouldn't let me. He threatened me that if I spoke about what happened between us, he would kill the people I cared about. He even threatened Ariel which scared me.

We continued our relationship for another few months. When me and him had sex, it wasn't the same. I felt used.

When I would argue with him, he would always hit and sometimes push me to the floor. I would have bruises and whenever my mom or someone in the house would question it, I would just say I fell or got them from sparing with someone in the gym.

Layna and my mom then caught him pushing mr down the stairs and then she kicked him out. I haven't seen him since.

My dad and Alex don't know because if they did, he would be dead, but I didn't want any issues with him. I just wanted to forget him. And with the help of my mom and Layna, I gladly did.

Dante and I met from this assassin academy my father took me to when I was younger and just started intense training. Then we soon started to talk more and more, and we then fell in love.

I'm also grateful I didn't lose my virginity to him. I feel like losing that is important now that I think about it. I lost mine when I was sixteen and it was to a guy with whom I used to be friends. But sadly, he died a year after due to suicide. He even wrote me a note. I remember crying while reading that note because what he said broke my heart.

He explained how he was feeling and why he killed himself. He didn't feel loved and he also was diagnosed with PTSD because of a traumatic event that happened with his father and mother when he was fifteen. But I guess everything became too much for him. I wish I could have done something to help him. I didn't notice any tendencies, but I wish I did.

Val comes out with the hamburgers he made and gives us a sad smile.

"Val, what's wrong?" Emma asks, noticing too.

"My mom and dad want to move," he states in an annoyed tone.

"Why?" I ask.

"My mom can't live in the house her best friend used to live in. Too many memories and too many bad ones she told me. My dad agreed," Val explains.

Emma looks devastated. "When do you guys have to leave?" she asks.

"Once Ace comes back. But we will also need to talk to him about it too."

"Do you want to leave?" I ask.

"No, but I understand why my mom and dad want to."

"Why don't you talk to them then?"

"I will. Mia doesn't know about this; I don't know how she is going to react. I'm scared to see, to be honest," Val admits.

"She won't be happy. But we will miss you no matter what. We love you, Val. So much," Emma states.

"I love you guys too." Val pulls us in for a hug while we all shed some tears. "But I won't be gone for long," Val winks.

I don't say anything, instead I just hug Emma and Val.

Twenty-One

Tomorrow is the day that Ana and her family will leave. It's been a few days since Valentino told us about them moving. They found a place pretty quick and they are also getting their furniture soon.

I'm honestly going to miss Val and Mia. But it's not going to be the same. Now it's just going to be me, Ace, Leo, and Emma in the house.

Well, I am soon going to leave too. I just need to get the update from Ace and the go ahead from my dad because he is the one who still wants me here.

Ace is also back, and we still haven't talked. He barely even looks at me. He just glares and ignores my presence.

When Ana told Ace, he was hurt. He wouldn't show it, but he was. He is mostly concerned about why they are leaving but I know he understands.

I'm surprised that Ace is still going to live here especially after everything that has happened. Mia was crying the day her mom told her. It's not like they are moving out of the country though. Ana said she still wants to be close to Ace in case he ever needs anything.

At least he has Lana.

I walk towards where Emma's room is held and knock before I hear her say "come in".

"Hey." I see Mia sitting on Emma's bed when I open the door.

"Hey." I walk over to the bed. "What are we talking about?"

"Nothing much. Just recapping some memories," Mia says.

"What's wrong? It looks like something is on your mind." Emma asks while observing me, which she seems to do a lot.

I furrow my eyebrows at her. "What do you mean?"

"You have that constipated thinking face," Emma sarcastically says.

"I don't have a constipated thinking face," I glare at her.

"Sure." Emma rolls her eyes. "What's up? You can talk to us."

"It's nothing. Just been thinking about stuff," I shrug my shoulders.

Emma looks at Mia and smirks before looking back at me. "Thinking about what?"

I narrow my eyes at Emma, because I have a feeling, I know what she is thinking about or assuming.

"I am guessing she is thinking about a person whose name starts with an 'A' and ends with an 'E'." Mia says while giving Emma a knowing smile.

I roll my eyes at them.

They keep assuming things, thinking Ace and I are hooking

up when it's the complete opposite. I don't think I would be able to handle Ace's tantrums.

"You guys are funny."

"You're not denying anything," Mia claims.

"Just because I'm not denying anything doesn't mean I'm in love with him."

"Dude, we know you're in love with him," Mia says while narrowing her eyes at me.

"Whoa. I'm not in love with Ace," I claim while widening my eyes at her statement.

"Yeah you are. He is too. Probably more though," Emma agrees.

"No, he's not. He hates me. Last time we talked he said he would be rather happy if I left or dropped dead."

"Dude, are you kidding? Ever since you came here, he has been much more different. He even stopped fucking around too," Mia says.

"Really? Isn't he screwing that Lexi bitch?"

"She's gone now. Ace kicked her out," Emma states.

"Well, he doesn't like me. He has been acting like an asshole every time I talk to him."

Again, I know he lost his mom but he isn't being rude to anyone else but me so that can't justify his actions towards me.

"Weren't you guys good at the night of the ball?"

"Yeah. We were okay" I shrug.

"And were you guys good when you left the ball?"

"Yes and no. We were good for a few minutes and then he started yelling at me and pushing me away. He just doesn't seem like the type to want to be in love. I'm not going to beg someone for their attention. I'm not that kind of person. If he wants to be, cool, we can be, but I haven't done anything wrong. I have only tried to help him."

"I have an idea," Mia states. "And it will be fun," a smirk lifts on her lips.

"And what's your idea?"

"Make him come to you. Play with him a little," Mia smirks.

"That's a horrible idea."

"No, it's not actually," Emma claims. "Dress in something a little less then what you normally wear. And since it's Mia's last night, we are going to go clubbing. You will for sure have his attention."

"I don't need his attention," I narrow my eyes at Emma.

"Aria, stop lying to yourself, it's getting annoying," Mia rolls her eyes and scoots closer to me on the bed. "Didn't you guys' kiss or something?"

I feel my cheeks heat up and I look down.

He also held me up against the door with his hand wrapped around my throat which I don't know how to feel about that.

"Do you know if he regrets it?"

"I think. He hasn't been talking to me," I shrug.

"Well make him come to you. Don't make the first move anymore," Mia says.

"I haven't been talking to him for the past few days."

"Okay good. Now we just need to up our game. Wear something a little bit more revealing. We are going to make him make the first move and come to you."

"Okay, easy."

Emma smiles. "Okay so it's a done deal. We're going to go to the club. Mia's last day is today so we are going to all go out and party," Emma says before jumping off her bed. "I will lend you a dress since I have the perfect one in mind and then we all can get ready and go to Ace's club," Emma says while walking to her closet.

"Okay. It is going to be Mia's last day so why not. Try to give me a dress that's not too showy though," I agree.

"Deal."

Mia, Emma, and I start getting ready.

Emma does my makeup, and I just straightened my hair.

I leave my room once I finish getting ready and head downstairs to wait for Emma and Mia. They still need to get ready because Emma was helping me with my makeup while Mia was in the shower.

When I walk inside the kitchen, I see Ace.

I can't help but roll my eyes and walk more inside the kitchen. I see him turn his head as I walk towards the fridge to get a water bottle. I can feel his eyes running up and down my body.

"What are you wearing?" Ace asks coldly as I open the fridge.

"A dress."

"Why?"

I close the fridge and look at him. "Because the girls and I are going out," I state before taking a sip from the water bottle.

Ace walks closer to me making me hit my back against the counter. "Not dressed like that."

"Who do you think you are? My dad?"

"Aria listen to me very carefully because I'm not going to repeat myself," he says before coming closer to me, and he did a once over at my attire again. "You're not going anywhere dressed like that, *amore*. Don't fight me on this."

I'm about to say something but then I hear Emma yell.

"Aria! Let's go!"

Ace looks behind me and then back down at me with a glare. "Fight me Ace so that I can fight back," I say before giving him a wink and walking away from him.

Last night was crazy.

Way too crazy.

I am pretty sure I drank at least more than one bottle of tequila. I am surprised I'm still here.

Mia, Emma and I partied like animals. We drank so much, and we danced the night away. Best club night ever.

When we got back to the house it was so late so almost everyone was asleep. I didn't see Ace last night thank god because I was too drunk to even function what I was doing, and I didn't want to deal with him.

But Mia, Emma, and I all slept in my room, and then when we woke up Lana made us a recovery breakfast. Then moments later it was time for the Ferrari's to leave. Val will still be over often, because he works for Ace but Mia will be busy with school.

It's almost five o'clock in the evening and it's been kind of boring in the house. Emma and I haven't been doing much. Mainly just watching movies and shit like that. I haven't seen Ace or Leo in the house, but Emma said it was because they had some things to deal with, with another family.

When Ace saw me this morning, he looked so pissed. Probably because of last night I'm guessing but I don't give a fuck. I just gave him a small smile and walked past him.

Currently, Lana is about to make dinner for everyone. She is making her Rigatoni with Vodka Sauce dish. I've never tried that before so I'm kind of excited.

While she is making dinner, I decide to FaceTime Layna. Her and I have been texting nonstop.

"What are you doing?" Layna asks as I stare at her from my phone screen.

"In the kitchen. What are you doing? Where is everyone?"

"I'm not doing anything. Cole went to go to the store to buy something for Ariel since she is sick. Calla is with her in the room and Alex is making her food with your mom. I think my mom is out and your dad is working."

"Oh, how are you and Cole?" I smirk.

"We're good," I see her blush through the phone.

They definitely did the deed.

"Layna," I urge.

"Shut up."

"Dude, you're so easy to read. When did it happen?"

"Last night," she mumbles and her face is full-on red.

"That's my girl!" I yell.

"Aria shut up. You're so fucking annoying."

"Aww is my best friend embarrassed?" I tease.

"Shut up. Don't you have someone to bother? Ace? Emma?"

"Emma is asleep with Leo and Ace is being a bitch."

"What time is it over there?" she asks while looking at her watch.

"Like five o'clock."

I then hear the door open and close on the phone.

"Baby!" I hear Cole yell.

Layna turns to look at Cole. "Oh, you're back," she says while getting up on the couch.

"Yeah who's on the phone," Cole says before I see his head in the frame. "Hey, Aria."

"Hey. I'm going to let you guys go because I know you went to the store for Ariel. Make sure to give her a big hug and kiss for me when she is better."

"I will. Bye love you."

"Love you guys," I hang up the phone.

"Ariel okay?" Lana asks as she walks up to me with a plate of food.

"Yeah she is just sick. She's a strong girl. Is the food almost done?"

"Yes, ma'am. Your plate is ready," she says as she hands me my plate.

"This looks good. Thank you," I give Lana a smile.

I start digging in while Lana makes more for the others. I like that Lana is here. She kind of feels like my grandma or mom.

"Hey," I turn my head and see Emma and Leo walk in.

"Hey. Lana made Rigatoni with Vodka Sauce," I say to them.

Emma sits next to me, and Leo sits across from her.

"Damn I love it when she makes that shit," Leo says.

"I know you do," Lana chuckles while placing a plate in front of him.

"Thank you, Lana," Emma says as Lana gave her a plate. "So how is the plan coming up?"

"What's the plan?" Leo asks, being as clueless as ever.

"Aria is trying to make Ace come to her," Emma smirks.

"Really?" I say to Emma. I look at Leo, "Not like that."

"Oh, that's why he has been in a pissy mood," Leo says while chuckling.

"What do you mean pissy mood?"

"He just looks annoyed and frustrated. It's actually quite amusing."

I roll my eyes.

Once I'm done eating, I go into the kitchen and start washing my dish. I hear footsteps coming towards me. I turn my head to my left and see Ace walk through the kitchen door. His jaw is clenched and eyebrows are furrowed.

"What's with you?" I ask, noticing he is in a bad mood but when is he not?

"Nothing," he spit as he walked past me towards the coffee maker.

"Okay no need to be a rude," I mumble.

He doesn't say anything. Instead, he continues to make his coffee while I finish washing up the dishes.

"*Merida*!" he swears in Italian.

"'Nothing', he says," I mock.

"Fuck! Do you always like pissing people off?" Ace mutters but doesn't look at me.

"Maybe you do need another cup of coffee dick."

He walks towards me very closely towering over my figure. "What did you just call me?"

I stand taller. "I called you a dick. If you don't like the name, then stop acting like one," I spit.

His lips lift into a smirk. "Why are you playing these games with me, Ari?" he asks leaning towards my ear.

I feel his chest against mine. I look up at him. His eyes are searching mine with that smirk still present on his face.

"I'm not."

I can feel his lips directly on the top of my ear. I feel my breathing become harder.

Fuck.

"Ari. Stop lying to me," he whispers. I don't say anything. I can't. "Why do you like to fucking play with me?"

"Play how?" I ask innocently, looking up at him.

"*Amore*. I want you. Stop making this difficult," he whispers.

"Doesn't seem like it." I look up at him. "You're the one making it difficult," I say trailing my finger up his chest.

Now our lips are close.

Very close.

If one of us moves its game over.

He wins. But that's if I lean in.

He has to make the first move.

Not me.

I feel his lips brush mine.

"What are you going to do Ari?" Ace whispers.

I kiss him on the side of his mouth and then lean towards his ear. "Nothing," I whisper before moving away from him.

Twenty-Two

I walk inside the gym while tying my hair up in a ponytail.

Today I have been feeling a little stressed out, so I want to let off some steam.

Yesterday I stumbled into Ace's torture room and I was looking at all of the weapons he had. Long story short he came in and we had a moment but then I ran out of there and spent the rest of the day in my room. Emma came in to check on me, but I just wanted to be alone.

I couldn't think straight. Being around Ace makes my head spin, both in a good and bad way. He is back and forth with me and it's frustrating. It feels good to blow off Ace though. I feel powerful. More than usual.

Ace is intimidating as hell, and I would never admit that out loud but waving him off makes me feel satisfied.

I walk towards the equipment box that has the boxing gloves and wraps. I grab a pair of clean gloves and I wrap my hands before putting the black glove on. I walk towards the punching bag and start punching it, throwing multiple punching combinations.

I do a jab and then a right cross three times before throwing another combination of punches. I repeat the punches over and over until I get bored and switch it up adding kicks and upper cuts.

I love punching the punching bag. It lets me get out all of my emotions and I can take out all of the built-up anger inside me that I don't usually showcase.

While punching I hear the door of the gym open making me look in the mirror in front of me.

I see Ace walk in.

He is shirtless and I can see his tattoos that are spread across his chest and trail up his tanned arms and biceps.

"Done eye-fucking me, *amore*?" Ace says making me look at him in the eye from the mirror.

"No, I was actually trying to see if that was a pimple on your nose," I say while squinting my eyes. "Yes, definitely a pimple. You're going to have to check that out."

I see Ace's lips lift a little and I turn my head around to look back at him.

Is he smiling?

"Trust me, I don't have a pimple. But if you really think so you can come closer and check to see."

I shrug my shoulders and take off my gloves, throwing them to the floor. I walk closer to Ace until I am right in front of him, our chests almost touching.

I lean closer to his face and bring my hand up to his jaw.

I look into his beautiful eyes instead of the imaginary pimple I told him I saw.

In fact, he has really good skin. His skin was clear of pimples. He did have a few scars from past cuts or scratches he got from fighting or other things. I also notice some acne scars on his nose area but to be honest they look like small freckles.

Don't get me started on his eyes. His beautiful green eyes that have that special sparkle in them. I love it when he has that sparkle in his eyes. They are probably the most beautiful pair of eyes I have ever seen. His eyes steal all of my words away.

I look down at his plumped lips that are a tad bit bigger because he probably just woke up and his face might be a little puffy. They are a beautiful pinkish nudish shade that look so soft.

I look back up to meet his eyes. "I guess I was seeing things. But you know what I do see?" I ask raising my eyebrows while giving him a small amused smile.

Ace's lips lift in a small smirk. "What do you see Ari?" Ace whispers.

I lift my lips in a smile. "I see a jackass who thinks the world revolves around him and who is always rude when people try to help him," I turn on my heel and walk back to the bag, not looking back at Ace's reaction to what I said.

"You got jokes, *amore*." Ace chuckles lightly.

"Yeah, I'm secretly a comedian. You didn't know?" I ask while putting the boxing gloves back on. Then I feel strong arms wrap around my waist making me feel butterflies. I look down at the tattooed arms that are wrapped around my stomach. I take a deep breath and look in the mirror across from us and see who is looking down at me. *Relax Aria.* "Get your baboon arms off of me, Ace," I state while trying not to show how much he affected me with his touch. The butterflies in my stomach flutter and I feel a tingle in my lower stomach making me want to cross my legs.

He's never touched me like this so I have no clue how to react.

"Why? You don't like me touching you?" Ace whispers in my ear making me feel chills everywhere on my body. I can't say anything. I can't. I feel frozen. I feel like I can't move. His arms are like the only place I want to be in. And I haven't felt like that in a long time. "Mmm?"

"Ace, let go of me," I demand.

"No," Ace turns me around. Ace looks down at me and I see his eyes trailing all over my facial features. "God, you're so fucking beautiful," Ace brings his hand up to my face and his thumb strokes my cheek. "I'm sorry for being a jackass," Ace mumbles.

"Not good enough. Why were you?" I raise my eyebrow.

"I'm not used to someone caring about me as much as you do. It's foreign."

"Doesn't mean you have to push me away, Ace," I deadpan.

"Well, I am done with that now," Ace leans his face closer to mine. "I want you." I pretend to think about it for a few minutes. "I have a proposition."

I narrow my eyes at Ace. "What is it?"

"Poker game. Whoever wins has to do whatever the other one asks."

I raise one eyebrow at him.

"Why would I do something stupid like that?"

"Because I know you secretly want to do something like that. Be grateful I'm not making it strip poker," Ace deadpan.

"Fine. If I win, I want to see all of the information you have on the Russians and planned attacks you might have on the Americans."

Ace raises an eyebrow. "You know how to make a deal."

"Learned from the best. What do you want?"

"One night with you. Not hooking up. Just hanging out."

"A date."

Ace almost winces when I said that. "Don't call it that."

"But that's exactly what it is," I state.

Ace's jaw clenches. "It's a yes or no."

"Fine. Deal."

"Let's go in the game room."

I furrow my eyebrows. "There's a game room?"

Ace nods his head and then steps away from me.

Ace and I walk to where the game room is located. In the game room there is a green card table, pool table, some small arcade games, and then a bar in the far end of the room.

"Over here," Ace states and I follow him to where the card table is. Once Ace and I sit down in front of one another he starts to shuffle the deck of cards. "You have played poker, right?"

"Yeah. It's not hard to learn."

"Well, I was asking since you didn't know how to wrap your own hands."

I glare at Ace. "I have trouble with it. I can wrap my own hands but it just takes me a while to get it right."

"Sure," Ace says with an amused smile. Ace starts to step the cards on the table. "Place your bets."

I take my blinds and play down seven.

I shouldn't be this confident but fuck it.

"Rise," Ace states.

I nip at my lip and place another few blinds down and then look at my cards. I have a Queen and a Three. Ace puts down a three, ace, and seven.

Ace and I play around for a few more rounds. When we have the last cards in our deck it's time for the showdown.

In my deck I only have a six, seven, three, and two.

Not that good of cards.

"Ready to lose?" Ace asks with a raised eyebrow.

"Are you?" I ask, sounding confident even though I'm pretty sure I'm going to lose.

"All blinds on the table. I'm getting bored," Ace says before putting his blinds on the table. I do the same. "Put down your cards, *amore*."

After a few seconds of just staring at one another, Ace and I put down our cards.

I almost choke on my spit when I see that Ace put down all four aces.

"What a coincidence," I state, trying not to think about the fact that I have to go on a date with Ace.

"Start getting dolled up *amore*, because we have dinner reservations we are going to be late to."

Once I finish getting ready I head downstairs to meet Ace outside.

I'm wearing a black mini dress with an oversized black leather jacket with black strappy heels.

When I walk outside the house I see Ace leaning against his car.

He is wearing a black dress shirt and slacks. It looks like a casual-formal outfit for him to wear.

"Ready?" Ace asks and I nod my head making him open the car door for me to get inside.

Once he is also in the car, he starts the engine and drives outside the gates of the estate.

"So why do you want to take me out?" I ask while looking outside the window.

"I can't just take a girl out to get some food?"

"You don't seem like the dating type," I state making Ace's jaw clench.

For the rest of the drive Ace and I don't say a word to one another.

When Ace finally stops and parks the car, I see we are in front of a building, and I look at Ace only to see him getting out of the car.

I open my door and am about to step out, but Ace holds open the door for me and takes my hands, helping me get out of the car. I thank him before he closes the door and locks the car.

"Where are we?" I ask him.

"You'll see."

Ace's hand is still holding onto mine as we walk through the building's glass doors.

We probably walk for like a minute or two before we go through another set of glass doors. When Ace pushes the doors open, I see a huge lake in front of us with the sun setting and boat at the end of the small deck that is outside.

Ace pulls me towards the deck. "With you being American, I figured you have never actually got the chance to do one of the popular things here in Italy."

Twenty-Three

Ace gets inside the boat and then looks at me. "Don't worry I won't let you fall," Ace says as he holds his hand out for me to take. I let out a sigh and put my hand in his as he helps me walk on the small motorboat. "Go sit down in the front. I'm going to pull more out."

I do as he says and sit at the very front of the boat where there is a red blanket and black pillows. There is also plates with covers on them and then a bucket with ice and champagne in it.

Eventually the boat is in the middle of the lake as the sun is close to disappearing from the sky. Luckily we aren't that far out from the city because all of the lights from the shore are reflecting to us.

"It's really pretty here," I say while looking at the scene around us.

"My mom used to take me out here once in a while when she wanted a night for just me and her. The first thing I ever ate here is

Carbonara and I have loved it ever since. That's why Lana makes it all the time. Every Sunday my mom would take Leo and me here and sometimes we would go to the park nearby. Those were the only times I ever felt like a kid. She made it easier."

"It's nice that you had those memories with her to remember. Those are one of the best memories anyone could ever have," I say with a small smile on my face.

"Yes," Ace says softly.

"I don't even remember if my mom or dad ever took me and Alex to the park or even out to dinner. We were always kind of locked in the house, " I say, trying to start a conversation.

I also wanted to change the subject because I don't want him to talk about his mom while getting sad. But if he is willing to talk about her, the good memories about her, then I am willing to listen fully.

"I never understood why your dad did that," Ace states and looks at me.

"He was scared people would use me for leverage, so he was careful with me for everything."

He nods his head. "Kind of hard when you get named best assassin," Ace chuckles.

"I think he sometimes forgets I know how to handle myself. He still sees me as his little girl," I explain. "Sorry for pretending to be your mole by the way. I feel bad because your family is so nice, and I was lying to them."

"It's fine. We are at a truce for now."

"For now?" I furrow my eyebrows.

"Don't piss me off anymore and it will stay a truce." I chuckle at what he said. "Well, I know you ate dinner because Lana made food, so I thought dessert was suitable," Ace says before taking the covers off the plates.

I see a really yummy looking chocolate mousse cake with a small strawberry on the top.

My favorite cake.

"How did you know I liked this cake?" I say with a small smile on my face.

"Lana. She told me out of the blue."

I take a bite out of the cake and almost moan from how good it tastes making Ace have a small, amused smile.

"You're really lucky to have someone like Lana in your life," I state.

"Lana is always there for me. Even when I am a dick to her, she still manages to handle my anger and attitude towards her."

"Lana cares for you a lot. Just like how other people do," I state.

Ace and I eat the cake while just talking about random things.

I learn that his favorite color is black, but I already knew that. He likes to box; it is his favorite sport. His favorite animal is a snake and he even used to have one for a pet. He got rid of it because he was always so busy and couldn't take care of it. He likes to race a lot. When he was eighteen he would always race with his friends at these dirt tracks nearby. He barely watches any movies because he is always working, but his favorite movies are Men in Black and The Lion King.

After we are done, we talk more about all of our likes and dislikes as he drives the boat back to the deck.

Before I met Ace, I never thought I would be able to look at someone and smile for no reason. Especially when he showcases his smile that he rarely shows.

His eye contact is very intense.

So intense that I have to look away, so I don't blush.

It feels weird to blush again; before I was scared of blushing but now it seems so easy.

When I first met him, all I wanted to do was strangle him and now I want to get to know him more.

The unspoken words between us are not awkward or uncomfortable.

After some walking, we end up on a grass field with a railing at the end overlooking the lake.

It is pretty dark outside, but the moon and small buildings around us gives some sort of light. There are so many stars in the sky, and I find myself getting lost looking at all of them.

"Whenever I got into an argument with my father, my mom would always take me here to clear my head. I would usually climb that rock and sit at the top whenever I came here by myself," he says as he points to the rock over the lake.

"Your dad . . .what happened with him?" I ask. I want to know. Ana told a small version of the story, but I want to know Ace's point of view. I'm not asking for my dad to know Ace's personal stuff. I'm asking because I'm genuinely curious and want to know his story. What happened the night Ace killed his father? "You don't have to answ-"

"No. I trust you," he sighs before talking. "I never really talk to anyone about it or things that happened with my dad. My mom knew almost all the things and the same with Leo. My dad wasn't the nicest man in the world. He was always taught to be very strict and disciplined. I didn't care for his rules though when I was a teenager."

He paused as if he was trying not to relive the memories.

"Long story short, he would always hit my mother and I for no reason and then he would punish us if we did any little thing wrong. It was around Christmas time, and I asked him if I could have this Batman Lego set and instead, he sent a group of his men to beat me because I asked to have something. That day he told me 'You don't ask for things Ace; you must earn them'. So, I took all of the punches and hits they gave me and I almost passed out because of that."

I can't believe Angelo did something like that to Ace. I know there was more to the story, but I don't want to push him to say more than what he is comfortable with.

Before I can say anything, he continues. "The night my father died was also the night I had my first ever kill. My mother and I were planning on escaping right after I got home from school. But when I arrived home, I saw my father hitting my mother while fucking her ruthlessly on the floor. She was crying for him to stop, and he wasn't. Instead, he just kept going and pulling her hair while calling her vulgar names while saying 'This is what you get for making my son turn against me.' I ran towards her and pushed him on the floor before punching him and kicking him. Long story short he died at my hands."

I feel my whole body spread with goosebumps after the story is finished. I can't even imagine what was going through Ace's head.

I don't know how I would react if something like that happened with my parents.

I look at him trying to see him going through all that.

That's why Ace is the way he is.

He went through both mental and physical abuse, but mental abuse is worse than physical because that sticks with you. His dad abused him on a daily basis, but he is stuck with those memories for the rest of his life.

"I don't know what to say. I'm sorry you had to go through that."

"Life's shitty," Ace mutters while turning his head away from me, as if he is ashamed.

"But you deserve better." I state.

"No. I'm not a good guy. If I was, I would feel guilty about killing him, but I don't."

"That doesn't make you a monster. You saved your mother."

"You don't know me, Aria."

"I know that you care a lot about your family."

Ace shook his head lightly before looking at me. "Have you ever wanted to live a normal life?"

I shrug my shoulders. "Yes and no. I like what I do but sometimes I imagine myself being a normal person living a normal life," I answer truthfully. "Have you ever wanted to live a normal life?"

"No. This is who I am, who I am born to be. It's the only life I know, the only life I wish for. For me to commit to a normal life, it would be like a lion living in a small cage at the zoo."

Twenty-Four

After Ace and I got home from the 'date', we went to my room to watch a movie.

It's morning now and Ace is asleep beside me with his arm around my waist and his head is on my chest.

He looks so calm and relaxed. As if nothing could touch him.

I trace the tattoos on his arms while he peacefully sleeps.

The tattoo was of a Gemini star constellation. I never knew when his birthday was but now, I know the frame of when his birthday could be. I'll have to remind myself to ask him.

It feels like a lifetime that I have known him but in reality, it's been more than two months.

I decided to stay in Italy for a bit longer.

I talked to my dad while Ace was changing out of his clothes last night.

I said that I wanted to stay in Italy for a little bit longer, but I didn't say anything about me wanting to get to know Ace.

But I really do want to see how things with Ace go, what this is between us.

Yesterday was a really good day. I felt happy and calm when I was hanging out with Ace.

I still haven't told Ace about what happened with my past and I feel guilty because he told me everything about his. I'm scared that he will see me as weak and that I'm not strong enough to handle myself. But when around Dante I am not. He is the only person I feel weak around and that is why I am so glad he isn't in my life anymore.

I notice Ace's eyes start to flutter.

"Morning," he says in his sexy morning voice.

"Morning," I say with a small smile on my face while trying not to blush or focus on the small tingles I feel in my stomach.

He rises to lean in to kiss me on the lips, but I lean away.

"The fuck? Give me a kiss," he demands.

Ace and I didn't kiss last night. We didn't do anything.

But if he is going to want a kiss I am going to have to brush my teeth at least.

"I have to brush my teeth," I state before getting out of his bed and walking towards the bathroom in the room.

"I have some work today but once I'm done, we're leaving," Ace states while still laying in the bed.

"Leaving?" I ask looking back at him.

"Yeah. Pack your bags. It's somewhere kind of cold."

"Where are we going?"

"Not telling," Ace gets up from the bed and walks towards me while I start to brush my teeth.

I roll my eyes and continue brushing my teeth as Ace stares at me from behind me. I try not to laugh because I probably look so stupid brushing my teeth.

Once I am done brushing my teeth, I put the toothbrush away and turn to look at Ace. "Yes? Do you like watching people brush their teeth?"

Ace has an amused smirk on his face. "No, but I like watching you." I roll my eyes and Ace walks closer to me and once he is right in front of me, he wraps his arms around my waist pulling me closer to him. "Can I have my kiss now?" I chuckle and shake my head no, making him glare at me. "Eh I was just being nice by asking but you're getting that kiss," Ace says before leaning in and kissing me on the lips.

His grip on my waist gets tighter and he licks my bottom lip before thrusting his tongue meeting mine. He pushes me against the bathroom counter and then trails his kisses along my cheek and then jaw, down to my neck. He bit the spot on the nape of my neck before sucking it and then giving one last kiss before leaning away.

"Be ready by four o'clock," Ace states as he backs away from me.

I open my eyes and furrow my eyebrows.

I can't tell if I imagined that kiss or if it was real.

"What kind of kiss was that?"

"I wouldn't call it a kiss. I would call it making you officially mine," Ace gives me a small wink before walking out of the bathroom, leaving me by myself with all of the wondering thoughts.

Once my bag is packed, I carry it downstairs. Ace's bag is already packed as well. I didn't pack that much because I didn't know how long we were staying for.

Emma said she knew where we were going, and I tried to force it out of her, but she didn't utter a word. But she helped me pack almost everything I needed. She also told me she knew Ace was planning this trip and trying to get me to be 'his'.

Ace was working almost all day. He said he had to take care of some new assassins he got and he has been doing a background check on them all. But he is almost done with work. He said he was just finishing up a phone call and then he will be out.

"Is he ready?" I ask Leo who walks inside the living room where Emma and I sit on the couch talking.

"Yeah, he's coming down right now,"

I have been thinking about the places we could be going to.

I was thinking Russia because it's cold there or maybe Iceland.

Soon I see Ace come out from the hallway and walk towards me. "Ready?" he asks, and I stand up from the couch. I nod my head and he walks towards me. "Let's go then," he says and grabs my hand.

We say goodbye to Leo and Emma, and they tell us to be safe.

Once we get into the car, Francisco drives us off to the airport. Francisco is going to be coming with us to this secret location wherever it is.

As soon as we get to the airport, Francisco opens my door and I step out and see a blacked-out jet. I've been on plenty of jets but this one was just beautiful.

We both walk towards the jet, and I see Francisco handing our bags to the jet workers who are putting them on the plane.

"Come on," Ace says as he leads me inside the jet. Once we walk inside, I feel the coldness of the air conditioning against my cheek making me shiver. I look around and see the interior of the jet. Almost everything is white, but it looks luxurious. "You like it?" Ace asks.

"Yes. Are you kidding? It's beautiful," I say walking fully inside the jet, looking around.

"Sit anywhere you want. Also, you can order food. They can make anything," Ace assures me.

I nod at him and find a place to sit. There is a lot of space on the jet. I take one of the middle seats on the plane. I also see a door in the back of the plane wondering where it leads.

"Where does that door lead?" I ask Ace, pointing to the door.

He comes towards me and sits down in the seat in front of me.

"A bedroom," he says as he stares at me with those intense green eyes.

I ignore the heat pooling in my stomach. "How long is the flight going to be for?" I ask Ace while crossing my legs and trying not to feel the butterflies in my stomach go wild.

Ace's eyes go to my legs and he smirks. "Around three hours. Not long."

Where the hell are we going?

"Have you ever been to this destination?"

"Yeah a few times. It's the perfect time to go right now."

"Why?"

"Not a lot of tourists." I nod my head and then take out a book that I am planning on reading.

As I'm reading the book, I look up at Ace to see what he is doing. He is on his phone typing.

He looks so calm and distracted. I see him furrow his eyebrows and bite his lip while on his phone. Probably thinking about something.

I see him lift his head to look at me, so I divert my eyes to look down at the book again and then look back up Ace who is still staring at me.

"Like what you see?"

"Please," I scoff. "I have a book to read," I say motioning to the book in my hand.

"Oh yeah. What book?"

"She's Strong but She's Tired."

"What's it about?"

"It's a poetry book."

"Read me one. I like reading poetry," Ace states as he put his phone down to give me his full attention.

I look down at the book. "He is not sorry. Forgive him, for the sake of yourself and walk away for the sake of your future." I look back up at Ace and I see him looking at me with a knowing look in his eyes.

"Sounds interesting."

"It is."

"Aria? *Amore*? Wake up!" I hear Ace say.

I open my eyes and see him hovering over me. I look around and see I am in a bed. He probably carried me here.

"What?" I ask in a weird morning voice.

"We're here," he whispers.

"We're here?"

"Yeah. Get up. Our bags are ready and in the car. Just change into something a little warmer 'cause it's going to be cold," Ace suggests.

I nod my head, and he leaves the room. I get up from the bed and change into a sweater and a large jacket that is hanging on the door.

I fix my appearance a little and put my hair in a ponytail before leaving the room. I walk out and see Ace on his phone waiting for me. He looks up and sees me and his eyes sparkle. My favorite thing ever.

"Come on *amore*," he says as he motions me to take his hand.

I slip my hand in his as he guides us out of the plane. The first thing I feel when I step out of the jet is the cold air hitting my skin.

"Holy s-shit," I shiver while covering my body with the large coat more.

Ace laughs. "*Amore*, welcome to Swiss Alps." He then kisses my cheek.

"Swiss Alps? Isn't that in Switzerland?"

Ace nods his head. "Let's talk in the car though because my balls are fucking freezing." Ace takes my hand and pulls us over to the car with Francisco holding the door.

"Why are we in Switzerland, Ace?" I ask once we get inside the car.

"I've only ever been here twice which was for work so why not?" Ace says, making a smile appear on my face.

"You're crazy," I say with a smile on my face and shaking my head. "Out of all places, Switzerland?"

"It's a beautiful place to visit."

He isn't wrong.

I've seen so many pictures of Switzerland and always wanted to go. I have been to a lot of places all over the world, but the Swiss Alps definitely isn't one of them.

After a thirty minute or so drive we finally arrived in the town that Ace says we are staying in. We get out of the car, and I see so much snow and locals outside.

"It's beautiful here, Ace."

"Good 'cause we are going to be staying here for a week or so."

"Really?" I ask him and he nods his head.

He motions Francisco to take our bags inside the hotel that is in front of us while Ace and I walk inside the hotel hand in hand. "Last time I went here I stayed in this hotel and it's beautiful inside."

Once we get all checked in, Ace leads us towards the elevator.

"So, what are we going to be doing here?"

"There's a lot we can do. I have some stuff planned but those are going to be kept as a secret," Ace smirks.

The elevator door opens so we both walk out, and Ace leads us towards our room. The first thing I notice when we walk in is the beautiful view in front of us.

All the lights of the town are lit, and the snow looks so clean and smooth.

"What's first on the agenda?" I ask, already wanting to go out and explore.

"Relax. We have a whole week here *amore*. I have plans for us tomorrow," Ace says and he walks past me into the room.

"Then what do you want to do?" I raise my eyebrow.

"Watch a movie...take a bath?" Ace asks with an amused tone.

I roll my eyes at him and walk towards him.

"Let's see what is for dinner first. I'm hungry," I say while ignoring the butterflies erupting in my stomach again.

I see that there is a laminated room service sheet on the side table, so I pick it up and look through every meal they have. They have many options and all of them sound delicious.

"Ready?" Ace asks while coming up from behind me.

"Yeah, I see that they have this dish with potatoes and some beef. They also have hot soup, that looks good."

"Well order whatever. I'm not picky," Ace shrugs.

I go to pick up the room phone so that I can order the food. Once I finish telling them the order and food to bring, I put the phone down and see Ace who is laying on the bed with his eyes closed.

I walk towards him and lay down in between his legs. "Tired?"

"Mhm," he mumbles while keeping his eyes closed.

I play with his hair as we wait for the food to arrive and when it finally does, I get off of Ace to answer the door.

The room service lady comes in and rolls in the food to the center of the room where there was also a small table with chairs for us to sit at.

I look at Ace and see him already standing up, but his hair is all over the place making me want to laugh and go fix it. He sees that I am looking at his hair, so he glares at me before fixing it. Once he sits down, we just start to eat and converse about many different things.

Mostly about some of the things we are going to do here.

It is super easy to talk to Ace. We never have things to run out of while talking to each other and when we do then it's not awkward. That's what I love so much about talking to him.

He also understands me in a way not many people do.

I am finding myself starting to like him more and more each day.

I have learned a lot about Ace during my stay with him. I learned that he can only really sleep when I'm playing with his hair or massaging his neck. I even watched him work on his Ferrari back at the house which was cool, and this was before he told me he used to work on cars.

Once we are done eating, we call room service so that they can take the table out of the room.

I start to unpack some of my stuff since Francisco put our bags in the closet. As I unpack my stuff, I feel arms wrap around my waist and Ace's head being placed on my shoulder. I can feel his lips touch the crook of my neck as I fix the clothes on the hangers.

I try to ignore him and continue to fix the clothes on the hanger as I feel his lips kissing along my neck and his hands gripping my hips and pulling me closer into him making me have goosebumps all over my body.

"Ace," I say in a warning tone while still putting clothes away, but he keeps me from moving by holding my hips tighter. "Can you stop? You're distracting me."

"Leave the hangers alone. They will be there tomorrow," he whispers in a husky tone. "Come take a bath with me," when I don't say anything, he turns me around so that we can see one another. "Are we going to do this the easy way or the hard way, *amore*?" Ace raises an eyebrow.

"I'm thinking we do this my way," I give him a smirk. "I'm kinda tired. I'm going to head to sleep." I raise on my tippy toes and kiss his cheek before walking away from him and walking towards the bed.

This is going to get interesting.

Twenty-Five

I HAVE NO IDEA WHAT WE ARE DOING TODAY. HE SAID he had something planned but I have no idea what it is.

This morning I woke up with his arms around me and the big, white blanket covering our bodies.

He got up first so that he could order breakfast for us and when it arrived, we both ate. He ordered crepes, orange juice, oats, fruit, and eggs. A ridiculously huge and filling breakfast.

After breakfast Ace said to start getting ready. He said to get dressed in something warm like he gave me a pair of cargo pants that were black.

So, I change into the black cargo pants and then into a black tank top with an oversized crew neck sweater and then oversized dark red jacket over it. I wasn't going to wear the jacket on right now though because we're still in the hotel room and we have the heater on, so I don't want to be hot.

I put my hair in a low bun and once I'm fully dressed, I walk out of the bathroom and see Ace who is tying his boots.

He lifts his head to look at me and I see him lift his lips a little. Not a smile but close.

"You look good."

I ignore the blush threatening to spill on my face. "So, what are we doing today?"

Ace looks up at me. "Ever been snowboarding?"

"A few times. Why? Are we going?" Ace nods his head and stands up. "Really?" I ask with a smile, and he nods again.

"Yeah. It's going to be fun. Francisco is already waiting downstairs for us."

Ace and I go downstairs where we see Francisco outside waiting near the car. He looks cold so I quickly run to him.

"You know we can open the doors ourselves, right? You don't need to wait outside," I tell Francisco.

"I don't mind Aria. It's part of my job," he says as he opens the door.

"Next time don't wait outside. You can get a cold or something," I say before stepping inside the car along with Ace behind me. The drive towards the ski lift is long since it was up on the mountain. "Wait, do we have snowboarding gear?" I ask Ace.

"Yeah. Francisco got you some gear while we were getting ready. I already have a snowboard, so he didn't need to get me one." Once we are on top of the mountain Ace and I get out of the car along with Francisco. There are a lot of people here. It looks super crowded. "Okay, so we are going to clip on our gear on the top of the mountain. But here are your gloves and goggles," Ace says, handing both to me.

I thank him and put on the gloves. I also zip up my jacket as well since it is freezing cold out here. I am not used to this kind of weather.

Once Ace and I are situated, we say our goodbyes to Francisco since he is going to stay in the car and wait. I ask if he wants to come but he says he would rather stay.

"When was the last time you went snowboarding?" I ask Ace once we get to the ski lift line.

"Probably when I was twenty-one. It was my birthday trip that Leo planned."

"That's fun." Now that reminds me. "When is your birthday? You never told me," I ask, remembering the Gemini tattoo he has on his forearm.

"It doesn't matter," Ace says sternly.

"Ace come on when is it?"

"May 21. It's nothing special-"

"Nothing special? Are you kidding, that's like a few months away?"

"Stop, Aria," Ace mumbles.

"What? You don't like your birthday?"

"It's whatever. It's just a day."

"Just a day? Well at least-"

"No, Aria!" Ace says cutting me off and turning to look at me. "Drop it."

I nod my head. "Okay, fine I'll drop it."

The rest of the time we are just waiting in line in silence. Neither of us utter a word.

A lot of people don't like their birthdays. Some people hate their birthdays and Ace is one of those people.

I don't care though because it's their opinion on their birthday. Everyone is different. I don't really care about my birthday or what I do for my birthday, but I definitely don't act like that when someone asks me about my birthday.

"I'm sorry, "Ace says once we get on the ski lift.

I look at Ace and raise my eyebrow. "What do you have to be sorry for?"

"I was being a dick to you. I just don't like talking about my birthday," Ace says.

"You don't have to be sorry. Everyone has different feelings about their birthday," I shrug my shoulders.

"Yeah, but I shouldn't have yelled at you like that."

"It's fine. I shouldn't have pried or continued-"

"Will you just let me apologize?" Ace says, cutting me off. "Look, I'm sorry. I just don't like my birthday. I never did."

"It's okay, Ace," I say and he scoots a little closer to me.

He grabs a hold of my gloved hand and looks down at it. He then brings it up and kisses the back of it. I blush and look at him. He just looks so calm and happy. I like it when he has that face where he wants to smile.

After a few more minutes of sitting and waiting for the ski lift to get to the top of the mountain, we are finally at the top.

Ace and I are putting on our gear as Ace tells me about the slopes.

"So they aren't that steep. You already know how to stop right?" Ace asks raising his eyebrow.

"Yes, Ace. I'll be fine," I stand up with all my gear on.

"Help me up," Ace says while holding out his hands.

I chuckle and go to help him up. "You're so heavy," I say, while struggling to help him up.

He stands to his full height towering over me as always. "Are you calling me fat?" Ace asks, coming closer to me.

"Maybe," I smirk.

I then see Ace lean closer towards my ear and I feel his hot breath touch my ear. "*Non lo dirò stasera quando ti scoperò, amore.*"

Ace then leans away and walks past me going down the mountain. I let out a breath I didn't even know I was holding and look down and see him sliding down the slope smoothly.

I let out a deep sigh and shake my hands to get all the nerves out and forget about the butterflies that were making my stomach tingle.

I let out another sigh but this time it is a frustrated one before going down the mountain.

"Fucking teenagers," I say as soon as I get inside the car.

Ace laughs at me and comes inside the car next to me. "*Amore* you still have snow in your hair."

I take off my huge snow jacket and start to try and get the snow I have in my hair out. Ace laughs again and then helps me take it out.

"Stupid ass teenagers think they're so funny," I mumble.

"They were just messing around."

"By throwing snowballs at me. All I was trying to do was put my hair in a ponytail," I say as Francisco starts the car.

Don't get me wrong I know we are around snow, but they really had to throw a snowball at my head? It hurt like a bitch too.

"Yeah, and then when they threw the snowballs at you, you went and tried to go and kill them."

"I could do it, Ace. I know you have a gun in this car somewhere," I say while looking around the car for a gun.

"We already left the site so there's no point in finding my gun, Ari."

"And you didn't even help me," I comment looking at him.

"No, I tried to help you by not making you kill them in public. I helped you get away from the situation."

"Whatever. Fucking idiots were laughing when they did that too. Didn't even say sorry."

The rest of the ride to the hotel was filled with me complaining about what happened at the Ski lift.

After Ace and I did a few slopes, we decided to take a small break by this booth they had nearby and while we were sitting, I got hit with a fucking snowball while I was pulling my hair back in a ponytail.

They didn't even apologize, they started laughing. So, once they started laughing, I tried to run over to them, but Ace grabbed my waist to stop me from doing anything. I know it's all fun and games but the snowball that hit my head hurt like a bitch.

"Thank you, Francisco," Ace says once we get out of the car. "You can head back to your room for the night. Also just leave the snowboarding gear in the car. We'll be good."

"Of course, sir. Thank you."

Ace closes the door and then takes my hand and leads us inside the hotel towards the elevator.

"You need to relax. Maybe have a bath?" Ace states once we get out of the elevator.

"Definitely in need of a bath. A warm one to be specific."

The elevator doors open, and I walk out and head towards the room with Ace behind me. As soon as I unlock the door I rush inside and start to take off my layers of clothing.

"Strip for me why don't you," Ace chuckles as he walks in and locks the door.

"I need to get out of these clothes. They aren't as comfortable as you think," I say as I take off my jacket.

Once I'm in my bra and underwear I walk towards the bathroom and turn the tub on to make it warm and ready for me to get inside. I also put bubbles because they had a bottle of bubble bath soap near the bath.

I don't know if Ace is coming in or not but I'm going in.

Once the tub is full, I get out of my underwear and bra. I put my hair in a quick bun before sitting inside.

Once I'm fully inside, I close my eyes and rest my head on the tub. I can already feel my muscles start to relax. I also love how the warm water touches my skin. It feels amazing.

I hear heavy footsteps coming near the bathroom, so I open my eyes. I see Ace just standing in the doorway with his boxers on while staring at me.

"Yes?" I ask while raising my eyebrow and trying not to look where his boxers are hiding his dick.

I then see Ace's lips turn into a smirk making me raise my eyebrows. He then takes off his boxers making me look away quickly. This is the first time I will be seeing Ace naked and just thinking about that makes me blush and have butterflies in my stomach.

He walks over to the tub so I move my legs so that he can come inside with me. Once he is fully in the tub, I look at him and place my feet on his chest.

"Did you have fun today?" Ace asks.

I nod my head ignoring the heat between my legs because of how close he is to me. "Yeah. It was super fun. I haven't been snowboarding in forever."

"Good. I'm glad you enjoyed it."

"What else are we going to be doing here?"

"I want to show you around the town a little and then maybe take you out to this restaurant I like."

"Mhm," I hum while looking at him as he touches my ankle softly.

I close my eyes and rest my head against the tub as I feel Ace start to rub small circles on the skin above my feet, right where my ankles are.

I hope he doesn't have a foot fetish though. Ace can't have a foot fetish.

Can he?

"Come here." I open my eyes and look at Ace to see if I heard him correctly but all he does is motion his head for me to come to him.

I lean closer to him so that I am now facing him, sitting in between his legs. I try to ignore how close our hips were next to one another. When I look up into his eyes, I see him have that same sparkle in his eyes that I saw way too many times to count. The same sparkle that Ana told me about.

I can stare into them forever. I want to stare into them forever.

"*Sei così bella,*" Ace whispers while taking a small strand of my hair that has fallen from my bun into his hands. I feel my cheeks heat up so I look away from him so that he doesn't see how I react, but he stops me and takes my chin in his hand and makes me look at him. "Why are you always so nervous around me?"

"I don't know. You just have this really intense stare, I guess. I don't know how to explain it," I shrug with a small smile on my face.

Ace is intimidating. Not only does he look like a Greek god, but he has this powerful aura around him. If I weren't Aria White, the American Mafia's best assassin I would be afraid of him and just feel shy around him. I sometimes do feel that way because, in reality, no one has ever made me feel this scared before. Maybe I was afraid when I was with Dante but it's different with Ace. I don't know if I am afraid of just what Ace can do or just Ace in general or if I am afraid of falling in love with Ace.

I feel like I am getting close to falling in love with him though. Because I have no clue what kind of power he would have over my heart. He could abuse me the way Dante did.

I don't want to admit it out loud or to myself how I truly feel.

"What kind of stare?"

"I don't know it's like some sparkle you have in your eyes. I see it sometimes. But I don't know maybe it's just me and I am being stupid-"

"No. You're not. I know what you're talking about."

"You do?" I furrow my eyebrows with a small smile spreading on my face.

"Mhm," Ace nods his head and moves his hand to my jaw so

that his thumb can stroke my cheek. "I only have that stare with one person, but she is gone now." I don't say anything. I just stare at him. "I know why too."

"Why?"

I see Ace bite his lip softly before speaking again. "Because I think I'm close to loving you."

Twenty-Six

"What?" I ask Ace who is still staring down at me with those beautiful green eyes of his.

Ace puts his hand on my cheek. "I never felt love or at least never felt this kind of feeling."

I don't know what to say.

I'm honestly scared to fall in love again. I have tried so hard to keep my heart protected but then Ace comes in and changes everything.

Do I love him?

Or do I love the idea of him?

I can't tell or give him an answer right now.

So, what I do is lean towards Ace and kiss him.

His hands grip the back of my neck while his other arm wraps around my waist and pulls me against his chest so that I'm straddling him fully. I can feel his cock right under me making me whimper and try to close my legs but since I'm straddling Ace I am just squeezing my legs around him.

I find myself wanting more and more from him. But I am scared. I am scared because I don't want my feelings to grow for Ace. No matter how much my body and heart want to, my head is telling me to be rational and leave him behind so that I don't get the chance to be hurt again.

I've been stuck with the pain Dante gave me for years but when I met Ace all that pain somehow washed away and I felt different, lighter, happier.

And when Ace touches me, only if it's a small kiss to the cheek or hand, or even when his wrist grazes mine when we stand next to each other I feel my stomach explode with fire, almost. It's the best feeling ever because I never felt those kinds of feelings before.

Ace removes his lips from me, and he looks at me, basically asking permission if we can continue and I don't say anything, instead I kiss him again and again and again. Anywhere and everywhere.

I think that the intimacy between Ace and I isn't about us taking off each other's clothes or kissing each other's skin, I think that it's when we saw each other at our worst, when we felt like the world was going to end. Like how I witnessed Ace the night of the ball when he was trying to push me away, but I found myself still wanting to stay and help him through everything. As I unraveled every imperfection of Ace from his personality to his scars, I saw something more to Ace than what meets the eye.

Ace trails his hands down my waist until they meet my hips. He grips them before pulling me closer making me feel his cock grow underneath me.

Ace removes his lips from mine and then looks at me.

His eyes are asking for permission which makes my heart melt.

I trail my hands up to tangle my fingers through his hair and I pull his face closer to mine making our lips connect at the same time I feel him thrust inside me.

"O-oh shit." Ace mutters and leans his head on my shoulder. I whimper as I feel him thrust up a little. I close my eyes and lean towards him to place my lips on his. I start to move up so that only his tip was all that I could feel before going back down. "Stay down." Ace said when I tried to lift myself again. I open my eyes and look down at him.

"Ace-"

"Stay down Aria. Don't move." He demanded as he gripped my hips in his hands and pushing me closer to him. "*Merda*, you feel so good." Ace thrusted up into me a few times making me whimper and squeeze my legs around him tighter. "You like that?"

"Yes." I close my eyes and my head fall back as I feel his dick move inside me. "I love it."

All of the heat in my body started to form in my lower stomach. I feel Ace's grip on his tighten again and I already know there will be bruises there tomorrow.

"*Dolce figa.*" Ace muttered in a breathy tone. "I'm finishing inside you."

"I have birth control." I place my hands on his biceps, holding onto him as I start to ride out my high with Ace finishing inside me before we start all over again.

Love.

It's such a strong word.

When I first used the word, I didn't really understand it. I never felt anything to the people I said it to, other than my family.

I had a couple of meaningless boyfriends before Dante but those lasted for probably no longer than a month. Those relationships were mainly flings and sometimes those flings that I had wanted more from me, but I couldn't give it to them. But I kept some of them around because I wanted to know what love felt like and why it was such a big deal to people.

With Dante, I thought I felt it but, in the end, it punched me in the face.

Literally.

He would only whisper 'I love you' as he slipped his hands down the waistband of my pants every night after a fight.

That is where I noticed and understood the difference between want and need. I may have wanted things to work out with Dante, but I definitely didn't need him. Dante wanted someone else but instead he got me and then took advantage of that.

Last night with Ace felt like love. It felt real and I wasn't afraid, and I didn't feel pressured. He made me feel loved and comfortable but I also felt like I was on fire everywhere. It felt natural, somewhat.

I think that intimacy is what people want when they have sex. They want to be touched and looked at, admired, smiled at, and feel safe with or feel like someone really got you instead of a part of you.

That is what I always wanted and finally I did with Ace last night. Now I want more and more of it, but with him only.

My mind kept swirling around the idea of telling Ace about Dante.

I want to but I am scared. I am trusting Ace with my heart, and I'm scared he is going to crush it. I didn't tell Ace I loved him last night because I wanted to make sure I really did love him and feel those things for him before admitting it. I wanted to admit it to myself before admitting to him and out loud.

But I do.

Ace was amazing with me last night. Whispering sweet nothings while also holding me afterward. I feel safe with him.

"What are you thinking about?" he asks while his arms are wrapped around my body tighter.

"Stuff," I answer.

I sit up next to Ace against the headboard while looking at the view in front of us. The Alps are just beautiful. I never thought I would come here.

Ace wraps his arm around my shoulder and pulls me closer and makes me lean my head on his chest. He kisses my head and starts stroking my arms making me have goosebumps everywhere.

"Aria. I don't want you to keep things from me. I want you to trust me. I know you have things you're afraid to tell me, but I don't want you to be afraid," Ace says softly.

I look up at him and think.

I can trust him. I'm trusting him with everything I have. I can trust him with my secrets and my weakness. I just hope he doesn't take advantage of that.

Because I don't think I could ever overcome my weakness, especially when that weakness is Dante.

I lean my head on his bare chest while staring at him.

"I had this boyfriend. I "was just thinking about how much I have changed since him," I start. "He was kind, caring, gentle. Everything I thought I loved. We met at this academy my dad sent me to so that I could start my training. I wasn't as strong as I am now."

Ace stares at me, taking in everything I say.

"I trusted him. A lot more than I should have. He was always there for me when I needed him to be. But after a few months of dating, we started having these meaningless arguments occasionally because I would always catch him checking other girls out and I would say something to him about it but then he would just say I am seeing things or that I am crazy. Then one night he and I were arguing over the same thing again but this time I said I wanted to break up because it all became too toxic." This is the part that gets to me. "Once I said that to him, he punched me. I fell to the floor, and he started kicking me while I was hopeless and couldn't do anything to protect myself. At my weakest point, he was fighting me. I couldn't push him away or fight him back. I would have fought back but he was stronger than I was at the time."

I try not to look at Ace while talking, I am just afraid to see his reaction.

"Before he left the room, he said that if I told anyone about what he did to me then he would kill my family, even go after Ariel. He is crazy and has so many connections through other groups." I say taking a deep breath and continuing.

"So, I stayed together with him for another five months.

Through those five months, he kept hitting me and taking advantage of me and no one knew. My mom and Layna saw the toxicity and the arguments, but I kept telling them that it was fine, and I loved him, and he loved me. The worst part is that I believed myself when I said all that. I wanted to feel loved and just wanted to have someone to care for me and love me. I thought what he was doing was love but I soon figured out it was the complete opposite."

As I start to remember all of those horrible memories, I feel a tear stream down my face. I feel Ace's finger on my cheek stroking it softly while also wiping the tear off, but I still don't make eye contact with him.

"One night, he pushed me down the stairs and Layna and my mom saw. They kicked him out. I don't know where he is now, but Alex and my dad don't know about it. Only Layna, my mom, and now you," I say softly, whispering the last part.

Ace clenches his fist that is by my side. He takes my chin between his fingers and forces me to look at him. He looks so mad, and I can tell his brain is thinking so many different things and just working like a machine.

"What's his name?" he asked in a deep voice.

"Dante Zelle." He didn't say anything after that. I'm scared he sees me as weak or gullible. I look away from him. "I shouldn't have told you. If you don't want me anymore or if you see me as weak-"

"Aria." Ace states making me shut up and look at him. "I see you far from being weak." He takes his hand and reaches it to his cheek wiping the tears that have fallen. "You're one of the strongest people I know. What you went through wasn't easy. I admire you for still being here and trusting me with all of this," he says softly while tucking a loose hair that fell from my face. "I love you. You understand? I will kill anyone who lays a finger on you. I want you to feel safe with me. I want you to know I won't ever touch you like that. Never." he says in a stern voice. "Tell me you know I won't?"

I look up at him and see him with a serious face. "You won't. I know you won't," I say softly.

He leans down and kisses my lips and I kiss back. "*Ti amo*."

"And I love you Ace."

Twenty-Seven

The rest of Switzerland was well spent. Ace drove us both around town and we went to the restaurant Ace wanted to take us to. We also went snowboarding again and it was super fun because we went on bigger slopes than before.

We also played in the snow. It may seem like a childish thing for some people, but it was still something I enjoyed. I wanted to stay there forever but Ace had to go back home because he had to check up on updates with the Russians. He just wanted to make sure that they are dead and there are no more Russian Bravta heirs or family members that are alive.

Once we landed, we got off the plane and there was a car waiting for us already. Francisco got all our bags and then once we were settled in the car he started to drive towards the house. The whole way to the house Ace had his arm wrapped around me making me feel safe and secure.

Once we got to the house Francisco parked the car and Ace

and I both got out and Francisco said he was going to get our bags so Ace and I just walked inside the house.

Other than Francisco rolling in our luggage, the house was super quiet. Something I still wasn't used to ever since Val and his family left.

That always made me wonder.

Was Ace ever going to move out of here?

"So, I have to get back to work," I look up at Ace. "But Emma is in her room. Leo texted me saying she wants to tell you something." I nod my head. "I'll see you later," he kisses my temple and squeezes my hand three times before walking away from me.

I run upstairs to where Ace said Emma was. I don't have to worry about the bags because Francisco said he got them. I offered to help but he didn't want help.

I knock on the door, and I hear her say 'come in'. I walk in and am attacked in a hug.

"Oh my god Aria! I missed you so much!" Emma exclaims while squeezing me to the point where I can't breathe.

"Okay, Emma, I get it. I was missed. Can you let go now," I struggle to say, since she is hugging me so tight.

"Sorry I was just so excited to see you," Emma lets go and goes to sit back down on her bed and covers her legs with her blanket. "So, I have exciting news that I need to tell you but first, tell me about Switzerland."

"Switzerland was amazing." I sit on the bed next to her. "Ace took me snowboarding and then we ate at this really nice restaurant. We also walked through the town. It was nice."

"That sounds amazing. I'm happy you and Ace went away. He really needed a break from everything. Was it cold there?"

"Very cold. But it was okay. I brought a ton of sweaters and jackets. Now enough with the questions about me."

"No, no, no; last one. I swear." Emma says with a big smile on her face. "Did you and Ace do the deed?" Emma wiggles her eyebrows at me. My face gets red, and I cover my face. "Oh my god! You so did!" Emma yells with a smile still present on her face.

"Shut up."

"Was he good?" she asks.

"Dude I'm not going to answer the question. Your husband is literally Ace's best friend," I chuckle.

"Yeah but still I have to act like a best friend since yours isn't currently here. So, spill."

I called Layna while I was in Switzerland. She told me that her and everyone else were doing good. She also asked when I would be coming home but I told her than I was planning on staying in Italy for a little longer.

Now that things are serious between Ace and I, I want to see how things between the two of us go. But I have a feeling that things will be great with Ace and me. No one has ever made me feel the way he has.

I laugh at her, "He was good and that's all I am going to say."

I wasn't going to tell her about the intimate details because that is between him and me.

Like the way he held me and told me I was beautiful or how well I took him.

"Anything else juicy happen?"

"He told me he loved me."

"What?! Did you say it back?" Emma squeals.

"At first no. I had to make sure that I truly did love him." I tell her with a smile on my face.

"Why?" Emma asks.

I never told Emma about my past because I never thought I trusted her, but I do.

"Because of what happened with my last boyfriend."

"What happened?"

"I had this boyfriend at the time and long story short he was super abusive towards me. I thought I loved him but, I didn't."

I trust Emma with this information. If I didn't then I wouldn't have told her so easily or feel comfortable with telling her.

"Wow," Emma sighs and sympathy showed across her face, but she always gives me a knowing look. "I'm so sorry you had to go through that Ari. I had that one time too. Before I met Leo actually. His name was Eli. I met him at a concert but later, in the relationship, he started to become rougher with me. But then I met Leo and now I am happy," Emma admits.

"Leo is good for you. He is respectful and knows when something is wrong with you."

"Yeah, I love him," Emma says with a soft smile.

"Now I know how that feels," I say while looking at her smile.

"I know Ace loves you. Fuck, everyone does!" she exclaims.

I laugh at her reaction. "Okay. Now, what is the good news that you wanted to tell me that was so exciting as you stated?" I ask.

Her face turns into a smile. "I'm pregnant."

"Oh my god!" I hug her, making her fall backward on the bed. "How many weeks or months?" I ask.

"Almost three months. We get to know the gender in a few weeks though. Leo and I are going to have a gender reveal then. I'm surprised I am so many months. I don't even look that big yet. If anything I thought I was just bloated."

I smile at her. "That's amazing Em. You're going to be such an amazing mom," I say while getting off of her.

"Yeah, we found out the day you guys left. It was kind of late but yeah. I'm excited." Emma says with a big smile. "I didn't even notice I was pregnant because I thought I was throwing up because of food poisoning and I don't have a period because of birth control so that's why I found out so late."

"You should be excited," I say, making her laugh. "This is amazing. I am happy for you."

"Also, I want you to kind of host it and help me with the party and everything like that. I also want you to know the gender."

"Of course, Em. I would be honored. Gosh, I'm so excited for you," I squeal and hug her again.

Today is the gender reveal for Emma.

I got the call from the doctor a week ago and I've been trying to plan the perfect party and announcement since Val, Mia, Ana, and Antonio are coming over for the party. I can't wait to see them all because it's been so long since I've last seen them.

My family is coming as well. Ace said I could invite them since I haven't seen them in so long.

My mom, dad, Alex, Layna, Calla, Elena, Ariel, and Cole, all of them are coming. I can't wait to see them. I haven't seen them in at least a few months since the ball, which is the last time they came to Italy. I also have to talk to them about what is going on and why I am staying in Italy.

They just got off their flight and they're heading here now so I am super excited. The party is starting around 1pm and it is the afternoon right now. Emma is currently getting ready right with a hair and makeup artist. I told her to wear a dress to show off her bump in whatever color she wanted. She said she would surprise me with the color.

I'm not going to wear blue or pink because I don't want people to think I'm choosing a color, so I'm wearing a black Chanel dress with white sneakers. I didn't do anything special for my hair. I just left it down and curled the ends. I did put some makeup on but didn't do a full glam look.

Ace knows the gender of the baby too. He wouldn't stop bothering me until I told him about it.

I'm excited for the gender reveal. I have a good and fun way of revealing the gender. I'm going to have Leo drive the Ferrari in the driveway and once he starts the engine the color of the baby is going to be revealed.

"Aria!" I hear from downstairs.

I leave Ace's room and run downstairs to see who called me. I was super busy in the past few days. I needed to make sure everything was perfect for Em. I reach the last step and look to see who called me. I see my whole family standing in the doorway. A smile made its way onto my face, and I run towards them and hug them.

"Oh my god! I'm so glad you guys are here and that you made it. Emma is going to be so happy!" I squeal as I hug each of them.

"Well, we wanted to see the epic reveal you have planned," Cole says with a teasing smirk.

"Well trust me it's going to be good," I say with a smile.

"What's the gender?" Layna asks.

"You really think I'm about to tell you guys the gender. Hell no," I laugh.

"Is it just you that knows?" Cole asks me.

"No, Ace knows too."

"Oh well, what time does the party start?" Calla asks.

"In like an hour. Emma is getting ready right now. Leo is with Ace doing god knows what and then Ana, Mia, and the boys are on their way right now."

"Oooo I can't wait to see Ana. I have so much I have to update her on," Elena says with my mom nodding her head.

"Well, they will be here soon. How long are you guys staying for?"

"A couple of days. Your father has some work to do back at home and Alex too," my mom says.

"Alright well you know where the rooms are, and you know where the food is but no going outside. I don't want anyone messing anything up before the baby momma comes out," I say making everyone laugh.

"So how are you going to do the reveal?" Layna asks once everyone was away.

"I'm going to have Leo start the engine on the Ferrari and it's going to show the color of the baby."

"Sounds cool."

"Yeah. How are you and Cole doing?" I smirk.

"We're good. I'm happy and in love. Cole took me to France a few weeks ago. It was the best trip ever. What about you and Ace?"

The first thing I did when Ace and I got together was tell Layna because she is my best friend and I have to update her on everything.

"Good. He took me to Switzerland and he told me he loved me. Since then we have been together hanging out."

Layna's eyes widen. "Really?"

"Yeah. I also told him about Dante."

Layna's eyes widen. "How did that go?"

"Good. He loves me and he said that he doesn't see me as weak or anything. He sees much more," I smile remembering the time we spent together.

It was the best trip of my life.

"That's amazing, Aria. I'm so happy you finally found someone who cares so much about you and who loves you."

"Yeah I am too. I finally understand what the hype is about love."

Layna chuckles. "Definitely. We are not no single bitches anymore." I laugh at what she said. "Well, I got to go see what Cole is doing and make sure he isn't unpacking my shit because he is a terrible unpacker."

I laugh as she walks away to her and Cole's room. I get up from the couch, Layna and I sat down on and go to the kitchen. I see Lana making Ariel food while Ariel is just playing with it.

"Hey, Lana," I say and sit down next to Ariel while picking her up and placing her on my lap.

"Hello, dear. Are you hungry? I made some pasta. Ariel keeps playing with it though," Lana says while fake glaring at Ariel.

Ariel laughs. "I did eat some of it."

"Really. Why is it so messy from where you were sitting then?" Lana asks while looking at the mess around her plate.

"I don't know," Ariel shrugs her shoulders and then starts playing with my hair.

"I'm good Lana. But save some for me later. I'll probably still get hungry after all the food we are going to be eating. Thank you for making some of the food by the way. It looks delicious."

"Of course, sweetie. Anything for you guys. Did you hear about house updates?"

Ace told me a few days after we came back from Switzerland that he is going to sell the house and build a newer and bigger one somewhere else. He said while he builds the house that we are going to stay at his safe house in the woods.

"Yeah. He said he might have an interested buyer."

"Really?"

"Yup. Are you going to be staying with us though? You know I can't live without your cooking." I laugh at her.

"Yeah, I'm still going to be with you guys. I can't live with you because I have my own family to be with, but you guys are like my children now. Especially you. You sometimes act like Ariel."

"Hey! What's so bad about me?" Ariel exclaims.

I laugh at her. "Nothing baby. You're perfect. I wish I were you," I say while pinching her cheeks.

Twenty-Eight

The party is in full motion. Val and Mia came over with Ana and Antonio.

Emma decided to wear a white dress that goes down to her calves, and it shows her bump perfectly. She is also wearing two different colored heels.

She told me she doesn't care what the gender is. She just wants the baby out of her asap. Leo is wearing a pink button-down. He told Ace and me that he wants a girl so he can protect her.

I know that Leo is going to be a great dad. I'm excited for when the baby comes.

Everyone is having a good time. Some of Emma's friends also came to the party. We took some pictures in front of the balloon set up I had done and in the sitting area of the backyard.

Emma introduced me to all her friends. Most of them she met in college or just on missions she went on with Leo.

I also got to meet some of Leo's friends. They were also some of Ace's friends too that I have never met so it was cool to meet some more people that Ace knew. He wasn't close with them though.

The food was also fantastic. Lana made some good mac and cheese which is now my favorite dish she has ever made.

"Hey." I feel a hand being placed on my waist and I already know whose it is.

I turn around and see Ace in a dark blue dress shirt and some trousers. He looks good. His hair looks freshly cut too. He looks exceptionally clean, and it makes me want to kiss him everywhere.

"Hey," I say back.

"How is everything going?"

"Good. I think I'm going to have Leo and Em reveal the gender soon or maybe announce some game-winners."

I had some games placed so that everyone could get the chance to win prizes. We had games like bingo, pacifier hunt, and gender predictions. There were some kids here at the party, so I had painting and drawing stuff set up for them.

"Well, you're the boss," Ace kisses me on the temple, and I then walk off to the front of the outdoor area.

"Alright, guys I'm going to announce the winners of our games, and then we can find out the gender of the baby," everyone cheers once I say that. I see Ace looking at me closely in the back of the room. "Alright now if I say your name you get to choose one out of the three gifts. So, the first winner is Valentino who won Bingo."

When Val won Bingo, he yelled out loud *"Bingo you bitches! I won!"* Everyone started laughing. I had to control him though because some kids started to cuss right after he said that.

"Yeah that's right. I won hoes. Who is the king of bingo? Me! That's who!" Val says as he gets up from his seat and runs towards the front where I'm standing.

I shake my head lightly at Val and laugh as well as everyone else.

The prizes in front are a mystery prize, a Louis Vuitton gift card with twenty-five thousand dollars on it, and a luxury coffee maker.

Ace said I could choose any gifts I wanted at any price. I thought these gifts were fair and Ace has a lot of money so why not.

"Okay. I'll get the mystery gift because all those gifts aren't good enough for *the* Valentino Ferrari!" Val says, making everyone laugh at him.

"Okay relax Val. Want to know your prize, your majesty?" I say sarcastically.

"Yes, please," Val smirks.

He is going to like this prize.

"Alright Val. Your prize is the Ferrari we are going to use for the reveal."

"Are you kidding!? Yes!" Val cheers for himself, and everyone watches laughing.

He then lunges onto me and hugs me tightly.

"Okay calm down. Go sit down so I can announce the other winner," I laugh and he lets me go. Val went to go sit down while also cheering for himself. Once I announce the last two winners, I decide it is time for the gender reveal. "Okay since there are no more winners, we are going to go do the gender reveal, so everyone follow me to the driveway."

I step away from the front of the backyard and walk towards Ace who is the only one who is waiting for me.

Once I reach him, he grabs my hand. "You did good, *amore*," he whispers in my ear making me blush.

"Thank you."

"I told you that you look beautiful by the way, right?" Ace kisses the back of my hand.

"Yes, you did."

"Well, I'm going to say it again. You look breathtaking," he says before leaning in and giving a small kiss under my ear making my cheeks heat up.

We walk towards the driveway where everyone is waiting and where Emma and Leo are in the front. I let go of Ace's hand and stand between Emma and Leo to explain what they are going to do.

"Okay so for the reveal I am going to have Leo start the engine of the Ferrari and Emma you're going to sit in the passenger seat while he presses the gas pedal. Sounds good?" They both smile and nod. "Great, go get in the car." The Ferrari I had for them was white with a beige interior. Once they are in the car everyone takes out their phones to record them. "Ready?!" I yell making sure they hear me. "Set! Go!"

Once I say go, Leo starts the engine making a bunch of dust come out from under the car.

"It's a boy!" everyone yells.

Twenty-Nine

"Leo, there's one more box!" I hear Emma yell.

"I know I'm going to get it right now! Hold on!" Leo yells back and then looks back at Ace, widening his eyes and sighing.

Today Leo and Emma are moving out. They wanted to move out a few weeks after the baby shower so that they could have more room for the baby. Emma told me they were moving the day she told me she was pregnant.

Most of their stuff is already at their new house. They are just grabbing some last things. Ace and I saw the house. It looked like the perfect house for them. It fit their aesthetic.

Ace is going to get rid of this house soon. He wants Emma and Leo to fully move out before selling the house.

I know he has some people coming tomorrow to check it out and if everything goes well with that then we are going to move into his other house until he gets the other one built. He already started drawing some blueprints for the new house and I am even helping him with the interior and exterior. He isn't going to keep any of the furniture. He is going to sell the house with the furniture and then buy all new furniture for the new house.

"Alright. I got to go before she goes batshit. I'll come tomorrow to see how the selling of the house is," Leo says as he comes out of the house with one last box.

"Well, you have to meet with me every day cause you work for me so don't think you're getting away from me so easily Leo," Ace says.

Leo laughs. "Alright, I'll see you guys later." Leo waves as he walks towards the car with Emma inside.

"Bye," I yell while waving as Leo and Emma drive out of the driveway.

I feel Ace's hand slide onto my waist, and I look up at him and see him looking down at me. "Finally, alone."

"Technically not all alone because we have Lana who comes over and some of your men, so no we aren't all alone," I tease. "Also, we have things to do so wait on relaxing." I then take his hand off my waist and pull him inside the house and walk towards his office.

"Who said I wanted to relax?" Ace questions as we walk towards his office.

I roll my eyes playfully as we end up in his office. He goes to sit in his chair. I am about to sit in the chair across from him, but he stops me.

"What?" I ask while furrowing my eyebrows.

He points to his lap.

"You're such a child," I tease and walk towards him and sit on his lap. His hand falls to my hips holding me and then he lays his head on my shoulder while looking down at his documents. "What are you working on?" I ask.

"I have some things to look over. Some deals other mafias sent and then some smaller groups we have in Italy that are asking for money and some more drug shipments."

"Are those smaller groups here a part of yours?" I ask.

"Yes, kind of. They are very loyal but don't really do the killings or jobs. I guess you could call them, what do you call them in America? Gangs?" he asks while scrunching his eyebrows together and I nod my head. "Yeah, but anyway, they help me make the money. Deal drugs, sometimes capture a few people but that's rare. I have my men do that work and other stuff."

I find this kind of stuff interesting. I never really got the chance to be a part of the business side of my dad's mob because I was always on dangerous missions.

"I never really understood the business side of things. My dad didn't really teach me," I say out loud.

"Why not?" Ace asks as he signs a few papers.

"I don't know. I was always on the missions where I had to kill and torture people, but I didn't do any business."

"What are you trying to say, Aria?" Ace looks up at me and raises his eyebrow while rubbing my upper thigh softly.

"I don't know. It kind of looks a little complicated," I say truthfully.

"Ehh, I guess it was a little hard at first but it's easy now. I know what documents and papers to assign. I like my stuff organized so that's another reason why everything is so easy for me," Ace says.

"What do you even do? I know that you said you assign missions but isn't there more?" I ask.

"I sign papers. I look through our stocks and check to see if we have enough money or the right amount of money in our bank. I look up different people and see who needs to be taken care of. I also make sure that no other mafia is trying to fuck around with me such as the Russians."

"I never understood how your mafia was always so powerful."

"You got a lot of questions, *amore*," Ace states while yawning. "You're not going to tell your dad any of my methods, are you?" Ace says in a joking manner. I laugh at him. "I constantly keep track of our stocks to make sure we have enough money, and we always have more than enough. For my men I always hand pick the best trained and most loyal assassins. I make all my men take a lie detector test before they join so I make sure we don't have any moles. I also sometimes go to the assassin academy they have in Germany. They have the best academy for assassins there. I visit and see who is the best and who isn't afraid to kill someone or lose a family member. Sadly, that's how it is in this world. I need to pick cold, heartless people."

I don't know if he is implying his loss of his mom or not. I don't want to bring it up though so I'm not going to.

"I love you, Ace. You know that right?" I assure him.

He looks up at me and I see the sparkle in his eyes shine again making my heart melt.

"I love you, Aria."

He leans in and kisses me on the lips, and I kiss back feeling fire fill my up my stomach with need.

Thirty

TODAY I'M GOING TO THE NEW HOUSE.

It's been a few weeks since the baby shower. Emma and Leo moved out a week after the shower. Luckily, it was an easy move for them because they didn't have a lot of things here.

Ace and I also moved into his safe house because the buyer that was interested in the house ended up buying it right after seeing it. There were a lot of things we had to do to get the house ready for the buyers. We had some of Ace's men pack our stuff. I didn't have a lot of stuff so there wasn't much they needed to pack for me.

Ace also donated all the furniture because he wanted to buy all brand-new furniture. And the buyers didn't really want the furniture. Ace said that he didn't want anything that reminded him of his dad, so he got rid of everything. He also went through his documents in his office and got rid of a lot of things.

While we were getting everything out of the house and in the process of selling the house, Ace had constructors build the new house he wanted to live in. He showed me the design of the house and the blueprints. It is going to be an excessively big house and I am excited to see how it comes along.

Ace even asked me if I can move in with him. At first, I was a little iffy about the idea because I didn't want Ace and I to move too fast with our relationship. We have only been together officially for a few months. Before he and I started dating we just spent time hating one another.

But the idea of Ace and I living together made my heart beat rapidly and I kept thinking about my future with Ace. So, I said yes.

I talked to Layna about it before making any last decisions and she said if I am happy with him then I should move in with him. I'm just hoping that I don't regret it.

Ace's men are working super-fast, and they have packed most of the stuff already. All there is left to pack is mainly the office and the kitchen.

I'm excited to see the progress they made. Ace wants me to design some parts of the house while he works so that's another reason why I'm going over to the house.

For Ace and I's room, he wants it to be like the one he had at his old house. For the bathroom, I know it's going to be black. I think almost all the room is probably going to be black. He said I can design some of the guest bedrooms and he is also having a library being put in the house, so I get to design that and choose what books to buy.

Another thing that I think is cool is that Ace is having a room dedicated to his mother. He is basically going to have a painting of her in the room and all her belongings, like clothes, perfume, makeup, and some pictures of her and Ace.

I never knew anyone who had a room like that in their house and I think it's great Ace is doing that for her.

Ace's office is almost done being decorated. He showed me a picture of how he wants it to look. I think he is excited about this house building process because it's his own house and he can change it and design it however he wants. He doesn't show he is excited, but I know he is.

Before I leave for the new house, I walk towards Ace's office to make sure he knows I won't be here. I might visit Emma afterward.

I have been going over every day to help her get around because her bump is now starting to get huge. Leo has been back and forth between Ace and Emma. Ace says that Leo should stay with Emma since he needs to make sure she is cared for, but Leo says Emma doesn't want him to do that.

As I walk towards his office, I hear Ace yelling.

Oh god.

I open the door slowly and see him yelling at one of his men.

"What the fuck do you mean you couldn't find him?!" Ace roars.

"Sir, he-he got away. We tried to block off the exit, but he found another way out," one of his men says while also shaking in fear silently.

"Well, then I guess I need to fucking get new men on this job since you three couldn't handle it!"

"*Capo-*"

Ace pulls out his gun and aims it at three guys before shooting them each in the head.

My eyes widen and I stay by the door, waiting for Ace to look at me.

Ace pulls out his phone and dials a number making the phone start ringing. "Fransisco come and get these bodies in my office and get fucking rid of them."

"Of course *capo*."

Ace hangs up and then puts his hand on his head and rubs his temples. I slowly walk towards Ace, going around the dead bodies on the floor where blood is starting to pool around their heads. Once I reach him, I touch his shoulder making him look up at me and move his chair out of his desk a little so I can sit down on this lap, and he instantly puts his hand on my hip to hold me.

"What happened?" I ask and wrap one of my arms around his neck.

"They were supposed to kill someone for me, but he got away. He has been snooping around the warehouse for the past month and a half and they can't fucking get him. So, I'm done with their bullshit," Ace says as he starts to look at random papers. "*Idioti del cazzo*," he mumbles. There is a knock on the door which makes Ace mutter, "Come in,"

I see Fransisco walk in along with two other guys. Once they grab the bodies they leave without saying a word.

I focus my attention back on Ace and play with his hair, rubbing circles on his neck to make him relax a little. "Do you know who this guy is?"

"No. In all my security footage, he is wearing a mask. This is the first time something like this has happened."

"Are they stealing stuff?"

"I had my men check and see if anything is stolen but it's not. It's weird because usually when someone breaks into something with these kinds of weapons, they would steal something, but they didn't."

"You will find him. Don't stress too much about it. You will get new men on the job. Better men. You'll catch this guy," I stroke his cheek as I tell him.

He looks up at me and he has a soft look on his face. "I love you."

"I love you," I say before he leans up and places his lips on mine.

He grips my hips making me let out a small moan. He slips his tongue in my mouth making me pull away from it getting any deeper.

It's like every time we kiss it feels like the first. It feels electric. I feel that spark. I can't ever keep my hands off him and when I do it's always hard to.

"How is it that whenever I am pissed off, you seem to be the only one who can put me in a good mood?"

"I have a special touch." I smile against his lips.

"Do we have time?" he mumbles while kissing me. I remove my lips from his and look at the clock while he kisses my neck. "We can make it. You have ten minutes to spare," he says before nipping at the skin on my neck. I smile a little before bringing his head back to mine and connecting our lips. "That's my girl. Sit on the desk," he spoke.

I do as he says and sit in front of him on the desk while he rolls his chair closer to me so that his frame is in between my legs as I stare down at him.

Ace slides his hands onto my thighs then hips before pulling me closer so that his head is at level with my bottom. "No screaming. I don't want anyone to know how my girlfriend sounds when she is with me," he says before he stars kissing my thighs going closer to where the ache is between my legs.

The heat in my stomach makes my cheeks blush as I watch him.

I feel him move my underwear to the side and he nips his bottom lip before leaning closer and pressing his lips against my pussy. I moan and thread my fingers through his hair while moving my hips as Ace licks and sucks me.

"Ace," I moan while rocking my hips. I feel him press a finger against me before rubbing and pushing it in. "God." I say as I feel myself clench around his finger.

"You're so beautiful Aria. All for me." Ace muttered and he leans in close making me thrust my hips towards his mouth.

I feel the heat in my stomach continue to build up until I climax around his finger and in his mouth while gripping onto his hair.

"Good girl," he kisses me on my pussy before leaning away and pulling my underwear up and fixing my dress.

"I need to go to Emma's to check on her, but I'm still going to the new house so that I can do some of the interiors. But maybe when I come home, we can watch a movie or do something," I say in a breathy tone.

"Yes, we can do something," he smirks at me, and I roll my eyes.

He kisses me on the cheek, and I get up from his desk.

Suddenly I feel a hard slap on my ass making my skin sting. I turn around and see a smirking Ace with amusement laced in.

"Ace!" I exclaim.

"I had to, *amore*. Your ass is just too perfect," he says before biting his lip a little. I start walking away and stuck the middle finger in the air so he could see. "I love you!" he yells as I walk down the hall, away from his office making me laugh a little.

I grab the keys to the car and once I get to the driveway I get into the car and start the engine making it roar to life.

Emma's house is twenty minutes away from the safe house, so it was a little drive. The new house is ten minutes away from her though. Ace wanted to live close to Leo.

Once I get to the new house, they let me in through the gate. I see a lot of people going in and out of the house. The house is starting to look good. I park the car and get out. I see one of the head contractors that is mainly in charge.

"Mrs. De Luca. Nice to have you here today. Shall we get started?" he asks as he comes up to me.

Almost all the workers call me Mrs. De Luca which is kind of weird because Ace and I aren't married. Don't get me wrong I would love to marry Ace but I'm way too young to be married right now.

"It's Aria, Chris, remember?" I chuckle, and he laughs nodding his head.

"My apologies."

I follow Chris inside the house. We go through all the rooms, and they are looking really nice. We go to Ace's office, and it looks like how Ace showed me in the pictures. They are doing a fantastic job.

I got to pick how the walls were going to look for the guest rooms. I chose a light gray because I thought that since most of the house is going to be black, grey, or white, I'll match the bedrooms.

"Okay now to Mr. De Luca's room, yes?" Chris asks.

"Yes," I answer nodding my head.

We get inside the room and his room looks perfect. The walls are just how he wants them to be and the room itself looks like the one from his old house.

He also has his ceiling to floor window on the side of his room where it overlooks all the city and even the beach nearby.

"The room looks amazing. You guys did such a good job," I compliment.

"Thank you, miss. The closet isn't quite done yet. There still needs to be a few more shelves but the bathroom is almost finished. It is connected to the room just like Mr. De Luca asked for. I can show you that right over here," Chris says pointing to the bathroom.

I am about to answer him, but I see a piece of paper on the floor by the window.

"Alright, I'll be there," I answer and walk towards the piece of paper.

It has my name on it. I bend down and pick the paper up and open it.

My heart stops and I feel my stomach drop.

The paper falls to the floor as tears start to prick my eyes.

. . .

'I'll see you soon, my love. Don't worry I will make it all better for us.'

-Dante

"Find Dante Zelle! I want everything you can find on him! If this job isn't done properly then I'll make sure to burn your entire fucking home to the ground," Ace yells through the phone before hanging up and shoving the phone in his pocket.

Just hearing his name sends shivers down my spine.

After I found that note, I had a crying session for like ten minutes. The head contractor constantly tried to calm me down, but he couldn't, so he called Ace.

I am usually never the one to cry but if anyone scares me, it's him. He is the only person who was able to hurt me so much that I would want to leave this life.

This house is thirty minutes away from the safe-house, but Ace got here in like ten minutes. It was dangerous and I scolded him for it, but he didn't care. Once he got here, he held me trying to calm me down while tears spilled from my eyes. Once he saw the note his whole body tensed, and his fist clenched. I saw him squeeze his hand twice making me want to hold onto his hand.

I calmed down a little bit while he yelled through the phone. I was standing by the window, and he was standing a few feet away from me.

"You," Ace says, looking at Chris, the head contractor.

"M-me? "Chris asks with a shaky voice.

"Did you see anyone come through the doors or was there anyone who tried to get in with security?" Ace asks the worker.

"N-no. I didn't see anyone. E-everything was running smoothly."

"Alright. I want more security installed and cameras everywhere. You should have had that done first," Ace demands. "I also want guards around the perimeter. No one and I mean no one except for me and her are allowed in the estate. Leo and his wife as well."

"Of course, sir," Chris says nodding his head.

"Get my security and get out," Ace growls, making Chris leave while shaking in fear. Ace rubs his temples and sighs before walking to me and wrapping his arms around me. "I'm not going to let him hurt you," Ace says putting his head on mine and rubbing my arms.

"He is going to kill everyone, Ace. My family. Emma and the baby, Leo. What if he kills you?" I ask looking at Ace making him look down at me.

"He is not going to kill anyone. Especially me," Ace replies cockily, making me laugh a little. "I won't let him hurt anyone. I won't even let him get near you. You hear me?" Ace whispers.

I nod my head and then bury my head in his chest. The moment is ruined when Ace's security comes in. Ace kisses my head and lets go of me to go talk to his guards. I turn around with my back facing them, so I look out the window.

What if he finds me and makes me regret leaving him?

He is going to kill everyone.

My mom, dad, Layna, Alex, Cole, Calla, Ariel.

Even Ariel.

God, I can't let her die.

And then Emma and Leo.

They have a baby on the way. I can't have her die. I would never forgive myself.

Dante is going to come and get me and take me away from Ace. He is going to be mad that I left him and kicked him out.

I felt small and hopeless around him. Dante is a psychopath. I will never forget all the times he hit me, punched me, pushed me, took advantage of me.

Everything.

I remember everything.

"*Amore*," I turn around and look at Ace. We are alone in his room. No one is here except us. "Let's go home. I got everything figured out. You'll be okay. I'll make sure of it. You're my priority now," he says and then takes me by the waist as we walk out of the room.

He rubs my back as we walk to the car. I feel weak and like my legs could give out at any moment. Ace opens the car door for me, and he then gets in the car on the other side after closing my door.

He starts the car and starts driving to the safe-house.

The whole way there it is silent. I just stare out the window as he drives while also keeping his hand on my thigh. Once we get there, he parks the car and then stops the engine.

He gets out of the car and then comes to my side and opens my door. I'm about to get out but instead, he picks me up bridal style and carries me. He walks through the front door and then heads towards his room upstairs. He puts me on the bed and then leaves to his closet. He then comes back with a black sweater and black boxers.

I just sit and watch him.

He raises an eyebrow at me trying to tell me to lift my arms. I smile a little and lift my arms. He lifts the dress I'm wearing and throws it across the room.

I'm just wearing a sports bra underneath. Ace gets his black sweater, and he puts it over my head, and I slip my arms through. I smile and he smiles back, and I adjust the sweater. He motions for me to stand up and I do. I hold onto his shoulders as he puts the boxers on me.

I could have changed myself. But Ace being Ace, he is stubborn and would still do it one way or another.

He then starts to make the bed more comfortable before I get in. I hop in bed and lay down. Ace leaves towards his closet and then comes out with just sweatpants on and then slips in bed beside me. He faces me as I face him. His arm is draped across my waist pulling me closer.

"I'm not going to let anyone touch you. You're mine and mine only. I'm the only one who can touch you," he demands. I nod my head. "I will find him, Aria. I promise."

"Okay," I whisper.

"Tell me you understand," Ace demands.

"I understand," I genuinely say.

"*Ti amo*," he speaks.

"I love you."

Thirty-One

Emma's delivery date is coming around. Leo is on his toes waiting urgently for the baby to arrive.

Lately, I haven't gotten any new notes from Dante. Ace has had Francisco follow me everywhere. He wants to make sure I'm safe at all times, but I have mostly been at Emma's house because one, I don't want to be alone and two, because I want to make sure she is doing okay with her giving birth soon.

Ace is still trying to find Dante. Ace didn't tell Leo and Emma about it because they have a baby on the way, and he doesn't want to worry them.

Her stomach is huge.

Currently, Emma and I are watching the movie Anastasia in the living room. We would watch it in her room, but her couches are so much more comfortable. They feel like you're sleeping on a cloud.

We are halfway through the movie when Emma decides to get

another snack. I was going to get it, but she is so stubborn, and she wants to get it instead.

"No. I'll get it. I'm the hungry one," Emma says, stopping me from getting up.

"Yeah, but your fat ass is pregnant."

"Yeah and my fat ass is going to go get me another snack. Not you, shut up," Emma says as she stands up from her place on the couch.

She is kind of struggling a little bit. I try to help her, but she stops me and continues to do it herself.

She is so stubborn.

She leaves for the kitchen to go get more snacks while I pause the movie and go on my phone.

'**What are you doing?**' Ace texted me.

'**Watching Anastasia with Em. She went to go get a snack.**' I reply.

'**Of course, you're watching that movie.**'

I can already imagine him laughing at me for watching it again.

Lately he has been smiling more often which I love. He has such an amazing smile.

'**Shut up. I know you're laughing.**'

I quickly text him back but then hear something drop.

"Aria!" Emma yells.

I jump off the couch and run towards her in the kitchen. I see her just standing with her legs a little apart with liquid coming out of her.

What the fuck?

"Oh my god," I say freaking out.

"Don't just stand there, stupid! Do something!" Emma yells.

"Okay um...where is your hospital bag?" I ask while walking closer to her with my eyes widened.

"Upstairs in the room."

"Okay don't move," I say and leave to go upstairs.

"It's not like I fucking can!" Emma yells.

I go inside Leo and Emma's room and find the hospital bag and grab it, carrying it downstairs.

"Okay, can you walk or something?"

"Yeah a little," Emma says while wincing.

"Okay then let's just walk slowly to the car," I hold her hand and she starts walking.

She is walking terribly slow. I don't have the patience for this. I grab my phone out of my pocket and dial Ace's number.

"*Amore?*"

"Emma's water broke. Where is Leo?" I ask.

"Next to me. Hold on."

"Aria?" I hear Leo.

"Hey, Emma's water broke. We are leaving the house right now," I speak.

"Is she okay?" he asks, sounding a little scared.

"She is fine. Don't worry. Just meet us at the hospital."

"Can I talk to her?" he asks me, making me look at Emma and see her face alter in discomfort and pain.

"She is a little busy. Just meet us at the hospital, okay?"

"Okay tell her I love her."

"Will do. See you guys there."

I hang up the phone as Emma and I walk outside. When we

get in the car, I start the engine and speed through cars to get to the hospital.

"It's okay, Em. Just a little longer. You can do it," I'm holding her hand as she tries to breathe. "Please don't have the baby here, Em. I don't know how to deliver a baby."

"Just fucking drive," she sneers.

After a few minutes more we finally get to the hospital. Nurses come outside and put her in a wheelchair while I get to the hospital bag and put it on my shoulder. They don't even wait for me, so I have to run after them.

"Okay honey, what's your full name?" I hear the nurse ask Emma as they wheel her down the hall.

"Emma Calvin Russo."

"Okay, and do you have a partner or someone who is the father of the baby coming?"

"Yes. He is on his way," Emma struggles to get out.

How big is this hospital? I feel like we've been walking forever.

"Okay, and what's his name?"

"Leo Pepe Russo."

"Alright, how many months are you?"

"Eight months and a week I think."

The nurse turns the corner and finds a room. "Okay since your partner isn't here, we will have the front desk let him in," she finishes talking to Emma and then other nurses start to get her situated on the hospital bed. The nurse turns to look at me. "Who are you?" she asks.

"I'm her sister," I speak.

"Okay well, you can wait here until her partner comes. Do you know who else is coming by any chance?"

"Uh, my boyfriend and then my aunt and her husband and kids."

I know that Val and Mia would want to be here.

"Okay, they have to wait outside since they aren't immediate family."

I nod my head and then she leaves to go check Emma's heart rate and how dilated she is.

Soon I hear Leo's voice echo through the halls. "I'm here! I'm here!" Leo comes out from the corner and then comes inside the room to Emma. "I'm here, baby. I'm here," he kisses her head and holds her hand whispering to her.

"Where's Ace?" I ask Leo while setting the hospital bag on the floor by the chairs.

"Parking the car," Leo says.

The nurse comes inside the room. "Okay, you're the father of the child, yes?" the nurses ask Leo.

"Yes," Leo answers.

"Okay well we are going to check how dilated she is and then we will move forward from there," the nurse says.

They check how dilated Emma is and she is nine centimeters, so they decide to start pushing now.

"I'm going to wait outside for Ace and call Val."

Leo and Emma nod their heads and I wish them good luck before leaving the room and going to sit on the chairs outside. I call Val while waiting for Ace and they say they are on their way.

"Hey, where are they?" Ace asks as he comes up to me.

"In the room. Emma is nine centimeters, so they are going to start soon." As if on cue we hear Emma grunt loudly making Ace and I grimace. I look at Ace and see him looking around where we were sitting. "What's wrong?"

"You guys didn't go to the top floor?"

"Top floor?" I furrow my eyebrows at him.

"Yea. I have a doctor who works for me. You guys should have just gone through the other parking lot and met with him instead."

"Oh. Well, I didn't know you have your own doctor here. If I did then I would have brought Emma to see him." I stated. "How was work?"

"Good," Ace states and sits down on the waiting chairs next to me. "We weren't that busy today. I had a meeting with the Mexicans, and we just talked about some shipments we got."

"Oh."

"And I also looked at some of the security cameras from the house and I haven't seen Dante in any of the footage." I look up at Ace. "But once I find him, I will kill him and make sure that he suffers for what he has done to you," Ace pulls me closer to sit next to him and he kisses me on my head.

After one hour Val, Mia, Ana, and Antonio arrive at the hospital, and Emma's grunting and crying stops. We are all waiting for the nurse to give us the go and come in.

Just then we hear the room door open, and everyone stands up.

We see a nurse that has some blood on her shirt making me grimace a little. "Emma Russo?" We all nod our heads. "You guys can come inside now."

We all start to walk into the room quietly, aware that the baby could be sleeping. We see Emma on the bed with tear-stained cheeks and a smile on her face as she holds the baby boy in her arms. Leo is next to her and has tears coming out of his eyes.

I walk on the other side of Emma making her look up at me. "Want to hold him?"

I nod my head and smile. She hands me the baby and I carry him in my arms and sway him side to side.

He looks just like Leo and has the same beautiful blue eyes just like Emma.

"What's his name?" Ana asks.

Leo and Emma look at each other before saying the name.

"Guys, meet Alexander Leo Russo."

Alexander is one of the cutest babies I have ever held.

Since Emma gave birth to him a few days ago I have been with Emma 24/7 to help her with him.

I don't want to call it baby fever or anything but it's making me want my own, but I know Ace and I couldn't. Even though we have been together for almost a year, Ace is busy and especially when he is also trying so hard to find Dante. It's just not good timing.

"Aria. Can I have my baby back now?" I hear Emma beg.

I am sitting on the couch with Alexander in my arms. I can't let him go. It's Emma's fault, she left.

"Why?! He is just too cute to not be held," I say looking down at him.

He has beautiful blueish, greenish eyes and has a little hair that looks like a dark blonde color.

"Yeah but I think you need to go home, and he needs to go to sleep."

"Why can't I just take him? Aunty Aria and Uncle Ace can take good care of him," I say to Emma.

Emma comes over to me and takes Alexander out of my hands. "No. You're going to end up kidnapping my baby. I don't need that."

"Ugh, fine. I think Ace is done with work anyway," I roll my eyes while standing up from the couch.

"Yeah, go home," Emma says while rocking Alexander.

"I'll see you tomorrow," I walk closer to the front door.

"Yeah. I'll see you tomorrow, too," Emma says in a sarcastic tone, making me look at her.

"What is that supposed to mean?" I furrow my eyebrows.

"Oh, nothing. Bye, Aria, see you soon!" Emma yells, making me chuckle as I walk out of the house.

Once I get in my car I start driving to the safe house.

The new house that Ace is building is going to be done in a week. I am super excited to see it. The last time I was there was when Dante left the note. I have been kind of scared to go back but I'm still excited to see how the house is going to look.

Once I get to the safe house, I lock the car and open the front door only to be picked up by Ace immediately afterward.

"Ace! What are you doing?! Put me down!" I exclaim.

"Nope," he says as he smacks my ass and makes his way upstairs.

I give up trying to get him to put me down because he isn't going to. We get to his room, and he then strolls into his bathroom.

Ace puts me down when he opens the bathroom door. He strolls over to his shower and takes off his t-shirt revealing his toned body. I can't peel my eyes away; I don't want to give him the satisfaction of him knowing he has a good body, but I bet he already knows that.

Ace turns the shower on and starts to take off his clothes. I do the same and take off my top which catches Ace's eyes.

I guess we are taking a shower.

He walks over to me and runs his hands down the side of my body, stopping at my waist. He licks his lips before biting.

"When did I decide to take a shower?" I speak softly, unhooking my bra as steam begins to fill up the bathroom.

"You didn't. I did," he smiles and then leaves the bathroom.

I slip off my bottoms and underwear then walk inside the shower. Ace comes back into the bathroom with two towels. He winks at me before putting them on the counter by the shower.

I smile at him as I feel the warm water hit my body, making me want to fall asleep. It feels so soothing. I lean my head back so that the hot water can wet my hair. I see Ace step into the shower and shut the shower door behind him.

"Hi," he says with a smirk.

I smile at him and shut my eyes, taking in the water that seems to bring me peace. Suddenly I feel a bunch of shampoo being put on my head.

"How much did you put?" I open my eyes and look at him with wide eyes.

"You need it," he shrugs.

"You're the one who kills people on the daily with blood on your suits," I point to his chest while talking to him.

He shrugs his shoulders. I scoop some of the shampoo off my head and plop it onto his. I glare at him while massaging his scalp as the shampoo fizzes up in his hair. He smiles slightly as he places his arms around my hips while I keep massaging his head.

After I finish washing his hair, he then washes mine, pulling the shower head out of its stand and washing the soap out of my hair.

"What's got you in a good mood?" I question him as he starts to trail his kisses down to my neck.

"I love you," he mutters to me, ignoring my question.

"Everyone loves me," I say before leaning away from him and getting out of the shower.

I get the towel off the counter and then throw one over to Ace. I wrap the towel around my body as he wraps the towel around his waist making it hang low on his hips.

He comes over to me and hugs me from behind.

He kisses down my neck and then back up to kiss the spot behind my ear. "You are so fucking beautiful, you know that?" I don't answer him instead I feel my cheeks heat up. He lets out a chuckle and leaves the bathroom and goes into his room. I feel so cold without him. "Oh, I already got your bags packed but we are leaving for France in the morning," he yells from his room.

Wait, France?

Thirty-Two

So, we're in Paris.

I didn't even know what time to wake up this morning, so Ace woke me up.

Right now, the jet is about to land. It has been a very long ride, but I slept for most of it. I'm sitting next to Ace while he has his hand on my knee and is looking out the window.

"Why did we come to Paris?" I ask Ace.

"You don't know, *amore*?" he says as he looks away from the window and looks at me. I stare at him with a confused face. "Our anniversary was like a few weeks ago. We didn't do anything. Yeah we got each other gifts but we didn't do anything."

This is true.

This is technically the anniversary of the day we met.

For our anniversary I had no idea what to get him. So, I decided to get a tattoo of an Ace card where my hip bone is. After he saw that let's just say it was a very long night.

Ace got me a huge rose bear. It was like ten feet tall. He did tell me that it wasn't all that he got me, but he wanted me to wait.

"You didn't have to take us to Paris though. I like staying home with you."

"Yeah well the house is almost done, and I wanted to get away for a bit." Ace shrugs.

"How many times have you been to Paris?" I ask him.

"A few times. Mostly for business though," Ace answers.

"I've only been to Paris twice. Once it was for the ball they hold every year and then when Layna took me here for my birthday."

"How long have you known Layna for?"

"All my life. We have been hip to hip since we were kids."

He nods his head.

"Mr. De Luca. The jet is about to land in less than forty-five minutes," the flight attendant says.

"Ok. You can go now. Tell my men to get our bags ready," Ace demands making the flight attendant leave.

"Harsh."

"You know me," he smirks.

Once the plane lands Ace and I get off and we don't wait for our bags. Francisco came with us like always, so he had a car waiting for us and he was going to go in another car and to take our bags to the hotel while Ace and I drive in another car. Once we get inside the car, he drives away from the airport.

"How long are we staying here for?" I ask.

"For a week. We can do whatever we want here. It's up to you. I have no plans for us because I know we both have been here before."

"Okay. Then I have a few ideas," I smirk at him, and he smirks back. The last time I was here Layna took me on this boat ride on the Seine River. It was absolutely beautiful. "I have an idea of what we can do tonight if you're not too tired."

"Tired? With you? Never," Ace smirks.

"Perfect. We will leave at eight o'clock."

"Perfect."

After driving through the streets of France we finally make it to the hotel. It is very luxurious.

"This is nice. Who chose it?" I ask while looking around the hotel room.

"Me. *Amore*, you should know I have the best taste in things," he smirks as he starts walking closer to me.

I smirk back at him once he reaches me.

He places his hands on my hips and pulls my body closer to him. He leans his head down to my lips and kisses me. His touch gets more addicting as he starts to lead his kisses down my cheek and then below my ear.

I lean my head back to give him more access. His fingers grip my hips harder pulling my lower region towards him.

But before things can go any further, we hear a knock at the door. Ace stops kissing me and leans his head down on my shoulder letting out a groan. He lifts his head, kisses me on the temple, and lets go of me before he walks towards the door.

"I'm going to go get ready," I say to Ace and walk into the bathroom.

Francisco got here before us and put our luggage in the closet. I grab my phone from my pocket and search up the number for the boat rides.

"Bonjour," I hear from the other line.

"Hello, do you have any appointments for eight-thirty tonight?"

"Yes. What's your name so I can write it down?" The person on the other line asked with a very thick French accent.

"Aria White."

"Thank you. We will see you at eight-thirty."

"Merci," I hang up and close my phone.

I start to get ready as I hear Ace talking to one of his men outside of the bathroom. I turn the shower on and hop right in. I have an hour to get ready.

Once I'm done in the shower I walk back inside the room, and I don't see Ace.

I decide to check my phone to see if he texted.

' I had to go take care of some things. I'll be back just in time for our date. I'll text you when I'm in the front.'

I text him back an 'ok' and also send an 'I love you' and he texts me back saying the same thing.

I go back inside the bathroom and take my towel to start drying my body and hair.

For my hair since it is still a little wet, I'm going to put it in a low bun. For my makeup, I'm not going to put any on. Maybe some mascara but that's it. After my hair is tied and mascara is put on, I change into a red summer dress.

Ace texts me once I am done getting ready, saying that he is downstairs waiting in the car.

Perfect timing.

I grab my phone and bag then leave the hotel room heading downstairs to where Ace's car is at. I see his car and the valet person opens the door for me. I thank him and was about to sit down but I see a bouquet of pink flowers on the passenger seat.

"Hello, *amore*," he says and I look at him instead of the flowers.

"You didn't have to get my flowers."

"I wanted to. Get in."

Ace takes the flowers and puts them in the back seat of the car so that I could sit down. He leans over to kiss me and I smile while feeling his lips on mine.

"Where are we going?" he asks when he takes his lips off mine and starts driving away from the hotel.

"Seine River."

"Ladies first," Ace says as he opens the car door for me.

I take his hand in mine and I hear Ace mutter 'beautiful' as I walk past him towards the boat.

"Aria White," I state my name to the man who has a clipboard in his hand.

Probably to make sure that no one is trying to sneak on stealing the boat.

I see him look through his papers on his clipboard and then look up at me. "ID?"

I pull my ID out of my phone case and show him. He smiles at me and motions me to start walking onto the boat. I smile back at him, and Ace's hand grazes my back as we enter the boat.

"Interesting choice, *amore*," Ace says in my ear making butterflies erupt in my stomach.

"I knew you would like it."

The boat horn makes a sound, and we see a waiter walk up to us.

"Bonjour. Welcome to the Seine River. Let me show you to your seats for the night," the waiter says with an accent. We follow him to the front of the boat where there is a beautiful set up on the deck. There is a red blanket with candles and roses. "There are menus for you, and you can order anything you want. Just let me know," the waiter says.

We thank him and then sit down on the blanket. The sky is pitch black and clear. You can see a lot of stars out tonight.

"So, what do you think?" I ask looking at him.

"I like it. It's quiet, romantic, private," Ace states and a smirk lifts on his lips.

I chuckle and then remember him leaving while I was getting ready. "Why did you have to leave earlier?" I ask. Ace looks like he is hesitant to answer. "You can tell me, Ace," I place my hand on his cheek and stroke it making him look at me.

He lets out a sigh. "My men found Dante in one of my warehouses. I guess he has been the one who was snooping around but not stealing shit as I told you in the office the other day." I nod my head urging him to continue. "I had to go see what was up with that."

"Are you worried?" I furrow my eyebrows.

"I just don't want him to get to you Aria. I won't let him. Not while I'm still breathing but it pisses me off that this dick is stalking you," he says, getting a little frustrated.

"Hey. You know I love you, though, right? I only want you."

He looks into my eyes and then down at my lips before

looking back at my eyes. "*Ti amo*, Aria." I lean forward and press my lips to his and he instantly kissed back. When we back away, I see him thinking about something. He looks conflicted about what he is thinking about, but he had a 'fuck it' moment. "Aria," he says in a hushed tone. "Stand up." I furrow my eyebrows and stand up while he holds my hand in his.

"What's wrong?" I ask, wondering why he looks so nervous.

He takes both of my hands in his. "Nothing. I just want to tell you something. First, I want to say thank you. You made me something that I never thought I could be. You made me feel again. I don't feel pain or anger anymore. Whenever I see you all of that washes away and it's filled with happiness. That's the first time I have ever admitted that out loud, too." I smile at him. "I love you. I want to spend the rest of my life with you."

I feel a tear fall down my cheek.

Fuck, why am I crying?

He can't be- can he?

Ace wipes the tear before going down on one knee in front of me and I widen my eyes.

Oh god.

"Ace-"

He takes out a black velvet box. "Aria White, will you marry me and carry the De Luca name?" he opens the box making me see a gorgeous diamond ring.

This can't be happening.

Ace De Luca is on his knee for me?

I stare down at the ring in awe. I don't think twice before nodding my head yes and pulling him up to his full height so I can kiss him.

"I love you. I love you. I love you," I say repeatedly while kissing him, making him chuckle.

He pulls away from me and takes my hand in his. He takes the ring out of the box and tosses it on the floor before placing the ring on my finger, gently.

I stare down at the ring in awe while trying to keep my emotions under control.

"I love it Ace. I love you," I say before jumping in his arms and kissing him on the lips.

I just hope that he isn't like Dante, because that thought is always in the back of my head. But I'm not worried.

Ace would never be like Dante.

Ace and I head back to the hotel after we stayed on the boat for another hour.

The whole drive to the hotel I have been impatient because all I want is Ace's hands on me. I want him to touch every single part of my body.

His hand squeezes my thigh a couple of times as he clenches the wheel in his other hand.

Once Ace parks the car, he cuts the engine and gets out before coming to my side of the car and opening my door. "Come on, *amore*. We are wasting the night."

I blush as I give him my hand. While we walk to our hotel room, he squeezes my hand until we get to the room.

Ace unlocks the door and then pulls us both inside the room.

I turn around so that my back is leaning on the door as I look at Ace in front of me. "Ace," I say while Ace just looks at me with a dark look in his eyes.

"*Amore.*"

"Why are you looking at me like that?" I ask innocently.

"Because I want to fuck you," he bluntly states as he walks closer.

When he is in front of me, he puts his hands on my waist and grips it a little before sliding them up my body, all the way to my hands to hold them up against the wall. He leans down and captures my lips, and he nips my bottom lip before shoving his tongue inside, deepening the kiss. After some kissing, he trails his kisses down my neck and slides his hands down my hips. "Keep your hands up. If you move them, it will only be worse for you," he mutters.

Ace starts to kiss more down my body while moving his hand to my back where the zipper of my dress is. He zips it down and the dress loosens around me. Once the fabric isn't covering my breast, he dips his head down and presses his lips on my nipple before doing the same to the other.

I hold his head to my chest as Ace starts to lick and suck on the skin at the same time, he grabs my legs and carries me to the bed. He puts me on the bed and at the same time I wrap my legs around his waist so that he is closer, but he pushes himself away from me.

I lean up and reach for him, but he takes my hands in his and presses them back on the bed and holds them there. "What did I say about your hands? They stay up."

"You said that they had to stay up when I was against the door. Not on the bed."

"Smartass," he mutters before leaning down and pressing his lips to mine. "Keep your hands there. Don't move them at all." Ace takes his hands away and he brings them to the bottom of my dress and takes it off in one motion. Ace backs away so that he can stare at me with my underwear only on. Ace unbuckles his belt and takes it off before walking towards me and putting his hands on my hips. The fire that I feel in my stomach almost makes my need for him uncomfortable. He strokes the tattoo I dedicated to him and then leans down to kiss it. "I love you.," he mutters and then slides my underwear off.

"Ace," I moan when I feel him move closer to me, to the point where his cock is teasing my entrance. "Please," I beg.

"Don't rush me, Aria," Ace demands and he kisses me a couple of more times on my hip bone and close to where my clit is. "God. Do you understand how breathtaking you are?" I try to close my legs, but Ace stands between them making me whimper. I see Ace stretch his arm to reach the side table.

When he brings his arm back I see ice in his hand making the heat in my stomach build. He puts the ice in his mouth while locking his eyes on me.

How did the ice even end up in the room?

He leans down and I feel the cold ice touch my torso as Ace starts to trail the ice downward.

I close my eyes when I feel the wet ice melting on my upper thigh. Ace trails the ice in his mouth down my leg and back up. I try to close them but he wraps his hands around my hips and looks up at me while dragging the ice across my thighs, slowly going closer to the spot in between my legs. I whimper and Ace looks up at me again. His eyes has fire in them as he looks at me with lust and love, wanting to commit the biggest sin on me.

As his face gets closer to the spot between my legs I close my eyes and lean my head back on the pillow.

I feel Ace blow cold air on my clit before feeling his lips on me. I moan while throwing my hands into Ace's hair. I feel the coldness of the ice touch my opening before feeling Ace's tongue.

"God."

"Wrong name *amore*." Ace muttered and I open my eyes to look down at him. His arms around wrapped about my thighs and he is looking up at me as he licked and sucked me while feeling the coldness of the ice on my sensitive skin. "Try again."

"Ace."

My eyebrows furrow when I feel the ice start to slip inside me. I rock my hips against Ace's face as I feel this new intense in between my legs.

It's different but it feels good.

I wrap my legs around Ace tighter as I climax on his mouth while moaning. Ace licks and sucks for another minute before he comes up and holds himself above me. He grab my hips to pull them closer to him and I moan when I feel his cock touch my entrance. His tip slips in for a second before he leans back and takes it out.

"Tell me what you feel Aria."

"If I do will that make you fuck me?" I ask getting frustrated with his teasing.

"Find out."

"In love," I say before I feel Ace thrust inside me.

Thirty-Three

France was absolutely amazing with Ace. He showed me so many places that I haven't even been to. I had a lot of fun with him. It was definitely a nice getaway.

As soon as we got home one of Ace's men said that the house was finally finished after months and months of waiting, we finally get to move in.

I'm not sure when Ace plans on officially moving in there. We have only been back for three days and we already have most of our crap at the house. Ace had his men pack up our belongings while we were in France, so we didn't have to worry about it when we got back.

I also showed Emma the ring. She was so happy for me and knew Ace would do it soon. I haven't told my mom or dad yet. I called Layna the day after, and she was screaming through the phone. I'm surprised Ace proposed to me before Cole got the chance to propose to Layna. I haven't thought about wedding planning at all. I want to start when Ace and I are all moved into the house.

I also want my mom here to help me plan it out because that's always something I wanted to do with her. I think it would be really fun to plan the wedding with Layna, my mom, and of course Emma.

I need to decide who is going to be the maid-of-honor because I have two amazing best friends now and I don't want to make either of them sad. I have to start thinking about so much.

I get out of the room and walk towards Ace's office. When I walk in almost everything is packed up. Ace sees me walk in and puts down his phone.

"Hey," I say.

"Hello, Mrs. De Luca," Ace smirks.

He keeps calling me Mrs. De Luca. It always makes my heart flip.

"Mr. De Luca," I state while walk towards him. "I have a question."

"And what is your question, Mrs. De Luca?" he asks.

"When are we moving to the new house?" I ask as I sit down on his lap and his hands go to my hips instantly.

"Today, actually."

"Wait, really?" I ask surprised.

"Yeah. We're going to leave in like 10 minutes. That's why everything here is packed up. Everything is already at the other house, so we don't need to worry about anything else."

"Perfect! Then let's go," I jump off his lap and he chuckles.

I run downstairs and get the car key. I have never been so excited to see the house.

"Slow down," I hear Ace yell as he walks downstairs.

I laugh and walk out of the front door and run towards the car.

Once I get in the car, Ace gets in the car as well a few seconds later.

I start the engine of the car making it roar to life. The drive to the house is calm and quiet. We get there pretty quickly since there is no traffic.

Security lets me and Ace in and I park the car in the driveway. I see all of Ace's other cars parked in the driveway as well. I get out of the car and look up at the house. It's beautiful. I have a huge smile on my face.

"You like it?" Ace asks as he walks towards me.

I have seen the house updates, but it looks officially done. They put the grass and flowers in and even some small trees in the front yard. The house looks ready for us to move in.

"Yeah. It's beautiful Ace. You did such an amazing job," I compliment him and put my hand on his chest.

"I've always wanted my house to look like this," he smiles at me and then starts walking, bringing me with him. We walk inside the house and all the lights are on. "So?" Ace asks once we finish looking at the house.

We are now in our room and it looks the same but bigger and more grand.

"It's amazing, Ace. I can't believe you did this. It's beautiful. Maybe you should have been a home designer instead of a crime boss," I smirk.

He laughs. "Yes, because I would be so good at designing homes."

"You would," I say in a serious tone. He shrugs his shoulders. "When is Lana coming?" I ask.

"She starts tomorrow. I gave her two weeks off since we weren't here and didn't need her to cook."

"Oh okay," I nod my head. "Is your office ready?"

He nods and takes my hand leading us upstairs.

I run to the bathroom for the third time today, sitting down on the floor and throwing up everything I ate. I flush the toilet once I am finished and then lean on the bathroom wall.

Fuck.

What's wrong with me?

I have been throwing up for the past week. I think it's food poisoning, but food poisoning shouldn't last this long.

Can it be- no it can't.

Not possible, I am on birth control.

It's been a month since Ace proposed to me in Paris and things have been going great up until this week since I have been puking so much and I just feel so weak.

I stand up and turn off the light in the bathroom and walk back into Ace and I's room. He is currently working. He caught me throwing up a few times, but I try to do it when he isn't looking or here so that he doesn't have to worry about me.

I pick up my phone from the bed and dial Emma's number.

"Hello," I hear Emma say from the other line.

"Emma," I groan.

"What's wrong? You sound awful, are you okay?" she asks.

"I need help."

"What happened?"

Fuck, am I actually going to do this?

Fuck it.

"Can you pick me up and buy a pregnancy test?" I mumble the last part quietly.

"What? I couldn't hear the last part."

I sigh, "Can you please pick me up and buy a pregnancy test?" I say with my voice as clear as day.

"Why the do you need a pregnancy test? Don't tell me you're-"

"I don't know. I just need to check. I've been throwing up so much for the past week, Em and I haven't eaten anything," I whine to her.

"Okay, I'm on my way. Does anyone else know?" she asks.

"No. Just you."

"Okay, I'm coming now. I'll text you when I'm in the front."

I hang up the phone and stand up from the bed going into the closet. I take out one of Ace's sweaters and put it on. I had shorts on, so I just left them on. I walk out of our room and walk downstairs towards the kitchen. I take out my phone while walking and dial Ace's number.

"*Amore,*" he says once he picks up the phone.

"Hey. I'm going to Emma's. I just wanted to let you know in case you're home before me," I say walking towards the kitchen where I see Lana making food.

Ace is at his headquarters which is a few minutes away.

I guess he had to look over new assassins because he needs to get rid of some of his workers since some of them suck and he doesn't think he can trust them since we now have Dante to worry about.

"Okay. What time do you think you'll be back by?"

"I'm not sure. I'm just going to hang out over there," I speak.

"Alright. How are you feeling? Still throwing up?" he asks, sounding concerned.

I freeze at the question. "No. I'm feeling better," I lie.

"Alright. I'll see you at home. I love you."

"I love you," I say and hang up.

"You don't look so good Aria. Are you okay?" Lana asks once I put the phone on the counter.

"What?" I knew what she asked but I don't know why I said what.

"You look pale, dear. Why?"

"Ummm, I don't know. I haven't gotten any sleep. Maybe that's why."

"Or it's because you just started getting that morning sickness."

I choke on the water I'm drinking. "What?!" I ask, still trying to control my coughing.

"Don't make me feel stupid. You know exactly what I'm talking about. Don't forget I had kids too," Lana says, giving me a knowing look.

"I have no clue what you're talking about," I say nonchalantly.

"Don't worry, I won't tell Ace," Lana smirks.

Just then Emma texted me saying she is outside.

"Well Lana this has been lovely as always, but I have to bounce but you enjoy your day. I love you and I will be safe, don't worry," I smile at her as I walk out.

"Don't be so nervous, you're going to do fine!" she yells making my face heat up.

I groan as I walk outside the door and run to Emma's car.

"Ready?" she says as I get in the car.

"As I'll ever be," I mumble, and she just chuckles. "Wait did you get the test?"

"I have some at home so you can just check there."

"Is Alexander home?" I ask.

"Yeah he is with Mia and Val. They came over today."

"And no one told me?" I ask, shocked.

Emma laughs and shrugs her shoulders. I think she noticed I look nervous because I am. I am so nervous.

"It's going to be fine," Emma assures me.

"What if he doesn't want it or me?" I ask.

"That's never going to happen. Don't worry. Ace isn't like that," Emma assures. "You need to relax,"

"I know but I'm still scared to see how he reacts," I say anxiously.

"You're going to be fine. Don't worry," Emma puts her hand on mine and rubs my knuckles.

I smile at her as she continues driving.

Soon enough we get to Emma's. I see Val's Ferrari parked in her driveway. Emma and I get out of the car and walk up the front door. We walk in and hear a ton of laughter.

"Emma!" I hear Val yell.

"Yeah I'm here! Aria is also here!" Emma yells back.

Then I hear running. I see Valentino holding Alexander in his arms while running towards me.

"Val! You can't run with the baby!" I hear Mia yell from the living room. Val hugs me with Alexander still in his arms. I hug him back and then I feel Mia come in and join the hug. They let go. "What are you doing here?" Mia asks.

I look at Emma and she shrugs and takes Alexander from Val's arms.

"I'm going to take a pregnancy test," I sigh.

"Why?" Val furrows his eyebrows.

"Morning sickness. Duhh," Mia says looking at Val and then turning to me. "Oh my god, I'm so excited. If it's a boy I think you should na-"

"Woah, woah. Relax. I just have morning sickness. I'm not even positive if I'm pregnant or not."

"Right, well then let's go check," Mia grabs my hand and pulls me to the bathroom.

"The test is in the guest bathroom under the sink!" Emma yells. "I'm going to go feed Alexander."

"Ok!" Mia yells.

Once we get to the guest bathroom, she finds the pregnancy test and gives it to me. She leaves me alone in the bathroom for privacy. I pee on the stick and leave it on the counter and wash my hands.

I leave the bathroom and see Mia, Val, and Emma sitting on the bed waiting. "So, I have an audience now?"

"I want to know if you're pregnant or not," Mia shrugs.

"You called me, soo..." Emma says trailing off.

I look at Val and see him smiling. "I want to be the uncle," he states making me laugh.

After we wait about three minutes, Emma says for me to go

check. I walk inside the bathroom and take the test and lifted it to my eyes.

Shit.

On the stick, it reads '*Pregnant*'.

Oh, Ace.

"What the hell am I supposed to do?" I say after a few minutes of staying quiet.

"Relax, Aria. It's not even bad," Emma says, trying to calm me down.

"Dude, what if Ace doesn't want it?" I worry.

"He will. Stop thinking so negatively," Mia scolds.

"Yeah Ace isn't like that," Val assures.

"When should I tell him?" I ask Val.

"Better to do it earlier than later. He doesn't like secrets. You know that."

Oh yes, I do.

"So today?" I ask.

"Yes," they all say.

I feel my phone vibrate so I look down and see that Ace is calling.

Great.

"Hello," I say as I pick up the phone.

'Who is it' I see Emma mouth.

'Ace' I mouth back, and she nods her head.

"Aria? Where are you?" he asks in a worried tone.

Oh god, what happened?

"Emma's still. Why? What's wrong?" I ask while also furrowing my eyebrows.

"I need you to come home. Now. Francisco is picking you up right now," he demands.

"Why? Ace, talk to me," I say frantically.

"I'll tell you when you get here. Just please listen."

"Okay, I'll see you in a few. I love you."

"I love you, *amore*."

Once he hangs up, Mia, Val and Emma have confused looks on their faces. "Stop being silent and fucking tell us," Val says standing up and moving his hands around.

"Uh, Ace said he needs me home right away. I don't know why though. Francisco is coming now to pick me up."

"Do you think it has to do with Dante?" Emma asks.

I told her about Dante after things started to get out of hand. She was so scared for me when I told her about what he has been doing.

"Who knows," I shrug my shoulders up.

"Okay well call me when you get home. I need to know you're safe," Emma says rubbing my shoulder.

"Wait who is Dante?" Mia asks, looking directly at me.

"Ex." I shrug.

"Tell us when you tell Ace too," Val says.

We all start walking out of the guest bedroom. "I will. Don't tell anyone. Not even Layna. I need to tell Ace first."

"We won't. Don't worry," Mia says and smiles.

"Where is Alexander?" I ask Emma as I start heading to the front door.

"Asleep. I put him down. Don't forget to text me," Emma scolds.

"I won't,"

I hug Emma, then Val, and Mia. I walk outside and see Francisco.

I go towards the passenger seat and sit up front next to him. When I first started to sit upfront with him, he was always confused about why I did that. I like Francisco a lot and I don't want to treat him like Ace's driver all the time.

"Hello, Aria. How was Mrs. Russo's house?" Francisco asks as he starts driving.

"It was good. I got to see the baby."

"How is little Alexander doing?"

"Good. He is getting big though," I chuckle as did he. "Hey, I have a random question."

"Yeah?"

"What's Ace's opinion on having kids or just kids overall?" I ask shyly.

Francisco looks at me and raises his eyebrow. I don't give any facial expression. "Well, I think Mr. De Luca likes kids. I know he wants some," Fran says. "Why are you asking, Aria?"

"Promise you won't tell Ace?" I ask. "I want to tell him before anyone else but since you know him the best, I want to get your opinion."

"I wouldn't even think about it."

I let out a sigh. "I may be pregnant. I found out at Emma's," I say shyly.

Francisco looks a little shocked, but he quickly hides it. "Congratulations, Aria. You're going to be a fantastic mother."

"Thank you, Francisco. But I'm scared of how Ace will react. I mean having a kid is a lot of work and I know he is busy with his work, and I don't want him to be frustrated."

"I think Mr. De Luca will be shocked at first. You have to remember how he was raised when he was a kid. You have to see it from his point of view. I think he is more afraid of being like his father rather than the though of having a kid. You know?"

"Yeah I get it. But I know he would be an amazing dad."

"Don't worry. Everything will work out fine. Just focus on staying healthy."

This is why I told Francisco so that he could give me advice on this, and he could tell me how he thinks Ace will react.

I smile at Francisco. I don't even realize we got to the house. Francisco parks the car, and he leaves the driver's side and helps me out of the car right when I start to open the door. I smile at Francisco and then walk towards the entrance of the house. I open the door and then hear Ace call my name.

"Yeah I'm here. What's wrong?" I ask.

I see him walk downstairs with Leo, Jared, and Josh. I haven't seen Jared and Josh since they left for the other house which was a while ago.

"Jared! Josh!" I run towards them and hug them tightly.

They hug me back and laugh.

"How are you doing, Aria?" Josh asks as I let go.

"Good," I smile not saying anything else. I then turn to Ace who has a straight face, but I can tell he is mad. "Ace. What's wrong?" I walk up to him and hold his arms.

He is so tense under my hands. I can't tell him about the baby now.

"Dante," he states.

"What about him?"

"He has pictures of you Aria. He said that he's going to come and get you soon. He left a letter again."

"What kind of pictures?" I whisper.

"What kind do you fucking think, Aria?" he says, making me a little shocked.

He is making it sound like it's my fault.

"Calm down. Okay. Do you have some sort of plan or what?" I ask him and then look at Leo.

He is the only one who looks calm. He is probably freaking out though.

"Uh well I was thinking to lure him out, but Ace doesn't want to do it," Leo says.

"Lure him out with what?" I ask.

"You," Josh says.

I look back at Ace and see his jaw clench.

"Don't even think about asking, Aria," he walks away making my arms fall to the floor.

I let out a sigh and close my eyes.

God, I'm tired and just want to go to sleep.

"It's okay, Aria. He is just a little stressed. He doesn't want to see you get hurt," Jared claims and I open my eyes and start at him.

"Well, I'm not the only one he is going to be worrying about now," I mumble.

"What to do you mean?" Leo asks.

I didn't think he heard me.

"Don't want to talk about it right now."

I need to tell Ace first.

I know Dante better than anyone and if we are going to kill him, we have to do it a certain way and one way or another it includes me.

I walk closer and closer to the gym and when I walk inside, I see Ace punching the punching bag repeatedly.

I walk over to where the weight benches are which is right behind Ace.

I see Ace lift his head to look at the mirror as he punches the bag and I see his eyes lift to me, in the mirror, before looking back at the bag.

Ace throws a few more punches before stopping and turning around to face me. He walks closer to me and takes his gloves off.

"If you're here to convince me then leave. It's not happening."

"You have never met Dante. You don't know what he is like Ace. The only way for this to work is to use me."

"There are other ways to go about this," Ace says while putting his hands on his hips where his gym shorts are hanging low on his hips making me see his v-line.

God Aria, keep it in your pants.

"No, there isn't." I state.

If he isn't letting me do this plan then what makes me think he will let me do it when he knows I'm pregnant?

"Aria-"

"Don't fight me on this," I stand up and walk up to Ace. "There is no other way."

Ace sighs and then goes to sit on the weight bench. "Are you still throwing up?" he asks and I feel my heart beat faster.

"Yes."

Tell him.

Tell him.
Tell him.

"You can do it, but I need you to tell me the truth," Ace states.

He knows.
He knows.
He knows.

"Tell the truth about what?" I question even though I know he knows because he isn't stupid.

"You know what. I'm not stupid," Ace raises his eyebrow at me. "It's one of the reasons I don't want you to do it."

I sigh and walk closer to him so that I'm standing between his legs. "At first I wasn't sure. I thought it was food poisoning but then I went over to Emma's to take a test and it was positive," I state truthfully.

"I knew you were," Ace says and he puts his hands on my hips. "I've had suspicions after you kept throwing up for more than a week and when I called you again today to see if you were ok, I just had a feeling that you were pregnant."

"Why didn't you tell me what you thought?"

"Because I didn't want it to become a reality," Ace says truthfully.

"Why?"

"Because I don't want to be like my father."

"You won't. You're nothing like him," I assure him while putting my hands on his face to make him look up at me.

"Like father like son, Aria. It will happen eventually."

"It will only happen if you let it happen."

"But-"

"No," I cut him off. "Don't think about the what if's or the but's. You can't think like that with a baby."

"You're thinking about trying to get kidnapped by Dante," he argues.

"I am not fully developed yet. If we do this now it will be better because I am not showing and he won't have any suspicions." Ace sighs and leans his head on my stomach and looks down at the ground. "Don't think about me getting hurt. I can handle myself."

Let's hope that's not a jinx because with Dante, it seems like he is the only one to have control over me.

"Fine. But there are going to be conditions."

I feel myself smile a little bit. "Tell me."

"One, you will be at least ten feet away from me. I have to have eyes on you the whole entire time. Two, under no circumstances are you allowed to tell anyone you pregnant. Who knows you are pregnant?"

"Francisco, Emma, Val, and Mia. Val and Mia were with Emma and I when I was taking the test," I state.

"Okay. But do you understand my rules?"

"I do. I'll be careful," I assure.

Thirty-Four

So, we're in Ace's office currently going over the mission.

It's been like a few days since we found out that he sent pictures of me.

Ace is saying that he wants to be the one to kill Dante. I don't know how I feel about Ace killing Dante. For some reason it's always been a dream as well as a nightmare to kill Dante. I'm carrying a baby as well so I'm conflicted on what I should do.

Ace and I also talked, we said we are going to wait on the wedding, and I just think it's a great idea because I don't want to be pregnant when walking down the aisle so it's better that we are going to wait. Ace said that what I thought was stupid and that I could walk down the aisle wearing a trash bag, and he would still get hard, but I want to feel and look my best.

But he agreed to postpone because he wants to have a smooth wedding where Dante can't randomly show up and mess it all up.

I still haven't talked to my parents. I feel guilty that I haven't told them I'm pregnant. I want to tell them. I am kind of scared to see what Alex's reaction will be, but I still want to tell him.

Yesterday, Ace and I went to get an ultrasound on the baby and to just see how many months in total I am.

I am about a month and a half pregnant. The doctor said we can find out the gender at four to five months.

I know I want to have a gender reveal party for sure, but I don't know if it's the best idea or not. I haven't talked to Ace about it. I'll talk to him about it probably a month before the gender reveal.

"So, Aria you're just going to stand here," Ace states while pointing on the map of his warehouse. We are going to be doing this plan in his warehouse because that's where Dante is going the most. "I will be behind this crate right here about to shoot him before he tries to attack or take you," I hear Ace say breaking me from my thoughts.

I nod at him.

Ace is sitting in his chair, and I'm sitting on his lap while all of his men including Leo, Jared, and Josh are in the room.

Before Ace can say something else, we hear a knock at the door.

"Come in," Ace says.

We see Francisco come in with a phone.

"For you sir," Francisco hands the phone to Ace, but Ace looks confused as Francisco hands the phone to him.

"Who is it?" he asks.

Francisco gives us a look as if saying 'Good luck'.

"Hello," Ace says as he put the phone to his ear.

"Ace," I hear a familiar voice say while I sit on Ace's lap.

It sounds like Alex's voice. But why would Alex call?

"Alex? Why are you calling? I'm kind of busy," Ace says, looking at everyone in the room.

"Where's Aria?" I hear him say from the other side of the phone.

He sounds angry.

Ace motions for everyone to leave the room so that he and I are alone. "Why?" Ace asks.

I look at Ace and raise my eyebrows at him and he just shrugs.

"I need to talk to her. Give my sister the phone. It's important." I hear Alex say in a demanding tone.

Ace gives me the phone and I put it to my ear. "Hello?"

"Aria?" Alex states.

"Yeah?"

"Okay first, are you okay?" Alex sighs in relief.

"Yeah, I'm fine why?"

"Okay good. Second, when were you going to tell me you're pregnant, and why the hell is Dante sending death threats to my wife and daughter?"

How the fuck did he know I was pregnant?

Death threats?

"Wait hold on. Backup. Explain."

"Dante sent a letter to me, dad, and Layna threatening that he will kill us all if you don't go with him whatever that means. Want to explain?" Alex says in a demanding tone.

He is angry. Definitely angry.

I don't say anything. I don't know what to say.

Ace takes the phone from my hand and speaks to Alex instead.

"What are you trying to imply, Alex? Sounds to me like you're blaming Aria?" Ace speaks.

He didn't sound so happy either.

"Ace, give Aria the phone. This is not any of your business. You don't even know Dante," Alex spits.

"You do realize I'm her fiancé, right? She tells me everything, asshole."

"Well, she's my sister and I don't really like my whole family getting death threats and last time I checked, she and Dante had a healthy breakup. Aria said there were no issues with their breakup. So, I'm confused about why I'm being forced to send my sister to Dante and his crazy ass."

"So, you don't even know why you're getting them? You don't know why they actually broke up? Did Layna and Lisa even tell you anything about Aria and Dante's breakup? Find out your fucking facts before you blame something on my fiancé, Alex," Ace demands.

This is getting too much.

"I was her brother before you were her fiancé Ace so don't come at me like that. Bet I can kick your ass in the ring," Alex bet.

Before Ace can scream at Alex more, I put my hand on his chest to calm him down and give him a look. Ace hates it when he is challenged. I know that if Alex were here right now Ace would have beat him to a pulp. I know Ace is stronger than Alex. Way stronger. Ace is not just muscle strong but also mentally and that's the best kind of strong someone can be.

Ace let out a deep breath before speaking. "Sure, Alex. You can think that."

"We're coming to Italy. Now. No questions asked."

Before Ace can answer Alex, he hangs up the phone. "Fuck!" Ace says as he throws the phone across the room breaking it.

I put my arm around his neck and rest my hand along the side of his head caressing his hair. "It's okay. He doesn't need to know what we are doing."

"But he just fucking ruined everything Aria. Like now I have to worry about your family not getting hurt," he sounds frustrated.

"It's okay. We'll figure it out. Also, my family isn't your responsibility. They can handle themselves. There's no need to get frustrated like that," I say softly and rest my head on his shoulder. Ace lets out a deep breath trying to relax. "Go to the backyard. Let your anger out a little."

He looks at me.

His face is now calm.

Jaw isn't clenched.

Having that same sparkle in his beautiful green eyes. He leans in for a kiss and I lean down and kiss him on the lips.

"Okay," he whispers against my lips.

I lean my head down against his. "Okay."

"The "control you have over me is crazy Aria."

I smile at him and wrap my arms around his neck and hug him.

"Your brother just landed and he is on his way. He just texted me," Ace says as he walks into the kitchen.

"What? I thought he was coming tomorrow?" I ask while also sounding shocked.

"Yeah but they decided to come earlier because Alex is getting impatient," Aced sighs. "Him, your mom, dad, Layna, Cole, everyone," Ace says in a frustrated tone.

Ace goes over to the coffee maker and starts making another cup of coffee. Before Ace came into the kitchen Lana and I were just talking. She was actually giving me tips for the baby and just being pregnant overall.

"I don't think a third cup of coffee is healthy for you dear," Lana says to Ace.

"Yeah well, neither is Alex constantly trying to piss me off while I do work. Aria I apologize in advance if I punch him square in the jaw," Ace says right before coming towards me and kissing me on the head and walking away.

I shake my head and Lana does the same.

"Ever since Alex called us, he has been so frustrated lately. Like Alex keeps pressing his buttons. Alex has also been blowing up my phone too, but I don't answer. It's just Ace is trying to fix this new plan for Dante since Alex is here. Like the plan was supposed to be just me, Ace, and his men but now Alex and my family are coming so they are going to want to get involved."

"Who knows about Dante?"

"Only Layna and my mom know. They didn't want my dad and Alex knowing because Alex and my dad would just go batshit."

"So, you're going to have to talk to them when they get here, I'm guessing."

"Yeah probably. All I wanted was to have a normal pregnancy, but I can't because I now have to worry about Dante, my family, and don't forget I still have to plan my wedding."

"Don't stress about all this dear. Besides you and Ace both agreed to have the wedding after your pregnancy."

"Yeah, I know. I was super excited though. But it's fine at least we will have our baby there."

"You know I have an idea," Lana says, giving me a look with a smile placed on her face.

"What is it?" I ask.

She smiles at me. "You can start planning the wedding right now. It will take your mind off of the Dante situation and it will also give you something to do. Your mom is coming so it's kind of perfect."

That's not a bad idea. I could start planning and set a date after my pregnancy. I want to look good in my wedding dress, so I have to also start working out again afterward.

"That's not a bad idea, Lana," I smile at her.

"I know. I can help you if you want of course. Just know Aria that you have a lot of support," Lana says and puts her hand on my arm in a reassuring way.

I smile at her. "I'm going to go tell Ace. He said that he could get me a good wedding planner."

Lana nods her head and I jump off the stool and start making my way upstairs. I may be pregnant but I'm not tired enough to run. I do have to be careful though or Ace will lecture me about it.

I open his office door and see him talking to one of his men.

"Okay, so Jose you keep locating Dante's location. Once you find him, tell me immediately. Leo, we're going to stick with the same plan, but I have to speak with Alex so that he doesn't fuck up everything."

"Of course, sir. I'll start right away," Jose says and then leaves.

"Ace what if Alex doesn't agree with the mission?"

"He will. I have a bet for him. If I win, he stays here while all of us go on this mission since we already have a perfect lineup."

"Alex won't let that happen. What kind of bet are you even going to place?" I ask, making my presence more known.

"Fighting match. The first one down loses. He said he is stronger. Then we will find out right now," Ace says smugly.

"Cocky much?"

Ace smirks. "*Amore*, it's not being cocky. He started it."

"You both sound like three-year-old's. Let me talk to him. I need to tell him and the rest of my family the truth anyway," I mumble the last part, but he hears.

"Why do you have to tell him? If you are not comfortable with telling them Aria you shouldn't."

I look at Leo. "Leo, can you give us a minute." Leo smirks and whistles his way out of the office. "Ace, I need to tell them. It's not fair I told Layna and my mom. My dad and Alex need to know. They are getting death threats. I need to tell him," I walk up and lean on his chair.

He pulls his chair out further motioning me to sit on his lap and I do. He puts his hand on my hip and stomach rubbing gently.

I don't have a bump yet, but he still likes to rub my stomach.

"I know but I don't want you to be forced Aria. You can't get stressed out right now, especially right now."

"I'm not. Don't worry," I stroke his cheek.

"Why did you come up here?"

"I want to get your opinion on something."

"What?"

"I want to start planning the wedding right now but obviously we won't have it until after the baby."

"Why right now? You can, but why?"

"It will give me something to do and look forward to. Plus, my mom will be here, and she can help me. Lana suggested it."

"Well then of course you can do it," I smile at him and kiss him on the cheek.

I'm about to get up, but he holds me down. "What?" I look at him confused.

"I want another one. That wasn't a proper kiss," he pouts. I roll my eyes and grab his face and kiss him on the lips. While he is trying to kiss back, we hear Ace's door open breaking us apart. He sighs and leans his head on my chest, and I put my head on top of his. "What?" Ace says frustratedly.

"Alex White is here. So is George White," the person who opened the door says.

Ace let's out a big sigh. "Let's go then."

Thirty-Five

"Are you just going to stay quiet or are you going to tell me, Aria?" Alex spits at me.

Me, Ace, Alex, my dad, Layna, my mom, Cole, Calla, and Elena are all seated in the living room.

"Don't talk to her like that," Ace says harshly while glaring at Alex.

Alex rolls his eyes and looks at me.

I let out a sigh before talking. "So, Dante and I broke up as all of you know. But I didn't tell you the truth about why we broke up. The only people who knew the real reason were Layna, mom, and I told Emma."

"So, you would tell Emma...someone you just met, over us? Cool, Aria. Really cool," Alex huffs.

"Alex! Hush now! Let your sister talk. You don't know what even happened," my mom defends and rubs my shoulder. "Keep going, Aria."

"You guys know that Dante and I had been arguing for a period during our relationship and it was because he mainly was checking out other girls. I talked to him about it, but he said I was crazy and that he wasn't. I trusted him. A lot more than I should have." I let out a sigh and look at Ace. He nods his head. "One night we argued over the same thing. I told him I wanted to break up and once I said that he punched me in the face."

"What?!" Alex says and stands up.

"Alex shut up and sit down!" Layna demands.

He stares at my dad and my dad gives him a nod as if saying to sit down. Alex rolls his eyes and sits down.

"He started to fight me, but I couldn't fight back. I don't know why but I felt like I was stuck and couldn't move. Before he left my room that day, he said, 'if you tell anyone about this, I will kill your whole family' and I believed him. So, after that, we stayed together for another few months. Through those months, he hit me, pushed me around, and even took advantage of me," I say softly, and Alex looks like he is going to blow. Cole looks pissed. "Mom and Layna saw me fall down the stairs one night. They knew something was wrong about my and Dante's relationship, but I said that it was nothing. But we didn't tell you because I didn't want you to do anything or worry about it. That's why I only told Layna and mom."

Everyone is quiet. I fear what they are going to think or what they thought.

"Aria. No matter what I want you to know we love you. We always will," Elena says and smiles at me.

"Thank you," I smile. I look at my dad and he has an unreadable expression. He is leaned down with his elbows on his knees. "Are you mad?" I ask my dad.

He lifts his head and looks at me. "No. I would never be mad at you, Aria. Especially with something like this," he says softly. "I'm just shocked. I wish you told me sooner so I could have beat the shit out of that kid. Fucking idiot," he mutters under his breath.

"I wish I told you sooner as well."

"I love you. You're my daughter. I will do anything and everything to protect you."

"I love you too," I smile at him, and he comes over and kisses me on the head then goes back to his seat next to my mom and wraps his arm around her.

I look in front of me and see Alex thinking extremely hard. He is looking at the ground not saying anything.

"Aria?" I look up at Calla next to him. "I want you to know I always have your back. No matter what. You're my family and always have been. That will never change. We're going to kill him," Calla says with a nod.

I chuckle. "Thank you, Calla."

"Same here, Ari. You're like my baby sister," Cole says. "I will always have your back. It doesn't matter what, I will always be there for you. Dante is going to pay for what he did."

"Thank you, Cole. You're like my brother too."

It is silent for a few minutes before my mom calls Alex's name. "Alex, honey? Say something."

He sighs and rubs his hand along his face before looking at Ace. "You have a plan?"

"Yeah but you need to follow it. I'm not going to allow you to do your own shit with this mission," Ace says with a straight face.

Alex stands up and nods his head. "Fine. I'll be back." Alex starts walking out of the living room but before Alex can turn the corner, Ace pulls him against the wall.

"What the fuck do you think you're doing?!" Ace roars.

"Ace let him go," I say once I'm right next to Ace.

"No, I have to make sure that this *stronzo* doesn't go around looking for Dante. We have a plan and we're going to stick with it, Aria," Ace says, looking back at me while still holding Alex to the wall.

"Can you get your fucking hands off me you asshole? I'm not going to get Dante. I just can't be here so fucking let go!"

Ace is still holding him against the wall. Staring into Alex's eyes. I already know what he is doing. He did it to me the first time we met. He is searching for a lie in his eyes. Ace lets Alex go and Calla immediately runs to him catering to him.

He gets to his feet. "I'm fine babe." Calla ignores him and still pulls him up. Alex looks at me. "Get your baby daddy under control, Ari."

Once he says that he has Calla let go of him and walks out the front door.

Great.

"He was mad. He couldn't even look at me," I say as everyone sits back down in the living.

"He isn't mad at you. He is mad at what Dante did to you.

What Dante did isn't something that Alex is happy about," my mom says sitting down next to me.

"He will come around, Aria. Don't worry," Calla says. "And if he doesn't, I'll make sure to kick his ass."

I laugh while also feeling my phone vibrate in my pocket. I take it out and see Emma texted.

'Why is Alex driving down the street really fast away from your house?'

'Are you here?' I text her.

Yeah. Ace said he needed Leo for some other work shit. I decided to come along because I heard Layna was there.'

'Oh okay. It's kind of tense here just giving you a heads up.'

She doesn't text back. Instead, I hear the opening of a door. I see Leo and Emma walk in.

"Where's Ace?" Leo asks when he walks inside the kitchen.

"Upstairs," I say.

Leo smiles at me before running upstairs to Ace's office. I see Emma come in with Alexander in her arms.

"Yay! I finally get to meet this little guy," Layna says and jumps up from the couch and runs towards Emma.

"Want to hold him?" Emma asks when she is next to Layna.

Layna nods her head at Emma and then Emma passes Alexander to Layna.

"He is adorable," Layna says while rocking him. "He has gotten so big too." She looks up at me and widens her eyes.

"What?" I asked.

Layna looks at my mom and then back at me. I look at my mom and she has a smile on her face.

What the fuck are they smirking at?

"Stop staring at me like that," I speak.

"Do you have something to tell us, Aria?" my mom says.

"Uhh no," I say before looking away from them.

Oh shit.

Thanks a lot, Alex.

"You sure? Forgot to maybe mention that you, I don't know, are having a baby?" Layna asks.

"Oh yeah. I'm having a kid, guys," I say as if it is the most surprising thing in the world. "Surprise."

"How many months are you?" my mom asks.

"Like two months," I feel a smile being placed on my face as I talk about my and Ace's kid.

"Wait when did you find out?" my dad asks.

Surprisingly, he doesn't look that mad.

"I found out about a month ago. We get to find out the gender in a few months."

"Are you going to have a gender reveal?" Layna asks.

"Yup. I haven't planned any of it yet. I was going to start planning maybe a month before," I answer.

"Oh my god, I can't wait. This is going to be so much fun," Elena says making my smile grow bigger.

"Yeah I'm super excited. I'm also nervous. Emma, you need to prep me on how my vagina is going to feel. You too mom," I say pointing to both.

Emma and my mom both laugh, and I see my dad and Cole grimace.

"Well, I'm not going to say positive things, but the pregnancy experience is the best part," Emma says.

"You're going to do fine, Hun. Don't think so negatively," my mom assures me.

"Do you already have name ideas?" Layna asks.

"I'm only two months pregnant. I barely have a bump."

"We're just excited that's all," Emma laughs.

"If it's a boy, you should name it Cole," Cole says cockily.

"Ew, why would I want to name my baby that. Imagine having the name Cole," I joke and he glares at me making me laugh.

"Whatever. Cole is a cool name," Cole says, making me roll my eyes.

"Congratulation's babe. You're going to be an amazing mother," Elena says, making me look at her and smile.

"Thank you. That means a lot," I say smiling at them.

"What was Ace's reaction?" my dad asks.

"He was shocked at first. I mean it's not the best time to have a kid right now with the whole Dante thing, but he is excited too."

"I'm so happy for you, Aria. You're going to be a great mother to the child," my mom says.

"Thanks, mom. I have you there with me to help."

"Oh, I didn't even see the ring yet in person. Show me!" my mom exclaims as she remembers about the ring Ace gave me.

"Oh yeah," I lean towards her and show her the ring.

Everyone else comes around my mom and me to look at the ring.

"It's beautiful, honey," my mom compliments.

"Damn, you snatched a good one A," Layna says, making me roll my eyes.

"Yeah. I got lucky," I say with a small smile.

I did get lucky.

"Have you thought about the wedding at all?" my mom asks, looking at me.

"Yeah I actually have. I want you to help me plan it, mom."

My mom now has the biggest smile placed on her face.

"When are you planning on having it?"

I haven't really told my mom or anyone about wedding plans. I mainly talk to Ace and Emma about the wedding, also Lana.

"A few months after I give birth, but I want to start planning right now so I have something to look forward to. There is going to be a planner here next week. Ace got one of the best planners he knows," I say with a smile on my face.

I am super excited.

"Oh, I can't wait. This is going to be so fun," my mom says while smiling widely. I know she is excited as well.

"You're going to look so beautiful, Ari," Layna squeals.

"I just can't wait. It's going to help me take my mind off things."

"And it will. But Dante isn't stupid. I wouldn't be surprised if he knew Ace is going to plan something," my mom says with a knowing look.

"Ace has a solid plan. I trust him to lead this mission."

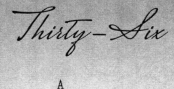

Today hasn't been that interesting. My mom and Emma have just been giving me tips and heads up on how pregnancy is going to go for me. Again, I'm only close to two months in.

Alex didn't come back the night I told everyone the truth about Dante. Calla was super mad at him when he did come back but that was at like five in the morning. She and him talked. Calla told me that he is just disappointed that I didn't tell him. Thank god Ariel isn't here. She is staying with our aunt again because Calla doesn't want Ariel to be involved with all of this.

I haven't talked to Alex at all, and it's been four days since then.

Ace says that the mission is going to be taking place in a few days and I'm so nervous, but I just can't wait to get all this to be over.

Ace says that he has someone working for Dante and the mole

is going to be telling Dante that I'm going to be at the warehouse, and it's perfect because Dante will be there in an instant.

Ace says that he is having the planner for the wedding come today so he can meet me and my mom.

The new house seems so full and somewhat brighter. It's full of life with everyone here. My mom said that she, dad, and Elena are going to stay in hotels. They want to give Ace some space. I don't want them to feel like Ace doesn't want them here, but they said that they wanted to. Ace doesn't care whether they all stay here or at a hotel. He wants them to be as comfortable as possible.

Layna and Cole are staying in one of the guest rooms. Mia and Val visit every day now that my family is here. Same with Ana and Antonio now because they want to make sure that everything is okay and that we are all safe and cared for.

"Honey, the wedding planner is here! Come downstairs!" I hear my mom yell breaking me from my thoughts.

I get up from my and Ace's bed and head downstairs.

Ace is on a warehouse check. He has to make sure that everyone is doing their job and that he doesn't have any moles. But before Ace left, he told me he would be back in time to meet the wedding planner. He has spoken to him on the phone, but I told him that he should at least meet the wedding planner in person and of course, he said yes.

I walk down the last step of the stairway and see my mom talking to a very well-dressed man. He has black curly hair and is almost a foot taller than my mother.

All I'm wearing are some loose shorts and one of Ace's black hoodies.

Shit, way to make a good impression, Ari.

"Aria, get over here. Stop being shy," my mom hisses.

"Sorry. I didn't have much time to get ready," I walk over to my mom and the wedding planner.

"Girl, you're fine. Anyway, I'm Mark Ashley. I'm excited to see what we create," Mark says and then smiles sweetly.

"Nice to meet you. I'm Lisa White and this is my daughter Aria White but soon to be *Aria De Luca*."

"Nice to meet you girls. I'm excited to get to know you guys." My mom and Mark smile. "Can I see the ring?"

"Oh of course," I take my hand and bring it to him.

"Wow, it's absolutely beautiful. You snatched a good one, Mrs. De Luca," Mark smirks and winks at me.

"Please just call me Aria. I hate the last name basis."

"Of course. Should we get started?" Mark asks.

"Yeah let's go into the kitchen. I'll be right back though I just need to call Ace to see if he is on his way."

My mom and Mark both nod their heads and I stay in my spot and pull out my phone.

I press Ace's contact and he picks up immediately. "*Amore*? What's up?" Ace asks once he answers the phone.

"Hey. The wedding planner is here. He is super nice."

"That's great," Ace says.

"Are you almost here or on your way? I didn't start anything. I let my mom and Mark go into the kitchen to talk."

Ace doesn't answer and I thought he hung up but then I feel strong arms wrap around my waist and hug me from behind. "Don't worry about a thing, *amore*. I'm right here," Ace whispers into my ear.

I turn around and hug him back. He leans his head down and kisses me on the lips. The kisses he gives me never get old.

I still feel a little shock when he kisses me.

I break the kiss. "Ready?"

"Of course, Mrs. De Luca. Lead the way," Ace says and I grab his hand and drag him to the living room to go to the dining room where my mom and Mark are sitting down.

"Hey. Did we start yet?" I ask as I drag Ace to the dining table and then sit down.

He puts his hand on my knee and his other is draped across my chair.

"No. You came right in time Mr. De Luca. I'm Mark. We have talked on the phone a couple of times but it's nice to meet you in person," Mark says. Ace nods his head. Mark smiles before opening the binder he has in his hand. "Anyway, now that we have introductions down. Can you guys tell me how you see your dream wedding?"

"Don't ask me. Aria's the boss with this. As long as she is happy with it then I'm happy with it." I smile at Ace and he starts rubbing circles on my knee.

"Well, then Aria, can you tell me a little about what you want?" Mark says and grabs his pen to start writing.

"Well, I really want an outdoor wedding. I saw inspirations on Pinterest, and I just loved the colors and the vibe I saw in the photos."

"Okay perfect. I love outdoor weddings. It just feels lighter and happier," Mark says while writing that down. He looks up at me. "What are some colors you want to see in the reception? Like the main colors that you want to have?"

"Um, I like a blush color. I saw some blush inspired weddings with gray or white so I really like how those looked," I answer.

"It's beautiful. I personally love working with those colors. When do you guys want the wedding to be?"

I look at Ace. "When is a good time for you?"

"It doesn't matter, *amore*. It's all up to you and when you're ready," Ace says.

"Okay, what's the date today?"

"It's January 12th," Mark answers.

"Then what about towards the end of October or beginning of November?"

I should hopefully be ready by then and have this baby out of me.

"Is there a specific place you want the wedding?"

I shake my head 'no'. "No, I haven't really looked into it, but I am going to start looking if you want me too."

Mark nods his head and writes more notes down. "Okay. That's all I need for now. I will come maybe two to three times a month. We can talk about guests and stuff like that the next time I see you," Mark says standing up.

"Perfect, I can't wait."

After Mark left Ace went to go finish some work in his office and all that. My mom is still in the dining room talking with Lana.

I however went upstairs to talk to Calla. Alex couldn't ignore me forever. He had to talk to me someday.

"Come in," I hear Calla say from the other side of the door after I knock.

"Hey," I say once I walk in.

"Hey," Calla says with a smile on her face.

"Where is Alex?" I ask.

She gives me a look that says, 'are you kidding me'.

"He is your brother. You'd know. Right?"

"Yeah, but he is also your husband," I argue.

"He is in the gym. Working off some sweat I guess."

"Is he still that mad?" I ask.

"He isn't mad, Aria. He could never be mad at you. You're his little sister. He is just disappointed that you didn't tell him and that you kept him in the dark these past few years about Dante," Calla scolds.

"Would you be mad?"

"I mean I wouldn't be happy but again he isn't mad. Just disappointed. Alex will get over it. Trust me. You two have huge egos and are both stubborn as hell. One of you needs to make the first move."

"Should I?"

"That's up to you. Do you want to wait? 'Cause you know Alex is going to stay being stubborn until he can't anymore."

"I hate it when you're right." I get up from the bed.

"Good luck," she hums as I walk out of her room.

Guess I'm doing this.

Alex better not be a bitch.

I walk downstairs and then stroll outside towards the gym. I see him punching the bag currently. His shirt is off, and he is sweating so much that it's dripping to the floor.

Ew.

"Alex?" No answer. "Alex?!" Still no answer. "Alex?!" I say a little louder and touch his shoulder.

He jumps a little bit and pulls a headphone from his ear. "What?"

"Can we talk?" I ask.

"I'm kind of busy, Aria. Maybe later," he says and is about to turn around.

He can't just fucking do that.

"No. Can we please just talk like mature adults? Stop running away from me and ignoring me. It wasn't even my fault."

"Dammit, Aria I know! I know it wasn't your fault," he says as he turns around to face me. "I'm not mad at you. I want you to know that first. That's something that I will never be mad at."

"Then why are you ignoring me?"

He comes closer and puts both his hands on each of my shoulders. I almost grimace because his hands are sweaty.

"Because I couldn't save you from him. I couldn't see the signs of him hurting you. He hurt you and got away with that. It makes me feel like a failure of a brother."

"Alex, you can't change the past, but you also can't beat yourself up about it. I am fine now. I'm happy," I say truthfully.

"I know Aria and I'm glad you're happy. I'm glad you are going to start a family of your own, too. But you can't make me stop feeling the way I do. It's going to take a while for me to just come to terms with it. That fucker deserves whatever Ace is planning."

"Are you helping with that?" I ask.

"Of course, I am. Ace said that he is going to be the one to kill Dante but I'm not going to let him. I'm killing Dante myself."

I roll my eyes.

Men.

"Ace isn't going to let you."

"Really?"

"Yup."

"Well then let's offer him something that he won't pass up. Shall we?" Alex smirks.

"Okay. But before we do, I just want to say I am glad to have a brother like you."

"And you're the best sister," he says trying to walk closer to me but I back away from him. "Stop being so anal and give me a hug," he says while opening his arms for me to hug his sweaty chest."

"I'm good," I chuckle and walk away from him to head inside.

Alex rolls his eyes. "Let's talk to your fiancé so I can prove you wrong," Alex says while following me towards the house.

"Yeah, okay sure, buddy," I snicker while walking behind him.

We leave the gym and go back inside the house. Ace is in his office so we both go upstairs. I don't knock on the door because I never do. I open his door and stroll in. I don't see him doing anything. He is just staring at something on his computer.

He looks up from his computer at me and then at a shirtless Alex. "*Amore*, why is Alex shirtless in my office while also sweating?"

"Ask him," I say and walk towards him.

As always, he scoots his chair a little out so I can place myself on his lap. He kisses my cheek and then focuses his attention on Alex.

"Alex, why are you shirtless in my office?" Ace raises his eyebrow at Alex.

Alex's lips lift into a smirk before talking. "Well, I want to propose something."

"Go on," Ace nods his head at Alex.

"So, you want to kill Dante. I want to kill Dante. But obviously, you're going to have your way no matter what, like always," Alex says with a little attitude.

"If you want to fucking say something Alex, then fucking say it. I hate people who beat around the bush."

"Yeah yeah, whatever. I want to have a little friendly competition," Alex says smugly.

Oh, Alex, what are you doing?

"Okay, and what is this competition?"

"Kickboxing match. The first one down loses, and the winner gets to kill Dante."

"We already discussed this, Alex. The deal was that whoever wins the kickboxing match gets to decide if you should even go on the mission or not."

"I'm going on the mission no matter what. But let's see who should be the one to kill Dante," Alex argues.

I want to intervene and tell them they are acting like children but they both have huge egos and will have this fight no matter what.

But I don't mind doing the deed of killing Dante. The thought has crossed my mind a lot but for some reason, something is stopping me from saying I should do it.

"You're playing an extremely dangerous game, Alex. You really think you can beat me?" Ace raises his eyebrow.

"Ace, I don't think. I know for a fact I can. I have more experience and I'm older," Alex smirks.

"You know age doesn't do shit for you. Also, you think you have more experience? That's ridiculous," Ace says with amusement laced in.

"Fine then, how about we settle it then? Ace versus Alex. It would be a hell of a match," Alex says while smirking and walking closer to Ace's desk.

"Tomorrow at noon. Sharp. Don't be late or it's over."

Thirty-Seven

All night I was super anxious for the fight with Ace and Alex.

I honestly have no idea who will win. Alex is a great fighter and has strategy and experience. I know Ace has a lot of experience, but I don't know how much and what he has been taught. But Ace is also mentally strong for a fight and has the muscle to win.

Ace and I are just in bed relaxing before we have to go downstairs for breakfast. Lana said she would call us down.

Ace is leaning his head on my stomach while tracing small circles on my thigh.

"What's wrong?" I hear him ask.

"Huh?" I look down at him.

"You look like you're thinking very hard about something," Ace states.

"Oh, I'm trying to figure out who is going to win."

He looks up at me and furrows his eyebrows. "You don't think I'm going to win?"

He sounds very offended and surprised.

"No, I don't know *who* is going to," I say, emphasizing who. "Alex has good strategy and is also really strong in defense. But you are mentally strong and never bring your guard down. You are also physically strong too which is an advantage, but I have also never seen you fight."

"You trying to hurt my ego, *amore*?" A smile appears on his face.

"Never," I say sarcastically. He chuckles as he starts to get off of me. "What are you doing?" I ask while laying still.

"We got a fight today. You didn't think I was just going to sleep in bed all day until Alex is ready. Quite the opposite actually," he says as he gets out of bed.

"So what? You're going to work out before the match?" I ask.

"Yeah. I told Lana to make me some porridge. It's good to eat before a fight and if Alex wants a fight, he is damn sure going to get one," he says walking over to me. "Get ready and come downstairs for breakfast," he pecks me on the lips and then gets up to leave out the door.

Oh, Alex what have you gotten yourself into?

So, while Ace did his workout, I just talked to all the girls in the kitchen. Everyone was here to watch this match Alex challenged.

I swear I can't handle the testosterone in this house anymore.

Lana is going to watch the fight with all of us. She said she wants to see some ass kicking.

Her words, not mine.

A few hours later, Ace and Alex are ready for the match. We all are in the boxing room. Ace had put a ring in one of the many rooms we had leftover. He told me he always wanted a boxing ring in his house and that he wanted to design his own gym.

Ace has Antonio be the referee because Antonio has boxing experience. I didn't even know Antonio had boxing experience.

Alex and Ace are both in the middle of the ring and Antonio is in the middle talking about the rules between the two.

"Okay, these are basic guideline rules for a regular match. You can't use ropes for leverage. Only combat moves are allowed. No weapons obviously. Play fair. Other than that, on my go, you can start," Antonio says from in between them.

"You scared, Ace?" Alex taunts.

"I have nothing to be afraid of. What about you Alex? Are you scared?" Ace raises his eyebrow.

Alex laughs instead of replying.

"Okay enough of the chit chat. One..." Antonio starts. "...two..." Both boys are starting to get into position. "...three!" Antonio moves away from them both.

Ace and Alex circle one another. They are studying, trying to observe one another's moves.

Suddenly Alex goes for a hit, but Ace blocks him and instead punches Alex in the throat.

"Oooo." Everyone winces.

Alex starts coughing repeatedly.

"Come on, Alex. Don't tell me you're all talk," Ace says as he circles him.

Alex doesn't answer, instead he lunges towards Ace.

Let the punches begin ladies and gentlemen.

Alex is on top of Ace punching the crap of him. I'm not worried 'cause I know Ace can take a punch. Alex's punches are flying against Ace's face. Everyone winces every time Alex lands a hard punch to his jaw or chin.

Ace is just defending himself, not making any moves to bring his defense down.

"What's wrong, Ace? Don't tell me you're all talk," Alex mocks.

Ace then breaks his defense pose and lifts his hips to send Alex flying off him. Ace stands up and starts jumping on his toes. Alex stands up and puts up his defense pose.

Ace lifts his leg and kicks Alex in the hips. Ace goes closer to Alex and punches him in the ribs and then brings his head down to contact his knee. Alex pushes Ace off him and then Alex starts to throw punches again. They both are punching the shit out of each other, and these punches aren't soft.

Ace lunges towards Alex and starts to punch him rapidly. Alex is getting a few punches in but not as many as Ace is throwing.

Alex tries to aim his leg for Ace's face, but Ace captures his leg and starts to throw punches at Alex's shoulder and face. Alex throws punches at Ace as Ace punches Alex in the ribs repeatedly.

Alex lets go of Ace and I can see a bruise forming on his torso from all the punches he has taken from Ace.

"Couldn't take a punch, Alex?" Ace taunts.

"You bitch. You made me bleed!" Alex whines while touching his forehead.

"All part of the match, Alex," Ace smirks before landing a right hook to Alex's face.

Alex pushes him back and they are back to just punching one

another. Ace captures Alex's head and then throws him on the floor while also getting some of Alex's blood on the floor as well.

Alex is holding Ace while on the floor making me laugh a little because of how they are groping each other.

"Aria. Hush," my mom hisses.

I roll my eyes, but my mom doesn't see it.

"Okay, I've had enough of this bullshit. I got shit to do," Ace says before lunging at Alex and sitting on top of him then punching him nonstop. Everyone was in their seats and then is suddenly out of them. They are up against the ropes watching it all unfold. "Give up, Alex. I'm killing that motherfucker," Ace says while still punching Alex. Every time Alex moves his defense pose; he gets a hard hit to the face. Alex isn't saying anything. He is probably thinking if it's worth it or not. "Alex, I'm not trying to kill you here so just give up already," Ace says.

"Fine. Fine. Stop. You win," Alex says, making Ace stop.

Ace gets off Alex and stands up. Antonio helps Alex up to his feet and holds him up with his shoulder. Calla moves the ropes out of the way for her to enter the ring. She goes over to Alex and supports Alex on her shoulder. Alex spits on the floor and I see red blood hit the white floor on the boxing ring. Alex looks up to meet Ace's eyes.

"You win. You can kill Dante."

Thirty-Eight

Today is the day.

The day Ace kills Dante.

It's been a week since the fight and of course Ace won. The past week he has been making sure everyone knows where they have to stand and watch. I'm going to be in the middle of everyone just patiently waiting for Dante to make a move and then boom. He's dead.

"Okay. Does everyone know where they have to go?" Ace asks.

Everyone nods their heads.

"Good. The plan is simple. Aria is going to basically wait in the back of the warehouse where there are crates and everyone is to hide in or behind one and not make a damn sound. There will be guards everywhere," Ace says while looking at everyone nodding their heads. "Everyone knows the plan now, so I won't have to repeat it a third time?"

Val, Alex, and Cole are here. Emma and Layna wanted to

come but instead, they stayed at home with Mia, Elena, Calla, Ana, and mom. They are all relaxing. My dad was conflicted about whether to come or not, but my mom wanted him to, to make sure I'm going to be okay.

Ace had found another letter saying that Dante wanted to meet up at one of Ace's warehouses and that's how we know where he is going to be at the exact time. With the letter, he didn't send other disgusting pictures of me. He just sent a letter.

But I knew that the mole plan would work.

We are currently at the warehouse. There are guards everywhere surrounding the perimeter.

Ace has his own office at each warehouse. It's nothing like his office at home. It's a little smaller but at least it's clean so can't complain. I shouldn't even be thinking about complaining.

"Good, then I want everyone to take their places. If a single hair on my fiancé's body is hurt, I will kill you. Simple," Ace bluntly says.

Everyone hurries out of his office. I walk towards Ace who is just standing and looking over the plans.

"Everything is going to be fine. Stop worrying," I assure while turning his head towards me so he can look at me.

"Aren't you nervous?" he asked.

"Of course, I am. But I know you won't let anything happen to me. I trust you. Remember?"

Dante is the only person I can be so scared of because he took advantage of me and made me feel weak. He still makes me feel weak.

He doesn't say anything, instead he leans in and kisses my lips and takes my hand in his. "Come on. Let's go kill this son of a bitch so I can go home and make love to my fiancé," Ace says, making me chuckle. When we get close to where I'm supposed to be standing Ace turns to look at me. "I'm going to be right behind that crate towards the left. If you need anything or it's getting too much, or you need me to-"

"I won't need you, Ace. I'll be fine," I say cutting him off before kissing his hand.

Ace kisses my temple and then walks to where he is supposed to be standing.

I walk to where I'm supposed to be standing and then just wait for Dante to reveal himself.

Only a few more minutes until he is going to be here.

I am currently wearing a big black sweater so you can barely see the bump but if I were to wear a tight shirt then you would see it. It's not big but if you looked closely, you could kind of assume I was pregnant or bloated.

As I am waiting, I'm starting to think about so many different things that could happen.

Should I kill Dante myself?

I know Ace wants to kill him but for the past few days, I have had this urge to kill him. I didn't care before but now I do. I don't know why-

"Aria." I hear from somewhere. That voice makes me feel goosebumps around my body. I turn around and look to see who called my name. "Don't be scared, beautiful."

Just then he walks out.

He is a little taller. He also shaved the scruff he had since the last time I saw him. He also looks older. His dark black hair is also freshly cut. He grew some more muscle. He looks dangerous. But Ace is way more dangerous than Dante. I already know that.

"Dante," I mumble.

"What's wrong? Like the view?" Dante says cockily while walking towards me.

I start walking back until my body hits the wall.

Shit.

"What do you want, Dante?" I ask as my heart rate picks up.

"Are you that naïve, Aria? I want you, of course. I've always wanted you," Dante says with a sinister smile.

"No. No. You hurt me. I could never forgive you," I reply while trying not to show how terrified I am of him.

Just because I am stronger now doesn't mean I don't feel weak around Dante. I don't know who this Dante is but if he is anything like the one a few years ago then I am terrified.

"Baby, no. I love you. You know that. That asshole Ace just brainwashed you," Dante tries to say in a comforting voice.

"No. He loves me," I assure.

"Sure, Aria. How is the morning sickness going?" Dante raises his eyebrows, and I feel my stomach drop. I forgot that he knows about my pregnancy. "What? Cat got your tongue?" Dante asks since I'm not saying anything.

"How do you know that?" I furrow my eyebrows.

"Aria, I know a lot. I'm not stupid," Dante chuckles.

"Sure, you're not," I mutter.

I grip the knife I have in my sweatshirt pocket. Ace knows that I have it and he said if I wanted to stab him I can. At first, I refrain from it but now that I think about it all I want to do is slice his neck open.

"Baby, can we please just make this transition easier?" Dante says and then he put his hands on my face making me want to throw up.

I move my face out of his hands and glare at him before taking out my knife and stabbing his hand and then taking it out to stab his stomach.

He screams in pain and then I see all of Ace's men and Alex come out of their hiding spots.

Alex points his gun at Dante and Ace comes to stand right next to me.

"You're done, Dante," Ace states.

Dante then starts laughing like a maniac. "You have no clue what I can do Ace."

"And you have no clue what I can do," Ace sneers.

"Ace, how are you doing?" Dante says as he turns around to look at Ace. Ace doesn't answer him. He just stares at Dante with a hard expression. "Well then if we are just going to skip the greetings then I will just get on with the fun," Dante holds his wound, and he winces. "This place is going to blow up in less than a minute. You see I have my escape plan, but do you have yours?" Dante raises his eyebrows. And before Ace or anyone can make a move to grab Dante, there is a smoke bomb he throws making smoke appear everywhere. "I'll see you soon, baby," Dante says and once the smoke clears, he is gone.

"Boss, we have to go. I'll explain-" One of his men came from around the corner and speaking.

"I know. Everyone, get out!"

"But Ace what about-"

"I'm not letting you die," Ace says before grabbing me and making me run with him to the nearest exit.

Everyone starts running towards the front of the warehouse leaving behind all the crates.

I run as fast as I can along with Ace. I don't look behind to see who is catching up and who isn't. I just want to get out of here and not get blown up.

Then suddenly, right when he pulls us both outside of the warehouse. I hear a loud bang, and everything blows up behind us. Ace covers me while we both fall from the impact of the explosion.

I can't hear anything. Just a very loud ringing sound in my ears. I open my eyes and see wood and parts of the building flying in the air.

I feel something hit Ace as he holds me tighter, trying to protect me.

"It's okay, Aria. You're going to be fine. Stay down. Close your eyes. There's nothing to see out here," he whispers in my ear. After a few minutes of just staying down, Ace gives me the single to stand to my feet. He stands up and he grabs my hand and lifts me. I stand to my full height, and he holds me up by my waist. "Are you okay?" he asks as he puts his hands on my face making sure I'm okay.

I nod my head before looking around. I see Val about to stand up. Same with Leo and dad. I try to keep looking around for Alex, but I don't see him.

"Where is Alex?" I ask, still looking around.

There is ash everywhere. I smell smoke all around us. You can barely see anything.

Ace lifts his head to look around. "There," Ace says motioning his head towards a body that is lying on the floor.

He looks lifeless.

I make a move to go to him, but Ace won't let me go. "Ace let me go. I need to see if he is okay." Ace looks at Alex and then down at my body and torn clothes. I know I have cuts on my body and probably bruises but I need to see if Alex is okay. "Ace let me go. Right now. I'm not playing." I shove Ace off me and start running to Alex's body on the floor. I kneel beside him. "Alex? Alex come on wake up!" I say while shaking him trying to get him to wake up but he won't move.

We are currently at the hospital. Ace has a doctor who works for him and he has an entire floor in the hospital for just Ace. So we had to go to the hidden parking lot and take the elevator that was only meant for this floor. Emma and the rest of the group are also here.

They took Alex into surgery and said they would let us know if he was going to be okay or not.

I'm anxious to see him and to just know if he is okay.

I know Alex and I fight a lot, but I love him. No matter what happens between us or even if he is being a total jackass, I still love him.

Ace is sitting down next to me in the waiting room. He barely said a word when we got here. He comforted me in the car on the way here. He has been silent though. I already know what he is thinking. He is thinking he failed me and that it was all his fault.

That maybe he should have been more discrete with the plans. I wouldn't be surprised if he is coming up with another plan inside his head right now.

I hate how he is so self-destructive.

While they took Alex in for surgery, I got checked too along with everyone else. Ace wanted to see if the baby was okay, and it was.

Leo is okay. He just has a broken arm from trying to stop himself from falling. Val is okay too and just has a few small cuts. Ace had to get stitches because a piece of wood got stabbed in his back. He didn't even notice or feel anything until I told him.

I don't really have any injuries because during the explosion, Ace was protecting me. I scolded him and he just kept saying stuff about how I need to be careful because we are going to have a baby and that I'm carrying it.

The baby is fine though. I'm not pregnant to the point where I can't do shit. I barely have a bump.

I look up when I hear footsteps walking closer towards us. I see the doctor coming closer with a clipboard in his hand.

I stand up along with Ace and everyone else.

Calla steps forward along with my mom and dad. My dad is limping though since he hurt his foot from the explosion.

"What's wrong? Is he okay?" Calla says anxiously.

I know why she is afraid.

If Alex dies, she not only lost the love of her life but the father of her child. Ariel wouldn't be able to have memories with her dad anymore.

"Alex is fine. He is awake now. He is incredibly lucky," the doctor states as he looks through his papers on the clipboard.

"What are his injuries?" my dad asks.

"He has a few broken ribs from the fall. He also hit his head hard and that's why he passed out. We don't know if he has memory loss, but I doubt it. Some other minor injuries but other than that he is okay. There's no need to worry," the doctor says giving us a reassuring smile.

"When can we see him?" I ask as I walk a little forward so the doctor can see me.

"Right now, if you want, but only a few people at a time."

"Calla you go. I'll wait with mom and dad." I say to Calla and she nods her head.

When Calla leaves, everyone goes back to sit in their seats.

I am standing until Ace takes my hand in his and guides me towards an empty hallway. We haven't really been alone much. We have been busy with this whole Dante thing and my family being over hasn't really given us enough time to relax with one another.

"Are you okay?" he asks as he leans me up against a wall.

He is super close to me. To the point where I can see all his beautiful features.

"I'm fine. The baby is fine. We're fine," I say nodding my head. "You need to stop worrying."

He puts his forehead on mine. "Kind of hard when we have your psycho ex-boyfriend after us."

"Yeah but we're going to be fine. I don't know how many times I have to tell you for you to get it, but I trust you, Ace. I know you're going to keep me and everyone else safe," I whisper to him.

"I love you," he whispers.

"And I love you," I kiss him on the lips and smile. "Come on, I want to see my brother."

"Oh yeah. Him," Ace sneers.

I hit his chest and he just laughs. We walk towards my mom and dad who look like they are waiting for me.

"Hey, the doctor says we can get more people to see Alex. Ready?" my mom asks as she gives me a small smile.

I nod my head and look at Ace.

"Go," he motions his head towards my parents. "I'll be right here," he kisses my temple and then lets go of my hand.

My mom and dad start walking, and I leave with them.

The nurses show us to Alex's room.

We hear laughing from outside the door.

My mom opens the door and we all walk in. Calla is standing next to Alex's bed while Alex is smiling at Calla.

His eyes full of love as he stares at her.

But then his head turns to look at me and I see a look of relief on his face.

"Oh, thank god, Aria," he speaks. I jog to him a little and hug him tightly. "Woah. Gentle. I'm a broken man," he says, trying to push me off.

I hit his shoulder and all he does is laugh and hug me back. "I'm so happy you're okay Alex," I whisper in his ear.

"Trust me, I am too. I'm glad you're okay though. You don't even look hurt," he says as he lets go of me.

"Yeah Ace was covering me the whole time things were flying. Do you remember what happened?"

"It's kind of blurry but I remember why we were there and

Dante blowing shit up. The last thing I felt before I passed out was a hard hit to the head and then I didn't see or hear anything."

"Well, I'm happy you're okay, Alex."

"Yeah is everyone else, okay?"

"Yeah everyone is fine," Dad says as he is limping towards Alex.

"Dad, don't tell me you're getting that old," Alex jokes at dad's walking.

"Better shut your mouth, boy," my dad says but you can see the smile on his face.

Mom, Alex, and Calla start laughing and the energy in the room seems lighter.

Thirty-Nine

Today is the gender reveal. I am super nervous to know what me and Ace are going to have. I don't care what we have as long as she or he is healthy.

Ace told me some boy and girl names that he likes.

If we have a boy, he wants the name to be Killian or Luca. I really like those names, especially Killian. For a girl, he wants to name her Thalia. I like the name Selena for a girl, but I love Thalia too.

"Aria! Are you ready for your hair and makeup?" Emma says as she walks into my room.

"Yeah," I look at her and smile.

"Perfect and you're already in your pajamas. Looks great by the way," Emma winks as she starts to get her makeup out.

Emma wants to do my makeup for today since she loves makeup, obviously. She said to just shower and get changed in random pajamas I have.

I tried on the dress Emma and I bought two months ago. It is a stretchy fabric so I knew it would fit me with the bump I have now. My bump is more vivid, and it looks perfect on me. I am trying to decide whether I should wear these white heels I have or these white Puma tennis shoes.

"Okay I already know what you're going to say but don't worry I won't put that much makeup on, but you still have to trust me," Emma narrows her eyes at me.

"Okay. But what are you even going to do?"

"You'll see," she smirks as she starts to do my makeup.

I am on my phone the whole time she does my makeup just looking through Instagram. I'm rarely on the app but I go through the explore page occasionally.

After she is done with my makeup she starts on my hair.

She decides to curl my hair since I never curl it which I was fine with. It will look nice with the dress.

"There! You look like a pregnant princess," Emma says as she puts down the curling iron.

"Thanks," I chuckle, and she just laughs along with me while I stare at myself in the mirror.

I don't know why I was freaking out about the makeup because she did a great job. She did a smokey eye which isn't something I normally do.

"Okay, so you need help with your dress, or you got it?"

"I think I'm good. I'll see you down there, Em."

"Okay. I'll see you down there," she says before walking out the door.

"Thank you."

"No problem."

Once she leaves, I go into the closet and get my dress out. It's stretchy so it will fit over my bump. Once I'm dressed and put on the Pumas, I spray some perfume on so that I can smell nice.

I hear a knock at the door while I'm looking at myself in the mirror. "Come in."

Then I feel a pair of strong, familiar arms wrap around my waist. "Hey," I hear Ace whisper in my ear.

"Hi," I say as I feel my cheeks heat up with blush.

Ace is the only person who can make me blush with such small gestures and make my heart flutter in ways no one else can.

He turns me around by my hand looking at my body, checking me out. "You look beautiful as always, *amore*." Ace then leans closer towards my ear. "Oh, the things I would do to you if there weren't people here."

Ace is wearing just a black suit with a baby pink tie. He told me he wants to have a girl and that if we were to get a girl, he would let no boys near her at all which made me roll my eyes.

"And you don't look too bad yourself," I say and rest my arms on his shoulders. "Is everyone here?"

"Yeah. You took a long time but it's worth the wait. Emma did a wonderful job, but you would look breathtaking if you just came in a fucking paper bag."

I laugh again. "Yeah well, we got people waiting so let's go."

Ace takes my hand and presses a kiss to my forehead before leading us downstairs.

I can already hear the music playing. There have been people coming in and out of the house setting up the party since morning, but it looks beautiful.

There are a lot of balloons in the pool, even some bigger ones that are bigger than me. There are also a lot of tables out for people to sit. The snack bar is already calling my name. The food and desserts on that table look good.

"Hey, baby." I turn around and see my mom and dad.

I let go of Ace and hug them before going back to standing next to Ace and his arm wrapping around my waist.

"Hey, mom. Do you know how Emma is going to do the reveal?" I ask.

I am getting super impatient.

"No, but she said it's going to be fun," my mom says as she smiles at me.

"I hope it will," I say. "Let's take pictures before we all get comfortable."

I don't want to be taking pictures all day. My mom and everyone are going to want to take pictures and I hate taking pictures so might as well get it over with it right now than later.

"Perfect. That makes things a lot easier," my dad laughs at my mom.

We all go over to the photo booth Emma has set up. It is super cute. It is a butterfly wall with pink and blue butterflies. I take pictures with everyone. It takes a long time. Probably a whole hour to just take pictures with people.

After the pictures, Emma starts to announce the games for all the kids. She has the same games I did for her shower and some other fun ones for the adults. There are a good number of kids here which I'm surprised about.

Some of my extended family flew to Italy for the party. Most of them are also coming to the wedding too.

I see Emma walk on stage for like the third time today. "Okay, because I can't wait anymore. I want to reveal the gender now. But first I wanted to say, Aria, you're going to be such an amazing mom and I can't wait to meet your baby girl or boy. I am going to make sure that this baby of yours gets spoiled since you always spoil Alexander." Everyone chuckles lightly at Emma. "Also, Ace I am excited to finally see that you will be having a kid of your own and I know for a fact you will be such an amazing father." Emma smiles and I see Ace smile back at her. "Okay, well everyone please follow me towards the pool, and we will reveal the gender there." Emma walks off stage and motions everyone to follow her.

"Come on," Ace whispers in my ear before kissing the spot below as he takes my hand to stand up and follow.

"Are you nervous?" I ask while walking with him.

"No. Are you?" Ace asks back.

"No. I'm excited," I say happily.

He kisses my cheek, and we get in front of the pool where Emma said.

"Okay, Aria, I want you to hold this gun," Emma says, handing me a black gun. Emma walks towards Ace. "And I want you to hold this gun." She hands Ace the same kind of gun I have. "And what I want you to do is just shoot the gun at that target in front of you," Emma says, pointing to a huge paper that says 'boy or girl'. "On three," she says, and Ace and I smile at each other as we stand side by side aiming our guns at the paper. "One, two, three!!"

Once she says that, Ace and I both shoot our guns and we see pink powder come out.

Ace hands the gun to Emma and smiles at the paper before turning to look at me and pulling me closer to him. Emma grabs my gun before Ace picks me up and hugs me and kisses me at the same time.

"I knew we were going to have a girl," he whispers into my ear.

I chuckle. "Better not be hovering over her," I scold.

"I'll make sure any boy who comes near her gets a punch to the face before dating her," he murmurs in my ear making me laugh.

Forty

I never thought it was so hard to get out of bed before but right now I'm having some issues.

I mean almost every fucking day I have an issue with this bump. I feel heavy and disgusting but Ace keeps reminding me that I look beautiful no matter what and sometimes he would show how beautiful I am by kissing every inch of my body. That would make me feel a little better, especially when he stares at me with that sparkle in his eyes that I adore so much.

It's been about five months since the gender reveal and the due date for the baby is coming soon. Time flew by amazingly fast.

Emma has been such a huge help too. I have a lot of people here with me at the house because they all want to make sure I am doing good. Mom always comes by and checks on me and sometimes hang out. Calla would come with Ariel as well as Layna. Layna is here all the time but that's because she is staying here instead of at a hotel like my mom and Alex are.

They all decided to stay in Italy until after I have the baby, but Alex and my dad have been back and forth going to California and then back here.

I have been having some aches these past few days too. Ace is worried and thinks we should go to the hospital, but I told him I can handle it.

Ace has been working a lot to find Dante's location and just working on other business stuff that I don't need to worry about as he says. He wants me to focus on getting this baby out of me.

He keeps me updated with all things Dante related. There has been no threats, fortunately.

Lana is also here helping me out too. She makes some good food for when I'm always hungry.

Right now, she is actually making food.

"Aria, are you sure you're okay? You look a little pale," Lana asks.

"I'm fine. I'm only tired. I've also been having such bad cramps. I don't get any sleep cause I'm always uncomfortable," I complain.

"Life as a pregnant woman. But at the end of the day, you get this right here in your arms," Emma smiles as she rocks Alexander in her arms.

He is getting so big. A funny thing is that Alexander's birthday is coming up. It's in two weeks which is such a coincidence because my and Ace's baby is going to be here in another week. Or maybe earlier depending on these fucking contractions.

Speaking of, I just felt another one making me wince a little.

"Maybe you should go to the hospital," Layna suggests as she sees the discomfort on my face.

Right after she says that I feel another one come.

Fucking hell.

"Where's Ace?" Emma asks while looking at Lana.

"Office," she states.

"We're going to the hospital. Sorry, but I know what a cramp feels like, and that face is screaming at me to take you to the hospital. I'll get Ace. Layna take Aria to the car," Emma demands.

Layna stands up and takes my hand. "Guys I'm fine. It's just-" I get cut off by another cramp.

It feels like someone keeps kicking me in the stomach, hard.

"Yeah, what were you saying?" Layna raises her eyebrows.

"Shut up and take me to the car," I say while trying to contain my anger 'cause these cramps are pissing me off.

Layna takes my hand and brings me to the car. I see Emma run upstairs to get Ace.

She better fucking hurry.

Layna helps me into the back seat of the car.

"I'm going to have Francisco drive you and Ace there," Layna says. She pulls out her phone and starts texting. "Okay, Francisco is coming right now. I also texted Alex and your mom. They're going to meet us there. I'll text Ana to come with Val and Mia in the car."

Just then I see Ace run out the front door with Leo, Emma, and Francisco behind him.

"Good luck. Try not to have the baby in the car," Layna says and she kisses my head and leaves.

Ace comes up to me and holds my hands that are in my lap. "Are you okay? What's wrong?"

"I'm fine. Layna and Emma are saying I should go to-" And another one comes again making me squeeze Ace's hand.

It feels like someone stabbed my stomach.

Ace sees me wince and he turns to look at Francisco who is getting in the car.

"Hospital, Francisco. And make sure you step on it," Ace demands and he closes my door and walks to the other side of the car and sits next to me. "It's okay, *amore*. Just hold on for a little longer. You can do it," Ace whispers into my ear as Francisco drives to the hospital.

Once we get to the secret parking lot at the hospital, Ace gets out of the car and runs to my side to help me out. The whole drive felt like it was an hour but it wasn't long.

"Do you want a wheelchair, or can you walk?" Ace asks.

"I can walk," I mumble as I hold onto him.

He nods his head and holds me close to him as we walk to front desk inside.

"She's in labor. I need to get her a room," Ace says as we walk up to the reception desk.

"Okay um..." The nurse looks confused about what to do.

"Do you even know what you're doing?" Ace spits.

"Hey, calm down. Just relax," I say to Ace as I rub his arm making him calm down.

"Just get us the doctor," he growls in a husky deep voice making the reception lady nod her head and run off. "The girl is probably new. Greg should have taught her how to do this shit."

"You need to calm down, Ace. Everything will be fine," I say in an assuring tone.

"I'm firing her when she comes back. I don't know why Greg

isn't here instead of that bitch." I shake my head at Ace and then I see the reception lady come back with the doctor. "You're fired. Get your shit and get out of my sight."

"Ace!" I yell while he just glares at the woman who runs to her desk to start packing her shit. "Such an asshole."

I am supposed to be the one who is angry with crazy pregnant hormones, not Ace.

Ace turns to look at me. "I'm not an asshole, *amore*. I'm being the boss. I need someone who knows how to do shit."

"Still an ass-" I get cut off by another cramp.

"Okay well how about we get you two to a room," the doctor says and Ace follows him while holding me.

Once we get to the room, Ace lays me in the hospital bed. I don't know if Leo and Emma are here but quite frankly, I don't care. I just want the pain to stop.

Ace helps me get in the bed and tries to make it comfortable for me. "You're going to do great," he says as he rubs my stomach trying to make the pain decrease but it doesn't do anything.

"Nice to see you guys again. How are you two?" the doctor says as he walks in. Ace glares at the doctor making him work faster. "Okay, Aria White?"

"Aria De Luca," Ace glares at the doctor again making me roll my eyes.

"Not married yet son." the doctor said making Ace glare at him

From the few times I have been here I can tell that Ace and his doctor have a strong bond because his doctor would always crack jokes, but Ace wouldn't do anything about it.

"Will you shut the fuck up and help her?" Ace spits.

"Oh my god, Ace, calm down," I say trying to make him calm down but obviously Ace just wants to be an asshole to everyone today.

The doctor doesn't say anything as he looks at his computer and all my vitals. The nurse came in earlier while Ace was making me comfortable.

"Okay, it looks like you are fully dilated so we can have you start pushing now. I'm surprised you didn't feel that much pain, Aria. Your contractions were extremely strong." the doctor says, and he motions the nurse to come forward and get to work.

Fuck, now I'm nervous and in pain.

"It's okay you can do it. I believe in you, *amore*," Ace whispers in my ear.

"Okay, Aria, I'm going to need you to do a big push for me," the nurse says and I nod my head.

I push while screaming at the same time. Ace gives me his hand for me to squeeze. He is brushing my hair away from my face as he whispers to me saying I'm going to be okay and that I am beautiful, but I wasn't really focused on that.

God, I'm going to be a mother.

This is crazy.

Fucking crazy.

After another thirty minutes, I'm starting to get tired, and my vagina feels like it is on fire.

"Okay, just a few more, Aria, you are doing amazing," the nurse assures me.

"You're doing good, baby, keep going," Ace whispers in my ear while rubbing circles on my arms and getting the hair out of my face.

I push again and again as much as I can.

"Okay, last one Aria. Give us one last big push," I do as the nurse says and push hard one last time before I hear a baby crying. "It's a girl!"

At exactly nine-thirteen a.m., my and Ace's baby girl was born. She is beautiful.

She has Ace's eyes which is something I adore the most about Ace. She has my small nose and ears. She already has some hair on her head which looks a little like mine because it's darker than Ace's.

"So, what are we going to name her?" Ace asks as he looks down at our baby girl in my arms.

"What about Thalia?" I ask and look up at him to see what he thinks.

"Perfect," he says and then kisses my head and continues to look at Thalia.

I know I said that Alexander was the cutest baby I've ever seen but now I'm going to be that mom and say that my baby is the cutest.

But she looks like a little alien but a cute alien.

God that sounds weird.

Me being a Mom.

But I wouldn't trade it for the world.

It's crazy that Ace and I made Thalia. How me and him made a human and how it was stuck inside my stomach for almost nine months.

Again, so crazy.

"She's beautiful just like you," Ace whispers in my ear.

I feel a blush spread on my cheeks. "Want to hold her?" I ask him.

He nods his head and I hand him Thalia. He grabs her from me and rocks her while she sleeps soundly in his arms.

His shirt is off and so is mine since the doctor recommended we do skin to skin contact.

"Sorry to interrupt but you have some people that are waiting for you outside. Do you want me to let them in?" the nurse says as she peeks through the door.

I look at Ace and he nods his head. "Yeah go ahead. Let them in," I say and she leaves.

Ace walks back towards me with Thalia still in his arms.

We hear the door open, and I see Alex and Calla come in first with mom, dad, Layna, Cole, Mia, Val, Elena, Emma, and Leo following along.

Jesus, everyone is here.

"Hey," my mom says first in a hushed tone.

"Where is my niece?" Alex asks.

Ace turns around to show him while holding Thalia sleeping in his arms.

"Oh, my-she is beautiful, Aria," my mom says as she comes up to look at Thalia closer.

Emma, Layna, and Mia follow along.

"What's her name?" Alex asks and looks back at me.

"Do you want to tell them or me?" I ask Ace as he is looking down at Thalia.

"You can. It doesn't matter."

"Thalia Judd De Luca," I say, and everyone smiles.

"Where did you get her middle name?" my dad asks.

I look at Ace for him to tell. "My mom. It was her middle name."

"That's beautiful, Ace," my mom smiles at him.

Ace and I had already discussed the middle name once we found out it was a girl. I love Judd for a middle name, and I think it fits perfectly with the name we gave her.

"Do you want to hold her?" Ace asks my mom.

My mom nods her head and Ace places Thalia into my mom's arms.

"She looks just like you, Aria," my dad says as he looks over my mom's shoulder.

Leo walks towards Ace. "Good job, dude." He does a small handshake with Ace.

"The fuck? I am the one who pushed the baby out," I say looking at Leo and he looks at me and laughs.

"Good job, Aria. You did amazing." Leo gives me a smile.

"Do you want to hold her, Alex?" my mother asks, looking at Alex who is staring at Thalia.

"Wait did you all wash your hands? I don't know what you have been touching and I want to make sure your hands are clean."

"Yeah, we also put on hand sanitizer," Alex says before taking Thalia from my mother.

"Where is Ariel?" I ask.

"She is at home with Lana," Layna says and she walks towards me. "Good job. You're going to be a great mother," Layna says, making me smile. She looks up at Ace who is next to me. "Ace, you're going to be a great father as well as a great husband to Aria."

Ace nods his head. "Thank you, Layna."

"Yeah Layna is right. I know I don't have to worry about Aria because you'll be there to protect her and now, you're going to protect another beautiful princess in the family," my dad smiles at Ace.

"That means a lot, George. Thank you."

Over the past few months, my father and Ace have been civil with each other. At first, he and my brother hated Ace but now they respect him. Alex and Ace are still acting like three-year-old's to one another sometimes.

"Of course. If you two need anything. You have my number."

"When are you guys even leaving?" I ask my family.

"Trying to get rid of us?" Cole smirks.

"Of course not. Why would I want to get rid of you guys?" I say sarcastically.

"We're going to stay until after the wedding. I have to go back home and work, but I want to be able to watch my baby sister walk down the aisle," Alex says looking up from Thalia.

"Emma, Leo. Come here," I motion for the two to come. Leo has his arm wrapped around her waist. "I want you guys to be the godparents," I say and they both look up at Ace. He smiles and nods his head. "I just know that you will always be present in our daughters life. Plus I know that Ace can only really trust Leo to care for our daughter."

"Thank you so much, Aria. I feel honored," Leo says.

"Yes, thank you. You guys are going to be such amazing parents," Emma says and she leans forwards to hug me. "You did such an amazing job, Aria. I'm so proud of you," she whispers in my ear. I feel a tear drop onto my shoulder.

I chuckle. "Pull it together, Em," I say as I pull her back to look at her.

"Dude, shut up. Be serious for once," Emma says and wipes her tears and looks at Thalia.

"Want to hold her?" I ask Emma.

She nods her head and goes to Alex and grabs the baby from him gently.

"Don't worry, baby girl. I'm going to be here to protect you no matter what," Emma whispers to Thalia.

Ace and I want to have Emma and Leo be the godparents because Alexander and Thalia are going to grow up together and we want them to be close. And since I am living here instead of the USA, I want the godparents to be closer to us and Emma and Leo are.

Forty-One

"Emma, you have your own baby. Hold on him," I say as I am trying to convince Emma to let go of Thalia so I can hold her.

Alexander is sleeping so she had to take mine.

"Aria, my baby is getting bigger each day. He is already starting to walk," Emma pouts.

"So? I want my baby. Give me her," I pout.

God, we sound like five-year-olds fighting over dolls.

Alexander's birthday was fun. It wasn't anything extravagant because he was only turning one. We just had a small party at Emma's house with close family only.

"Well, I kind of need to feed her so I can put her to bed so give me," I take Thalia from Emma's hands and hold her in my arms.

"Want me to come with?" Emma asks as I stand up from the couch.

"You want to watch me feed Thalia?" I ask trying to see if she understood what she just said.

"Yeah," she says happily.

"No, Emma." I leave the living room and walk upstairs to where Thalia's room is which is next to ours.

We have her room next to ours so we can hear her. We also have a baby monitor in there too. Ace has one in his office just in case anything happens, but I shouldn't be thinking about 'ifs'. It makes me anxious.

I open her room door and sit down on the chair next to her bed. I then start to feed her while I just watch her silently. I always get distracted when I watch her do anything. It's like she captures your soul when you stop and stare at her.

Her beautiful green eyes sparkle just like Ace's which I am in love with because I think that is my favorite feature of Ace's.

I notice she is done so I stand up from the chair and try to burp her before putting her down for a nap. "Goodnight, Thalia. I love you," I say softly, and lightly kiss her head.

I turn off the lights and leave the room, softly closing the door. I walk further down the hall to Ace's office and open his door. I see him looking at the computer. He looks like he is reading something.

He looks up from his computer and sees me walking towards him. He doesn't say anything, except he scoots his chair for me to sit on his lap.

He kisses me deeply when I sit on his lap. He gives me a few more pecks before looking up at me.

"What are you working on?" I ask before looking at his computer.

"Just looking at deals some other organizations sent out. What about you? What did you do before you came here?" Ace asks.

"I put Thalia down for a nap. She is sleeping now," I start to play with his hair while talking to him.

"You're so good with her. She sleeps perfectly when you put her down. With me, it's a mission sometimes," he mumbles, sounding annoyed.

"Well, I just got that touch you know," I say and wink at him.

"Yes, definitely, *amore*," he says sarcastically.

He types some stuff on his computer while I watch and play with his hair lightly.

His hair is so soft but that's probably because he uses my conditioner sometimes.

This is usually what happens during the day. After I put Thalia down for a nap I either workout or come to Ace's office to hangout or bug him. Sometimes we do other things, but we won't talk about those details.

"Have you found any updates on Dante?" I ask Ace.

I feel Ace tense beneath me. "No. We checked Naples but he wasn't there. It's like he is always one step ahead. It's fucking frustrating."

"I know, but you'll find him. Don't worry," I assure. "Did you find any moles yet?"

"No, but right now that's not what I am worried about Ari. I am scared that he will come after you or Thal-"

Ace gets cut off by the sound of Thalia crying on the baby monitor.

I sigh at the same time as him. "It's okay, I'll get her," I say and get up from his lap and walk towards Thalia's room.

I open her door and am about to turn on the light, but I see a dark shadow near Thalia's crib.

The figure turns around and I see Dante's face.

"Get the fuck away from her now!"

"Aww, Ari it's ok, baby. I won't hurt her. I would never think of it," he reaches down to touch her.

"Don't touch her," I look around the room for some weapons to use but can't find anything.

I run towards him and aim a hit at his face making his face turn to the side. I push him down to the floor, but he captures my leg in his hand and pulls me down with him.

I feel terror spread through my body.

It's familiar and I don't like it.

"Ace!" I call for him.

"Shut the fuck up," Dante growls as he puts his hand over my mouth.

I try to kick him off, but I can't. I knew I was never strong enough to go against Dante.

I am always weak around him.

He is going to hurt everyone.

I start to hear footsteps running towards the door and Dante gets off me. Before I can react and get up, Dante picks up Thalia and Ace opens the door.

He has a gun in his hand and aims it for Dante. "Careful, Ace. One wrong shot and it's bye-bye, Thalia," Dante smirks.

Ace aims a shot at Dante but misses. Thalia cries as Dante gets out of the room by going out of the open window.

"He's on the roof. I can still get him," I say as I quickly stand up and jump out the window and start running towards where Dante went.

I don't turn around to look if Ace is following. I keep following Dante's dark shadow. I see him hop down the side of the wall. I follow him quickly to where he hopped off and see a ladder. I don't even use the ladder. I just jump off and run towards him.

"Dante! Stop!" I yell as I run towards him.

We enter the driveway and I see Ace come out of the front door.

Dante is running towards a big black car and once he opens the door, I feel my heart break.

How could he do this to us? We trusted him with everything, and he just betrayed us.

I run closer and closer to Dante as he opens the door and puts Thalia in the backseat before closing the door and opening the front door where I see Francisco in the driver seat.

I get up to Dante but before I can make any move or kick or hurt him, he pushes me against the car and punches me in the stomach and face but then I feel him get ripped off of me and I see Ace on top of him punching him. I get up and turn to get Thalia but before I can I see Francisco aiming a gun at her.

"Tell Ace to get off Dante before I shoot her."

I back away from the car a little, afraid he might shoot the gun. "Francisco don't do it. I thought you were family," I say as a tear streams down my face.

"Sorry, but Ace just isn't doing it for me anymore," Francisco shrugs.

I hear Ace wince making me look at him and see that Dante stabbed him in the neck making my heart stop for a second.

I don't know what to do. Stay with Thalia or go to Ace who may be dying.

Dante walks away from Ace and towards the car passing me. "If you want to ever see your daughter again Aria, then you know what to do. Take a step closer and Francisco will kill Thalia," Dante warns as he walks closer to the car. I walk to Ace once I hear him scream in pain trying to get the knife out of his neck. "I'll see you soon, baby," Dante says once he gets in the car and drives away.

I run to Ace and hold him while putting pressure on his wound. "It's okay, I'm here. It's okay."

"Thalia," is the last thing Ace says before his eyes fall.

I am currently in the waiting room at the hospital.

My dad and Alex are on their way here right now because they heard what happened with Ace and Dante but everyone else is here, showing their support and making sure I'm okay.

God, I don't know if Ace is alive or not, but I am scared. I don't know what I'll do if he isn't.

It's all my fault.
I let her go so easily.
How stupid could I be?

"Aria?" the nurse says, and I stand up immediately and stand in front of her. "He is in stable condition. He lost a lot of blood from the stab and that is why he fainted. He is alright though. He won't have any damages to his voice but I suggest he rests for a couple of days. He is sleeping right now but I can only have a selected group of people," the nurse states.

Ace's regular doctor isn't here because he had a family emergency so he had his assistant help us instead. I did call him and he told me what the nurse is going to be doing.

I look back at everyone behind me.

"It's okay, go. We will be here," Layna says and I nod my head and wipe a tear that had fallen.

I follow the nurse to Ace's room, and she opens his door. "I am sorry for what happened," the nurse says, making me look at her. "I really hope you catch this guy. I know Ace and you will do whatever you can," the nurse smiles and I give her a small smile back but don't say anything.

I walk inside Ace's room and the nurse closes the door. I look at Ace who has a bandage on his neck and his eyes are closed as monitors are all around him and he has IV's hooked up to him.

I let out a sigh and walk towards him on the side of the bed.

"I'm so sorry," I say while trying not to let out a whimper or cry. "It's all my fault. If I had just done something or just wasn't being a pussy and just killed Dante, none of this would have happened," I say and I see Ace's eyes flutter a little. "I can lose everything, but I can't lose you or Thalia. You both have consumed me in such a short amount of time, and I love you both endlessly."

I can't hold it in anymore.

All the things I have been wanting to cry out just come out. I cry about Ace almost dying, Thalia being taken, Dante, everything Dante has done to me.

I let it all out and close my eyes while resting my head on Ace's chest that is moving up and down.

After a few minutes of crying into Ace's chest I feel an arm being placed on my back. "It's not your fault. This could never be your fault."

I feel more tears come before I wrap my arms around Ace and hug him. "I was so scared you were-"

"It's going to take a lot more than a stab to the neck to kill me, *amore*," Ace mumbles.

"Ace, he got her. D-Dante got her. She's gone," I sob into Ace's chest.

"We'll find her. Don't worry, we'll find her," he says reassuringly.

"I'm so scared Ace. I have never been this scared before," I say while trying to contain my tears.

Ace lets out a heavy sigh and lets me go. "I'll do everything I can to get her back, Ari." Before I can say anything, I hear my phone ring and I take it out and see Francisco's number. Ace looks down at the phone. "Answer it. Speaker."

I do as he says and put it on speaker. "Aria." I hear Dante say from the other side of the phone.

Ace grabs the phone before I can say anything. "Where the fuck is she, Dante?"

Dante then chuckles. "She is safe, don't worry I have someone who is taking care of her, but I was calling to give you a chance to save you daughter."

"What?" I ask.

"I want you Aria. No doubts about that. So, I want you to meet me at a location where Francisco will text you and you meet me there and then we have a little trade," Dante says calmly.

I look at Ace and I already see the gears in his head turning. "When and where?" Ace asks.

"Day after tomorrow at ten-thirty in the morning. Don't be late. Francisco will send you the address the day of," Dante says before hanging up.

Ace tosses the phone on the bed and rubs his hands along his face. "Fuck," Ace mutters. "Okay. We need a plan," Ace states.

I raise my eyebrows at him. "Are you crazy? You almost died and now you are ready to just get up and go?" Ace starts to take the IV's out of his arms and all the other stickies on him. "Ace-"

Before I can continue to scold him, he cuts me off. "Don't argue with me, Ari. I'm finding her. I am fine," Ace stands up from the bed and walks towards the bathroom that is in the room.

I sigh and shake my head lightly. "I'll be in the waiting room."

I walk out of the room, and I see Leo down the hallway.

I walk in front of him and next thing I know he hugs me. "I'm sorry this happened to you, Aria. You and Ace don't deserve this. Please talk to him," Leo whispers in my ear. "He is probably thinking so much crazy shit in his head right now."

"He's awake and definitely going crazy," I mutter. "He is changing right now but you can go in and talk to him."

Leo nods his head and I walk back into the waiting room where I see everyone sitting down.

Emma looks up at me. "How is he?"

"Crazy," I roll my eyes. "He is up and changing so that we can go back to the house."

I see Val furrow his eyebrows. "Shouldn't he be resting?"

"We got a call from Dante saying to meet him at this location."

"Doesn't mean Ace should not relax," Antonio says.

He sounds super mad, but he understands how Ace is.

"You know how he is," I shrug.

We then hear footsteps coming towards us making all our heads turn and see Ace and Leo.

"Are we going to find my daughter?"

Forty-Two

I AM SCARED.

My stomach feels like it's going to drop.

What if things don't end up well?

What if Dante ends up killing Thalia?

I don't want to think about all the things that could go wrong but there are so many.

Dante is always smart with whatever he does. He would always help my dad with missions and planning them so no wonder he was able to succeed each time.

"Okay, I don't want anyone to shoot. I want to get Thalia out of Dante's hands before firing towards him. I want all guards around the perimeter," Ace says. We got the location from Francisco just a few hours ago and Ace is reviewing the entire plan right now. We are all in his office while he is explaining what not to do and what to do. "Jared and Josh, I want you inside along with

Alex, Leo, Val, Antonio, Cole, Layna, and George," Ace looks at Jared and Josh.

They have been around the house frequently just checking in and to see how we were doing. They have just been busy going on missions while also checking on the Russians to make sure there are no heirs or anyone who would come for us all.

Emma isn't coming on the mission because she has a kid and Leo doesn't want her to get hurt. Same with Calla but with Alex.

I hate that this is all happening right before the wedding too. I don't even feel like having a wedding.

Dante ruined it all. I want to have Thalia at the wedding. It will be complete if our daughter is there. The wedding is supposed to be in two months.

Mark is supposed to come over a few days before the wedding to just do a final check of everything. Mark met Thalia. He was smiling nonstop.

For the past day Ace has barely gotten any sleep. He has been trying to find the location on his own and try to see if he can find out where Dante is while also trying to heal the wound on his neck.

"Okay, we're good?" Ace asks. Everyone nods their heads. "Good, now let's go get my fucking daughter."

Everyone leaves Ace's office and makes their way to the cars downstairs.

Ace walks towards me. I haven't really been talking much because of that night. I am still in shock.

"*Amore*, stand up," Ace says. I stand up and he steps closer to me and hold my hands. "We got this. I have extra precautions everywhere. There is no way he will be able to escape this time," Ace reassures me while touching a strand of my hair that fell.

"I'm scared. What if he does ki-"

"Don't say that. I won't let him. We will kill him before he even gets a chance. No hesitating," I nod my head. "Good, now let's go get our daughter so we can come back home and fucking watch a movie or something."

I give him a weak smile and he guides us both out of his office and towards the car.

Ace takes his own car while everyone else goes in other cars.

Ace drives the streets very fast while some of his men drive behind us. Everyone is going to be parking a mile away from the location Dante wants Ace and I to meet him at.

Ace and I drive to the location, and it looks like an incredibly old warehouse. It looks burnt down and some of the walls are cracked.

I know Dante expects me to bring my family. He wouldn't expect anything less. So, I did. But I'm still trying to take precautions.

"Come on. We can do this. We are going to get our daughter back. Okay?" Ace whispers to me while he looks at me with his intense eyes.

"Okay."

"I love you."

"I love you," I say back, and he leans forward and kisses me on the lips softly.

I feel a small tear escape my eye, but I wipe it as Ace leans away from the kiss.

"Let's go," he says and then opens his door and shuts it.

I open my door and get out of the car. I already see Alex and them walking towards us.

"So, we aren't going to shoot or anything until he gives us Thalia? Right?" Val asks.

"Yeah don't shoot and if you do and you hit my daughter, Val, I'll put a bullet into your head so please listen," Ace says in a dangerous tone. Val nods his head. "Good, now let's go before he thinks we won't show up," Ace says and starts walking.

I follow him as everyone does.

The door is already unlocked when we get to the warehouse. Ace and I walk in hand-in-hand. Everything in the warehouse looks very old and dirty. There is equipment, crates, and boxes everywhere.

I see Dante walking out from the burnt crates and boxes.

Francisco has Thalia in his arms, and I instantly start to feel better from seeing her, but I am also scared and anxious. I walk a little forward to try and get her.

"Tsk tsk tsk. Not so fast, Aria," Dante says, stopping me from walking further. "Glad to see you here."

"What do you want, Dante?" I say trying to get straight to the point.

"You already know, Aria," he smirks.

"But why would you go this far just for me?"

"Think of it this way. Why do you think Ace would kill thousands of people just for you? Because I know he would," Dante smirks.

"Dante, you can't say you love me. You never did."

"You don't know that Aria," he spits. He starts to get angry which makes me afraid because he is close to Thalia. "You know what I want Aria, I want you to come over here and I will have Francisco put Thalia down and then Ace you can come and get Thalia once Aria and I leave the building. My men are going to watch you to make sure you don't disobey."

I gulp. I look at Ace and he looks down at me.

He gives my hand three tight squeezes and then I let go and walk towards Dante.

When I get in front of Dante, I look at Francisco. "I am disgusted with you," I sneer at him, and he just chuckles. I look at Dante. "Can I just hold her before not being able to see her again?" I say with some tears coming out of my eyes.

Dante pulls me towards him and grips my arm. "If you try anything, I'll kill her and Ace while you just sit and watch," Dante hisses in my ear.

I nod my head and Dante lets go of me so I go to Francisco and take Thalia from his arms.

"Hey," I say right before sniffling. "You're okay, baby. You're going to be okay. Mommy's here," I whisper to her. "I just want you to know that I love you so much and that you will never be alone. Especially not in a family like ours. Daddy is over there waiting for you." And now the waterworks are starting. "I'll miss you. I'll miss you so much but just remember I'm always going to be here for you."

I know this is all a show, but it still feels like a goodbye that I am not ready for. Thalia is sleeping so she isn't even listening. Even though this is all part of Ace's plan I still feel scared. *What if I really don't see her again?*

"Okay enough. Give her to him," Dante says and snaps his fingers towards Francisco. I hand Thalia over to Francisco. He takes her out of my arms gently while I wipe my tears. "Okay good. Now, remember what I said, Ace. You move before Aria and I leave, then you're dead along with your daughter," Dante says right before grabbing my forearm roughly pulling me with him.

I look back while Dante is pulling me. Ace's fist is clenched hard and so is his jaw. He can't do anything though 'cause that's not part of the plan.

Once I can't see him anymore, I turn my head towards Dante. "I don't know why you would want me, Dante. I will never love you," I spit.

"See Aria, that's where you're wrong. You will want me. You will love me. You want to know why? Thalia and Ace will die if you don't."

"Fucking asshole," I say and afterwards he pushes me to the ground.

I hiss as I get a small cut because my arm fell on top of a sharp piece of glass. I sit up and I take a glass shard out of my skin.

"Curse at me again Aria and I will just keep teaching you a lesson. Now get the fuck up," Dante says.

If he didn't want me on the floor, then he shouldn't have pushed me.

I stand up and put my hand behind my back touching the gun tucked into my waistband.

"Not so fast," I hear from behind me. I turn around and see Lexi. *What the hell is she doing here?* "Hey, Aria. Long time no see. How's the baby?" Lexi smirks.

"What the fuck?" I look back at Dante and see him staring with an amused smile on his face.

"What? Surprised to see me?" Lexi says smiling.

"Lexi, what the hell are you doing? Are you really working with this maniac?" I ask surprised.

"Oh, Aria. You don't understand, do you?" *Understand what? Is she like that desperate or something?* "I want Ace and the only way for that to happen was to get rid of you and here we are. Plan falling into place," Lexi smirks.

"You're crazy. The both of you are," I say as I pull my gun out and aim it at her.

She aims her gun back at me. "You really want to do this Aria?" Lexi asks.

I don't say anything, I just stare at her.

"Alright if none of you are going to shoot then I will," Dante says before I hear a gunshot.

But it isn't Dante's.

I then hear multiple gunshots go off. Lexi hears them and turns her body to the warehouse. I shoot her in the head and turn around aiming my gun at Dante.

"Put the gun down, baby," he says once he sees me aim the gun towards him. "I don't want to have to shoot you just for you to put the gun down."

"You know what really sucked about our relationship? I thought I was loved. You made me think that what you did to me was love. But it was just fucking abusing me and hurting me. You deserve nothing but hell."

Dante makes a move to grab me, but I shoot him in the shoulder. He still pushes me down to the ground and as he is holding me, I feel a sharp sting on the side of my neck.

I whimper before pushing him off of me.

I feel my eyes start closing and when they do, I see nothing but darkness.

No.

I have to get up.

I open my eyes again and Dante is sitting on the grass while holding his wound. I stand up but almost fall because of how weak my legs feel.

I aim the gun at him, and Dante looks over at me. "I did all of this for us, Aria. You're finally mine now," I hear him say.

"Goodbye, Dante," I say as I walk closer to him. "You may be smart, Dante, but not that smart. I really wished things ended up on a good note but obviously, you're too fucking psychotic to do that."

I shoot him before he can say anything.

One in the heart for breaking mine.

One in the head for messing with mine.

And one in the throat because that was the worst place where he ever touched me.

And he's dead.

He is finally gone.

"*Aria!*" I hear someone yell.

I turn around and see Ace running towards me. I start running towards him. This feels like something out of a movie. Something super cliché but I don't care. I just want him to hold me and tell me that we did it. That we can be happy now and not have to worry about Dante.

Once I reach him, he wraps his arms around me, and I jump into his arms.

He is holding me up by my thighs carrying me. His head is buried into my neck just taking me in.

"We did it," he says as I start to sob a little into his shoulder.

"He's dead," I say into his shoulder.

"I know. I'm so proud of you, love. I knew you could do it. You really think I would let you and Thalia leave me?" Ace says before pressing a kiss to my neck.

"No."

"Good. Cause you and Thalia are never leaving me now that *I got you both.*"

Forty-Three

We all walk out of the limo and the girls all head towards the building while my father and I stay back.

It's been about a month or so since I killed Dante. For this past month Ace, Thalia, and I have been together relaxing and making sure we are all okay. Ace took us to the hospital so that I could get checked out and get whatever serum Dante gave me out of my system. They also checked Thalia to make sure she was okay.

But Dante is dead, and I feel relieved but also feel like this is somehow a *dream* that I will wake up from soon.

"You look beautiful, Aria," my dad says as he kisses my cheek and hugs me.

"Thank you, Dad," I say and hug him back.

"You're going to do great, kiddo. Stop worrying. You chose a good one," my dad says.

"I remember when you didn't like him."

"I don't remember that," my dad laughs.

"I love you, Dad," I whisper.

"I love you, too. Now let's go. Ace is waiting for you," my dad says and releases me from the hug and holds my hand to walk us to where the ceremony is being held.

Ace and I decided to have it take place in front of Lake Como. It is perfect.

We walk towards the aisle and wait until the music starts. Once it does start, my dad walks, and I follow holding onto his arm.

I see a lot of flashes go off making me feel nervous. I look straight and there he is.

Ace De Luca.

He is wearing his all-black suit with a bow tie and a white flower tucked into his pocket. His hair has been freshly cut too and his stubble is gone. He looks like a god as always. I also notice his eyes are tearing up making me think he is going to cry.

My dad turns me around so I'm facing him. He leans in and kisses my cheek. "I love you," he says before giving my hand to Ace. He looks at Ace. "If you break her heart. I'll kill you, Ace," my dad smiles as he says that.

"Wouldn't even think of it, George," Ace says and takes my hand in his big soft ones.

I am standing in front of Ace and staring at him and all his features. The priest starts talking while Ace and I just stare at each other. He has that sparkle in his eyes once again. The sparkle that has me feeling like *it is all a dream that I will wake up from.*

"You look beautiful, Aria," Ace says at a low whisper.

Everyone doesn't see that sparkle in his eyes, but I do. He looks at me with so much love and admiration. The priest keeps talking but I'm not listening. I just keep looking at Ace. I see all his flaws. The scar on the top of his eyebrow. The small tattoo he has next to his ear. His beautiful green eyes that are bright and sparkly. The small scar he has on the top of his head from when he and Alex fought that one time.

He has so many flaws, but I love him no matter what.

"Now for the vows," the priest says looking at Ace.

Ace nods his head and takes a piece of paper out from his pocket.

"*Aria*. There are so many emotions that I'm currently feeling right now. Right here looking at you is making me crazy. I never knew what love or anything close to that felt like but when I look at you, I feel so much love that it makes me fucking crazy. When I first laid eyes on you, I knew you were different," Ace says and I feel myself tear up. "I obviously thought you were beautiful. Who would be stupid and say you're not? I knew that I loved you the day I saw you in the chair cursing at yourself. It was funny to watch. That was the first time I have laughed before my father ruined that for me. You made me feel again, Aria. You made me smile and laugh. You made me capable of loving. I will continue to tell you how much I love you and our daughter, Thalia, every day till the day I die and when I do it, will be for you."

I smile at him while nipping my lips trying to stop myself from crying.

"I love you and all of your imperfections as much as I love your perfections. I love everything that you brought into my life. I will take care of you. I will cherish each day with you for as long as I live. *Ti amo Aria De Luca da quando vivo. Finché morte non ci separi.*" he says as a small tear falls from his cheek.

But he wipes it before looking at me and away from the paper.

The last part makes me cry a little, but I don't have a full-on breakdown.

"*Aria*," the priest says.

I take a deep breath before I start. "Ace. I have never met someone like you in my life before and I have met and killed a lot of people," I laugh and so does everyone else. "I never thought I would be able to love again. You make me feel like I am the only girl in the world. You make me feel I'm in a dream every time you look and stare at me. I'm glad that I got kidnapped by you. Sort of," I chuckle. "I have never experienced love like this before. You taught me how to love again, how to trust, how to enjoy life to the fullest. I'm happy with where we are right now. We're happy. We're finally able to breathe and live. You gave me such a beautiful baby girl and hopefully many more."

"Definitely," he chuckles lightly and the crowd laughs.

"I have never wanted to kill and love a person so much at the same time before. I am so grateful I met someone like you Ace. The world doesn't deserve you. I don't deserve you. I love you," I finish, and Ace extends his arm and wipes my fallen tears.

I take the ring that Ariel is holding, and I hold onto Ace's hand and slide it on his finger. Ace takes the ring for me and holds my hand so that he can slide the ring on my finger.

"With the power vested in me, I now pronounce you husband and wife. You may now kiss your bride," the priest says.

I look at Ace who is smiling. He places one of his hands on my waist to pull me closer. His other hand holds onto my cheek and then he presses his lips against mine. The kiss is passionate and takes my breath away. I feel like if I died then and there, I would be happy.

He pulls away before it gets too heated. "My beautiful wife," Ace says and I giggle.

The crowd cheers and stands up smiling.

Ace and I are having our fist dance.

We have a slice of cake and did the speeches which almost made me want to cry.

Everything is just perfect. I can't explain how unbelievably happy I am right now.

Ace takes my hand. "Are "you still there?" he asks.

I nod my head and laugh. "Just thinking about how lucky I am."

The music continues playing and I lean my head on his shoulder, smiling as we dance slowly.

"Thank you for saving me," I whisper to Ace.

"I think it's you who saved me, Aria."

"Wake up!"

What?

I look at Ace in front of me, but I just see him smiling at me. He isn't blinking or anything just staring at me.

"Wake the fuck up!"

I hear someone yell but when I look around, everyone is calm. Everyone is laughing and smiling, having a good time.

"Wake up, my love!"

I start to feel reality settle in and terror spreads through my body when I open my eyes. I look around and see I am in a dark room. I am laying on a bed and there is minimal light.

Where is everyone?

Where am I?

"Glad to see you're finally awake, Aria." I look in front of me and see my worst fear smiling down at me.

"Dante," I mumble as I feel my heart speed up and terror all throughout my body.

"Welcome back to me, baby," Dante says before he walks closer to me as I start screaming and crying.

Acknowledgement

Thank you, guys, so much for all of the love and support you have shown me throughout this entire book. I can't thank you guys enough for how kind you all have been. I would have been able to publish this book without you. Writing is my passion and I'm so happy that I am able to write amazing stories for you guys. I also want to thank my uncle for helping me publish this book and being there for me while publishing and I couldn't be more grateful to have him in my life. I would also like to thank my editor, Antonia Salazar for helping me edit this manuscript and my cover editor, Acacia Heather who created this beautiful cover that I am obsessed with. I can't wait for you guys to see what will happen in Ace and Aria's next story.

Aria De Luca (De Luca Series Book 2) coming soon . . .
Follow _jaclinmarie_ on Instagram for more updates.

Printed in Great Britain
by Amazon